'Gerhard Self is a find. He is likeable, eccentric and on the lookout for women, although romantically he cuts his coat according to his cloth' *Spectator*

'A missive from the last years before re-unification, with a lingering Cold War atmosphere . . . here the crime novel becomes the vessel for a more raw, immediate and violent response to the demands of guilt and reparation'
Scotland on Sunday

'As in *The Reader*, the Nazi years cast their shadow but the darkness of the plot is offset by Self's entertaining character, with an appetite for women, cocktails and Sweet Afton cigarettes' *Daily Mail*

'Self is a likeable man with some genuine eccentricities. Every year, he decorates his Christmas tree with different objects – this year it is sardine cans – and he has truly awful chat-up lines. When he sees a woman reading an article about sterilisation in a magazine, he first asks if she comes here often and then leaps straight in: "Are you sterilised?" The novel is weighty and well-built, like an old Mercedes, and it comes with a three-year guarantee for parts and labour' *Daily Telegraph*

Bernhard Schlink was born in Germany in 1944. A professor of law at the University of Berlin and a practising judge, he is the author of the major international bestselling novel *The Reader*, *Flights of Love* and several prize-winning crime novels. He lives in Bonn and Berlin.

Walter Popp was born in Nuremberg in 1948. He studied law at the University of Erlangen and spent postgraduate and research time at Cambridge University and in the USA, where he worked alongside Bernhard Schlink. In 1978, he started a law practice in Mannheim before moving to France in 1983. He now lives in a Provençal village with his teenage daughter and works as a translator.

By Bernhard Schlink

Self's Punishment (*with Walter Popp*)
Flights of Love
The Reader

Self's Punishment

BERNHARD SCHLINK & WALTER POPP

Translated from the German by Rebecca Morrison

PHOENIX

A PHOENIX PAPERBACK

First published in Great Britain in 2004
by Weidenfeld & Nicolson
This paperback edition published in 2005
by Phoenix,
an imprint of Orion Books Ltd,
Orion House, 5 Upper St Martin's Lane,
London WC2H 9EA

A CIP catalogue record for this book
is available from the British Library

ISBN 0 75381 889 2

Typeset by Deltatype Ltd, Birkenhead, Merseyside

Printed and bound in Great Britain by
Clays Ltd, St Ives plc

www.orionbooks.co.uk

Contents

Part One

Part Two

Part Three

Part One

I

Korten summons me

At the beginning I envied him. That was at high school. The Friedrich Wilhelm in Berlin. I was getting the last bit of wear out of my father's old suits, had no friends, and couldn't pull myself up on the horizontal bar. He was top of the class, in PE too, was invited to every birthday party, and when the teachers called him Mr Korten in class, they meant it. Sometimes his father's chauffeur collected him in the Mercedes. My father worked for the state railway and in 1934 had just been transferred from Karlsruhe to Berlin.

Korten can't stand inefficiency. In gym, he taught me how to do the upward circle forwards and the full-turn circle. I admired him. He also showed me what makes girls tick. I trotted along dumbly at the side of the little girl who lived on the floor below and attended the Luisen, just opposite the Friedrich Wilhelm, and gazed adoringly at her. Korten kissed her in the cinema.

We became friends – studied together, national economy for him, law for me – and I was in and out of the villa at Wannsee. When his sister Klara and I got married, he was our witness, and presented me with the desk that is still in my office today, heavy oak, with carved detail and brass knobs.

I hardly work there these days. My profession keeps me on the move, and when I drop in to the office briefly in the evenings, my desk isn't piled high with files. Only the answering machine awaits, its small window letting me know how many messages I have. Then I sit in front of the empty surface and, fiddling with a pencil, listen to what I should take on and what I should avoid, what I should sink my teeth into and what I shouldn't lay a finger on. I don't like getting my fingers burnt. But they can just as easily get jammed in the drawer of a desk you haven't looked in for a long time.

The war was over in five weeks for me. A wound that got me home. Three months later they'd patched me together again, and I completed my legal clerkship. In 1942, when Korten started at the Rhineland Chemical Works in Ludwigshafen and I began at the public prosecutor's office in Heidelberg, we shared a hotel room for a few weeks before we found our own apartments. The year 1945 saw the end of my career as a prosecutor in Heidelberg, and he was the one who got me the first cases in the financial world. Then he began his rise, and he didn't have much time, and Klara's death heralded an end to the Christmas and birthday visits. We move in different circles and I read about him more often than I see him. Sometimes we bump into each other at a concert or a play and we get on. Well, we're old friends.

Then . . . I remember the morning clearly. The world was at my feet. My rheumatism was at bay, I had a clear head, and I looked young in my new blue suit – I thought so anyway. The wind wasn't carrying the familiar chemical odour in the direction of Mannheim, but towards the Pfalz. The baker at the corner had chocolate croissants and I was having breakfast on the pavement in the sun. A young woman was walking along Mollstrasse, drew closer and grew prettier, and I put my disposable container on the window sill and followed her. A few steps later, I was in front of my office in the Augusta-Anlage.

I am proud of my office. I've had smoked glass put in

4

the door and windows of this former tobacco shop, and on the door in elegant golden letters:

'Gerhard Self – Private Investigations'.

There were two messages on the machine. The company chairman of Goedecke needed a report. I'd proved his brand manager guilty of fraud, but the manager had contested his dismissal before the labour court. The other message was Frau Schlemihl from the Rhineland Chemical Works requesting her call be returned.

'Good morning, Frau Schlemihl. Self here. You wanted to talk to me?'

'Hello, Doctor Self. General Director Korten would like to see you.' No one apart from Frau Schlemihl addresses me as 'Doctor'. Since I stopped being a public prosecutor, I've not used my title. A private detective with a Ph.D. is ridiculous. But being the good personal assistant Frau Schlemihl is, she's never forgotten Korten's introduction when we first met at the beginning of the 1950s.

'What about?'

'He would like to tell you over lunch at the executive restaurant. Is twelve-thirty convenient?'

2

In the Blue Salon

In Mannheim and Ludwigshafen we live beneath the gaze of the Rhineland Chemical Works. It was founded in 1872, seven years after the Baden Aniline and Soda Factory, by Professor Demel and Entzen, His Excellency, both chemists. The Works have grown since then, and grown and grown. Today they encompass a third of the developed land of Ludwigshafen and boast around a hundred thousand employees. In collaboration with the wind, the rhythm of RCW production determines whether the region, and which part, will reek of chlorine, sulphur, or ammonia.

The executive restaurant is situated outside the grounds of the plant and enjoys its own fine reputation. Besides the large restaurant for middle management, there is a separate area for directors with several salons still decorated in the colours that Demel and Entzen synthesized in their early successes. And a bar.

I was still standing there at one. I'd been informed at reception that the general director would unfortunately be somewhat delayed. I ordered my second Aviateur.

'Campari, grapefruit juice, champagne, a third of each.' The red-haired, freckled girl helping out behind the bar today was happy to learn something new.

'You're doing a great job,' I said.

She looked at me sympathetically. 'The general director's keeping you waiting?'

I'd waited in worse places, in cars, doorways, corridors, hotel lobbies, and railway stations. Here I stood beneath gilded stucco and a gallery of oil portraits where Korten's face would hang one day.

'My dear Self,' he said, approaching. Small and wiry, with alert blue eyes, grey crew-cut, and the leathery brown skin you get from too much sport in the sun. In a band with Richard von Weizsäcker, Yul Brynner, and Herbert von Karajan he could take the Badenweiler, Hitler's favourite march, play it in swing, and he'd have a worldwide hit.

'Sorry to be so late. You're still at it, the smoking and the drinking?' He frowned at my pack of Sweet Aftons. 'Bring me an Apollinaris! How are you?'

'Fine. I'm taking it a little slower these days, not surprising at sixty-eight. I don't take every job any more and in a couple of weeks I'll be sailing the Aegean. And you're not relinquishing the helm yet?'

'I'd like to. But it'll take another year or two before anyone can replace me. We're going through a sticky patch.'

'Should I sell?' I was thinking of my ten RCW shares deposited at the Baden Civil Servants' Bank.

'No, my dear Self,' he laughed. 'In the end these difficult phases always turn out to be a blessing for us. But still there are things that worry us, long term and short term. It's a short-term problem I wanted to see you about today and then put you together with Firner. You remember him?'

I remembered him well. A couple of years ago Firner had been made director, but for me he'd always remain Korten's bright-eyed assistant. 'Is he still wearing Harvard Business School ties?'

Korten didn't respond. He looked reflective, as though

considering whether to introduce a company tie. He took my arm. 'Let's go to the Blue Salon. It's ready.'

The Blue Salon is the best the RCW has to offer its guests. An art-deco room, with table and chairs by van de Velde, a Mackintosh lamp, and on the wall an industrial landscape by Kokoschka. Two places were set. When we were seated a waiter brought a fresh salad.

'I'll stick to my Apollinaris. I've ordered a Château de Sannes for you. You like that, don't you? And after the salad a *Tafelspitz*?'

My favourite dish. How nice of Korten to think of it. The meat was tender, the horseradish sauce without a heavy roux, but rich with cream. Korten's lunch ended with the crunchy salad. While I was eating, he got down to business.

'I'm not going to get well acquainted with computers at this point. When I see the young people sent to us from university these days, who take no responsibility and are incapable of making decisions without consulting the oracle I think of the poem about the sorcerer's apprentice. I was almost glad to hear the system was acting up. We have one of the best management and business informa- tion systems in the world. I've no idea who'd want to know, but you could find out on the terminal that we're having *Tafelspitz* and salad in the Blue Salon today, which employees are currently training on the tennis court, which marriages among the staff are intact and which are floundering, and at what intervals which flowers are planted in the flowerbeds in front of the restaurant. And of course the computer has a record of everything that was previously housed in the files of payroll, personnel, and so on.'

'And how can I help you with this?'

'Patience, my dear Self. We were promised one of the safest possible systems. That means passwords, entry

8

codes, data locks, Doomsday effects, and what have you. All of this is supposed to ensure no one can tamper with our system. But what's happened is just that.'

'My dear Korten . . .' Addressing each other by our surname, a habit from schooldays, is something we'd held on to, even as best friends. But 'my dear Self' annoys me, and he knows it. 'My dear Korten, as a boy even the abacus overwhelmed me. And now I'm supposed to tinker about with passwords, entry codes, and data what-do-you-call-them?'

'No. All the computer business is sorted out. If I understand Firner correctly, there's a list of people who could have created the mess in our system. Our sole concern is finding the right one. That's exactly where you come into it. Investigate, observe, shadow, ask pertinent questions – the usual.'

I wanted to know more, but he fended me off.

'I'm none the wiser myself. Firner will go into it with you. Let's not spend all of lunch talking about this miserable situation – there's been so little opportunity to meet since Klara's death.'

So we talked about the old days: 'Do you remember?' I don't like the old times, I've packed them away and put a lid on them. I should have sat up and paid attention when Korten was talking about the sacrifices we'd had to make and ask for. But it didn't occur to me until much later.

So far as the current day went we had little to say to each other. I wasn't surprised his son had become a member of parliament – he had always seemed precocious. Korten seemed to hold him in contempt but was all the prouder of his grandchildren. Marion had been accepted into the Student Foundation of the German People, Ulrich had won a 'Young Research' prize with an essay about the twinning of prime numbers. I could have told him about my tomcat, Turbo, but let it go.

I drained my mocha, and Korten officially ended the meal. The restaurant supervisor bid us farewell. We set off for the Works.

3

Like getting a medal

It was only a few steps away. The restaurant is opposite Gate 1, in the shadow of the main administrative building, a twenty-floor banality that doesn't even dominate the skyline.

The directors' elevator only has push-buttons for floors fifteen to twenty. The general director's office is on the twentieth floor, and my ears popped on the way up. In the outer office Korten entrusted me to Frau Schlemihl, who announced my arrival to Firner. A handshake, my hand clasped in both of his, an 'old friend' instead of 'my dear Self' – then he was gone. Frau Schlemihl, Korten's secretary since the fifties, has paid for his success with an unlived life, has faded elegantly, eats cakes, wears a pair of unused spectacles round her neck on a thin gold chain. She was busy. I stood at the window and looked out over the jumble of towers, sheds and pipes to the trading port and to a hazy Mannheim. I like industrial landscapes and would be hard pressed to choose between the romance of industry and the forest idyll.

Frau Schlemihl interrupted my idle musings. 'Doctor Self, may I introduce you to our Frau Buchendorff? She runs Director Firner's office.'

I turned around. There stood a tall, slim woman of about thirty. She wore her dark-blonde hair up, which lent her youthful face with its rounded cheeks and full lips an air of experienced competence. Her silk blouse was missing the top button, and the one below was open. Frau Schlemihl looked on disapprovingly.

'Hello, Doctor.' Frau Buchendorff reached out her hand and looked at me squarely with her green eyes.

I liked her gaze. Women only become beautiful when they look me in the eye. There's promise in such looks, even if it's a promise not kept, nor even proffered.

'May I take you through to Director Firner?' She preceded me through the door, with a pretty swing to her hips and bottom. Delightful that tight skirts are back in fashion.

Firner's office was on the nineteenth floor. At the elevator I said to her, 'Let's take the stairs.'

'You don't look like my idea of a private detective.'

I'd heard this often enough. In the meantime I know how people imagine private detectives. Not only younger. 'You should see me in my trench coat.'

'I meant it in a positive way. The guy in the trench coat would have his work cut out for him with the dossier Firner's going to give you.'

Firner, she'd said. Was she involved with him?

'You know what it's all about, then?'

'I'm one of the suspects even. In the last quarter the computer paid five hundred marks too much into my account each month. And via my terminal I do have access to the system.'

'Have you had to pay the money back?'

'I'm not the only one. Fifty-seven colleagues are affected and the firm is considering whether to ask for it back.'

In her office she pressed the intercom. 'Director, Herr Self is here.'

Firner had put on weight. The tie was now from Yves Saint-Laurent. His walk and movements were still nimble, and his handshake hadn't grown any firmer. On his desk lay a bulging folder.

'Greetings, Herr Self. It's good that you're taking this on. We thought it best to prepare a dossier with the details. By now we're certain we're dealing with targeted acts of sabotage. We have managed to limit the material damage thus far. But we have to reckon with new surprises at any time and can't rely on any information.'

I looked at him enquiringly.

'Let's start with the rhesus monkeys. Our long-distance correspondence, unless it's urgent, is saved in the word-processing system and the fax is sent out when the cheaper night rate applies. That's how we deal with our Indian orders, for example, and every half-year our research department requires around one hundred rhesus monkeys with an export licence from the Indian Ministry for Trade. Two weeks ago, instead of a hundred, an order went out for a hundred thousand monkeys. Luckily the Indians thought this odd and double-checked with us.'

I imagined 100,000 rhesus monkeys at large in the plant, and grinned.

Firner gave a pained smile. 'Yes, well, the whole thing does have its comic aspects. The mix-up with the tennis court bookings caused a lot of amusement too. Now we have to check every fax one last time before it's sent out.'

'How do you know it wasn't just a typo?'

'The secretary who wrote the message gave a printout of it as usual to the responsible party to have it proofed and initialled. The printout contains the correct number. So the fax was tampered with while it was in the queue on the hard-drive waiting to be sent. We've also examined the other cases in the dossier and can discount errors of programming or data gathering.'

'Good, I can read about that in the file. Tell me something about the circle of suspects.'

'We approached that in a conventional way. Among the employees who have right of access or access possibilities we eliminated those who've proven their worth here for more than five years. As the first incident occurred seven months ago, we can also discount all those who were only employed after that time. In some cases we could reconstruct what happened the day the system was meddled with; for example, the day of the fax message. Those absent that day are scored off. Then we examined virtually all input on a selection of terminals over a specific period of time and dug up nothing. And finally,' he smiled smarmily, 'we can rule out the directors.'

'How many does that leave?' I asked.

'A good hundred.'

'Then I've got years of work. And what about outsider hackers? You read about stuff like that.'

'We were able to eliminate that with the help of the telecom office. You speak of years – we can see it's not an easy case. And yet time is pressing. The whole thing isn't just a nuisance: with all the business and production secrets we have in the computer, it's dangerous. It's as though, in the midst of battle—' Firner is a reserve officer.

'Forget the battles,' I interrupted. 'When would you like the first report?'

'I'd like you to keep me constantly up to date. You can avail yourself of the men from security, from the computer centre and the personnel department, call on their time as you like. I needn't tell you that we ask for utmost discretion. Frau Buchendorff, is Herr Self's ID ready?' he asked over the intercom.

She entered the room and handed Firner a piece of plastic the size of a credit card.

Firner came round the desk. 'We took a colour photo of you as you entered the administration building and scanned it in straight away,' he said proudly. 'With this ID you can come and go in the complex as you please.'

He attached the card with its plastic clip to my lapel.

It was just like getting a medal. I almost felt obliged to click my heels.

4

Turbo catches a mouse

I spent the evening hunched over the dossier. A tough nut to crack. I tried to recognize a structure in the cases, a pattern to the incursions into the system. The culprit, or culprits, had managed to worm their way into payroll. For months they'd transferred 500 marks too much to the executive assistants, among them Frau Buchendorff, had doubled the vacation benefits of the low-wage groups, and deleted all salary account numbers beginning with a 13. They had meddled with intra-company communication, channelled confidential messages at the directors' level to the press department, and suppressed the automatic reminders of employees' anniversaries of service that were distributed to department heads at the beginning of the month. The programme for tennis court allocation and reservation confirmed all requests for the Friday most in demand so that one Friday in May, 108 players assembled on the sixteen courts. On top of that there was the rhesus monkey story. I could understand Firner's pained smile. The damages, around five million, could be handled by an enterprise as large as the RCW. But whoever had done it was able to saunter through the company's management and business information system at will.

It was getting dark. I turned on the light, switched it off and on a couple of times, but, although it was binary, no deeper revelation about electronic data processing came to me. I pondered whether any of my friends understood computers, and noticed how old I was. There was an ornithologist, a surgeon, a chess grandmaster, the odd legal eagle or two, all gentlemen of advanced years to whom the computer was, as for me, a terra incognita. I reflected on what sort of person it is who can work with, and likes, computers, and about the perpetrator of my case – that it was a single perpetrator was becoming pretty clear.

Belated schoolboy's tricks? A gambler, a puzzle-lover, a joker, pulling the leg of the RCW in grand style? Or a blackmailer, a cool-headed type, effortlessly showing that he was capable of bigger coups? Or a political action? The public would react sensitively if this measure of chaos came to light with a business that handled highly toxic material. But no. The political activist would have thought out different incidents. And the blackmailer could long since have struck.

I shut the window. The wind had changed.

The next day I wanted first to talk to Danckelmann, the head of Works security. Then on to the files of the hundred suspects in the personnel office. Although I was hardly hopeful that the trickster I had in mind would be recognizable by his personnel files. The thought of having to examine one hundred suspects by the book filled me with utter horror. I hoped that word of my hiring would get around and provoke some incidents through which the circle of suspects could be narrowed.

It wasn't a great case. It only struck me now that Korten hadn't even asked whether I wanted to take it on. And that I hadn't told him I'd think it over first.

The cat was scratching at the balcony door. I opened up and Turbo laid a mouse at my feet. I thanked him, and went to bed.

5

With Aristotle, Schwarz, Mendeleyev, and Kekulé

With my special ID I easily found a parking place for my old Opel at the Works. A young security guard took me to his boss.

It was written all over Danckelmann's face that he was unhappy about not being a real policeman, let alone a proper secret serviceman. It's the same with all Works security people. Before I could even start asking my questions he told me that the reason he'd left the army was because it was too wishy-washy for him.

'I was impressed by your report,' I said. 'You imply there could be hassle from communists and ecologists?'

'It's hard to get your hands on the guys. But if you put two and two together, you know which way the wind is blowing. I have to tell you that I don't quite understand why they brought you in from outside. We'd have managed to sort it out ourselves.'

His assistant entered the room. Thomas, when he was introduced to me, seemed competent, intelligent, and efficient. I understood why Danckelmann could hold sway as head of security. 'Have you anything to add to the report, Herr Thomas?'

'You should know that we're not simply going to leave the field open for you. No one is better suited than us to catch the perpetrator.'

'And how do you intend to do that?'

'I don't have the least intention of telling you that, Herr Self.'

'Yes, you do. Don't force me to point out the details of my assignment and the powers conferred on me.' You have to get formal with people like that.

Thomas would have remained resolute. But Danckelmann interrupted. 'It's okay, Heinz. Firner called this morning and told us to offer unconditional cooperation.'

Thomas made an effort. 'We've been thinking about setting a trap with the help of the computer centre. We'll inform all system users about the provision of a new, strictly confidential and, this is the decisive point, absolutely secure data file. This file for saving specially classified data is empty, however, it doesn't exist, to be precise, because no data will be entered. I'd be surprised if the announcement of this absolute security doesn't challenge the perpetrator to prove his ability by infiltrating the data file. As soon as it's entered, the central computer will show the coordinates of the user and our case is over.'

That sounded easy. 'So why are you doing it only now?'

'The whole story didn't interest a soul until one or two weeks ago. And besides,' his brow furrowed, 'we here at security aren't the first to be informed. You know, security is still regarded as a collection of retired, or even worse, fired policemen who might be capable of setting an Alsatian on someone climbing over the fence, but who have nothing in their heads. Yet these days we're pros in all questions of company security, from the protection of objects to the protection of people, and data. We're currently setting up a course at the technical college in Mannheim which will offer certification in security studies. In this, as ever, the Americans are—'

'Ahead,' I finished. 'When will the trap be ready?'

'This is Thursday. The head of the computer centre

wants to see to it himself over the weekend, and on Monday morning the users are to be informed.'

The prospect of wrapping the case up on Monday was enticing, even if the success wouldn't be mine. But in a world of certified security guards guys like me don't have much of a place anyway.

I didn't want to give up immediately, however, and asked, 'In the dossier I found a list with around a hundred suspects. Does security have any further information on one or another of them, something that's not in the report?'

'It's good that you mention that, Herr Self,' said Danckelmann. He heaved himself up from his office chair and as he came over to me I noticed he walked with a limp. He followed my gaze. 'Vorkuta. In nineteen forty-five, age eighteen, I was taken to a Russian prisoner-of-war camp. Came back in fifty-three. Without old Adenauer I'd still be there. But to return to your question. We are in fact privy to some information about the suspects that we didn't want to include in the report. There are a couple of political cases that the Secret Service keeps us up to date on. And a few with problems in their private life – wives, debt, and so on.'

He rolled off eleven names. As we worked through them I quickly gathered that the so-called political ones concerned only the usual trifles: signed the wrong leaflet as a student, stood as candidate for the wrong group, marched at the wrong demonstration. I found it interesting that Frau Buchendorff was among them. Along with other women she had handcuffed herself to the railings in front of the house of the Minister for Family Affairs.

'Why were they doing it?' I asked Danckelmann.

'That's something the Secret Service didn't tell us. After divorcing her husband, who apparently coerced her into such things, she stopped attracting attention. But I always say, whoever was political once can't shake it off from one day to the next.'

The most interesting person was on the list of 'Losers', as Danckelmann called them. A chemist, Frank Schneider, mid-forties, divorced several times. A passionate gambler. He'd grown conspicuous when he started going to the wages office too often to ask for advances.

'How did you latch on to him?' I asked.

'It's standard procedure. As soon as someone asks for an advance a third time, we take a look at him.'

'And what does that mean exactly?'

'It can, as in this case, involve going so far as shadowing a person. If you want to know, you can talk to Herr Schmalz, who did it at the time.'

I had a message sent to Schmalz that I'd expect him for lunch at twelve noon at the restaurant. I was about to add that I'd be waiting for him by the maple at the entrance, but Danckelmann brushed me aside. 'Leave it. Schmalz is one of our best. He'll find you all right.'

'Here's to teamwork,' said Thomas. 'You won't hold it against me that I'm a bit sensitive when our responsibility for security is removed. And you are from the outside. But I have enjoyed our pleasant chat, and' – he laughed disarmingly – 'our information on you is excellent.'

On leaving the redbrick building where security was housed, I lost all sense of direction. Maybe I used the wrong stairs. I was standing in a yard along the lengths of which the company security vehicles were parked, painted blue with the company logo on the doors, the silver benzene ring and in it the letters RCW. The entrance at the gable end was fashioned as a portal with two sandstone pillars and four sandstone medallions from which, blackened and mournful, Aristotle, Schwarz, Mendeleyev, and Kekulé regarded me. Apparently I was standing in front of the former chief administration building. I left the yard, and came to another, its façades completely covered with Virginia creeper. It was oddly quiet; my footsteps resounded exaggeratedly on the cobblestones. The buildings appeared to be disused. When something struck my back I whirled around in fright. In front of me a garishly bright ball gave a few more bounces and a young boy came racing after it. I retrieved the ball and approached the boy. Now I could make out the windows with net curtains in the corner of the yard, behind a rosebush, next to the open door. The boy took the ball from my hands, said 'thank you', and ran into the house. On the nameplate by the door I recognized the name Schmalz. An elderly woman was looking at me suspiciously, and shut the door. Again it was absolutely quiet.

6

A veal ragout on a bed of mixed greens

When I entered the restaurant, a small, thin, pale, black-haired man addressed me. 'Herr Self?' he lisped. 'Schmalz here.'

My offer of an aperitif was declined. 'No thank you, I don't drink alcohol.'

'And what about a fruit juice?' I didn't want to forgo my Aviateur.

'I have to be back at work at one. Happy if we could directly . . . Little to report anyway.'

The answer was elliptical, but without sibilants. Had he learned to eradicate all 's' and 'z' words from his working vocabulary?

The lady at the reception area rang the bell for service, and the girl I'd seen serving at the directors' bar took us up to the large dining hall on the first floor to a window table.

'You know how I love to begin a meal?'

'I'll see to it straight away,' she smiled.

To the headwaiter Schmalz gave an order for 'A veal ragout on a bed of mixed greens, if you would.' I was in the mood for sweet and sour pork Szechuan. Schmalz eyed me enviously. We both passed on the soup, for different reasons.

Over my Aviateur I asked about the results of the investigation of Schneider. Schmalz reported extremely precisely, avoiding all sibilants. A lamentable man, that

Schneider. After a row over his demand for an advance, Schmalz had tailed him for several days. Schneider gambled not only in Bad Dürkheim but also in private backrooms and was accordingly entangled. When his creditors had him beaten up, Schmalz intervened and brought Schneider home, not seriously injured, but quite distraught. The time had come for a chat between Schneider and his superior. An arrangement was entered into: Schneider, indispensable as a pharmaceutical researcher, was removed from work for three months and sent to a clinic, and the relevant circles were informed that they were not to allow Schneider to gamble any more. The security unit of the RCW used its influence around Mannheim and Ludwigshafen.

'A good three-year gap while the guy lay low. But in my opinion he remained a ticking bomb, even ticking today.'

The food was excellent. Schmalz ate his at a rush. He didn't leave a single grain of rice on his plate – pedantry of the food neurotic. I asked what, in his opinion, should be done with whoever was behind the computer shambles.

'Above all, interrogate him thoroughly. And then make him get in line. He can't be a threat to the plant any more. Bright guy. He could . . .'

He flailed around for a non-sibilant synonym for *certainly* or *surely*. I offered him a Sweet Afton.

'Prefer my own,' he said, and took a brown plastic box from his pocket containing homemade filter cigarettes. 'Made by my wife, no more than eight a day.'

If there's one thing I hate, it's homemade cigarettes. They are way up there with crocheted modesty covers for toilet paper. The mention of his wife reminded me of the janitor's apartment with the nameplate 'Schmalz'.

'You have a young son?'

He looked at me guardedly and deflected the question with a 'Meaning what?'

I told him about how I'd lost my way in the old factory, of the enchanted atmosphere of the overgrown yard and the encounter with the little boy with the brightly coloured ball. Schmalz relaxed and confirmed that his father lived in the janitor's flat.

'Member of our unit, too. The general and he knew one another well from the war. Now he . . . keeping an eye on the old plant . . . In the morning we take the boy to him, my wife being an employee here in the company, too.'

I learned that lots of the security people had lived in the compound and Schmalz had more or less grown up there. He'd been through the rebuilding of the Works after the war and knew its every corner. I found the idea of a life spent between refineries, reactors, distilleries, turbines, silos, and tank wagons, for all its industrial romance, oppressive.

'Didn't you ever want to look for a job beyond the RCW?'

'Couldn't do that to my father. His motto: we belong here. Did the general throw in the towel? No, nor do we.' He looked at his watch and leapt up. 'Too bad, can't linger. Am on personal security' – words he spoke almost error free – 'duty at one o'clock. Kind of you to invite . . .'

My afternoon in the personnel office was unproductive. At four o'clock I conceded I could quit studying the personnel files once and for all. I stopped by to see Frau Buchendorff, whose first name I now knew to be Judith, also that she was thirty-three, had a degree in German and English, and hadn't found a job as a teacher. She'd been at the RCW for four years, first in the archives, then in the PR department where she'd come to Firner's attention. She lived in Rathenaustrasse.

'Please don't get up,' I said. She stopped feeling for her shoes with her feet under the table, and offered me a coffee. 'I'd love one. Then we can drink to being neighbours. I've read your personnel file and know almost everything about you, apart from how many silk blouses you own.' She was wearing another one, this time buttoned up to the top.

'If you're coming to the reception on Saturday, you'll see the third one. Have you received your invitation already?' She slid a cup over to me and lit a cigarette.

'What reception?' I peered at her legs.

'We've had a delegation from China here since Monday, and as a finale we want to show them that not only our plants, but also our buffets are better than the French. Firner thought it would be a chance for you to get to know a couple of interesting people for your case, informally.'

'Shall I also have the chance to get to know you informally?'

She laughed. 'I'm there for the Chinese. But there is one Chinese woman, I haven't figured out what she's in charge of. Perhaps she's a security expert, who wouldn't be introduced as such, so a kind of colleague of yours. A pretty woman.'

'You're trying to fob me off, Frau Buchendorff! I shall have to lodge a complaint with Firner.' Scarcely had the words left my lips than I regretted them. An old man's hackneyed charm.

7

A little glitch

The next day the air lay thick over Mannheim and
Ludwigshafen. It was so muggy that, even without
moving, my clothes stuck to my body. Driving was
staccato and hectic, I could have used three feet to work
the clutch, the brake, and the gas pedal. Everything was
clogged on the Konrad Adenauer Bridge. There'd been a
collision, and immediately after it another one. I was stuck
in a traffic jam for twenty minutes. I watched the
oncoming traffic and the trains, and smoked to avoid
suffocating.

The appointment with Schneider was at half past nine.
The doorman at Gate 1 told me the way. 'It's not even five
minutes. Go straight on, and when you come to the Rhine
it's another hundred metres to your left. The laboratories
are in the light-coloured building with the large windows.'

I set off. Down at the Rhine I saw the small boy I'd met
yesterday. He'd tied a piece of string to his little bucket
and was ladling water out of the Rhine with it. He emptied
the water down the drain.

'I'm emptying the Rhine,' he called, when he saw and
recognized me.

'I hope it works.'

'What are you doing here?'

'I'm going to the laboratories over there.'

'Can I come with you?'

He shook out his little bucket and came. Children often

attach themselves to me, I don't know why. I don't have any, and most of them get on my nerves.

'Come on then,' I said, and we made our way together to the building with the large windows.

We were about fifty metres away when several people in white coats came rushing out of the entrance. They raced along the banks of the Rhine. Then there were more, not only in white coats, but also in blue overalls, and secretaries in skirts and blouses. It was an odd spectacle, and I didn't see how anyone could run in this heat.

'Look, he's waving at us,' the little boy said, and indeed one of the white-coats was flailing his arms and shouting something at us I couldn't understand. But I didn't have to understand; it was obviously about getting away as quickly as possible.

The first explosion sent a cascade of glass shards raining down the road. I grabbed the little boy's hand, but he tore loose. For a moment it was as though I were paralysed: I didn't feel any injury, heard a deep silence in spite of the continuing rattle of glass, saw the boy running, skidding on the glass shards, regaining his balance then finally falling two steps later and somersaulting forward from the impetus of movement.

Then came the second explosion, the scream of the little boy, the pain in my right arm. The bang was followed by a violent, dangerous, evil-sounding hissing. A noise that struck panic into me.

It was the sirens in the distance that made me act. They awakened reflexes inculcated in the war to flee, to help, to seek cover, and give protection. I ran to the boy, tugged him to his feet with my left hand, and dragged him in the direction we'd just come from. His little legs couldn't keep up, but he pedalled his feet in the air and didn't let go. 'Come on, little one, run, we've got to get out of here, don't slow down.' Before we turned the corner I looked back. Where we'd been standing a green cloud was rising into the leaden sky.

In vain I waved at the ambulance tearing past. At Gate 1 the guard took care of us. He knew the little boy, who was clinging tightly to my hand, pale, scratched, and frightened.

'Richard, in the name of God what happened? I'll call your grandfather right away.' He went over to the phone. 'And I'll call the medics for you. That doesn't look good.'

A splinter of glass had torn open my arm and the blood was staining red the sleeve of my light-coloured jacket. I felt dizzy. 'Do you have a schnapps?'

I only faintly recall the next half-hour. Richard was collected. His grandfather, a large, broad, heavy-set man with a bald head, shaved clean at the back and sides, and a bushy, white moustache, gathered up his grandson effortlessly into his arms. The police tried to get into the Works to investigate the accident, but were turned away. The doorman gave me a second and a third schnapps. When the ambulance men came they took me with them to the Works doctor, who put stitches in my arm and wrapped it in a sling.

'You should lie down for a while next door,' said the doctor. 'You can't leave now.'

'Why can't I leave?'

'We have a smog alarm, and all traffic has been stopped.'

'What's that supposed to mean? There's a smog alarm, and no one can leave the centre of the smog?'

'Your understanding of it is completely wrong. Smog is a meteorological overall occurrence and has no centre or periphery.'

This I considered complete nonsense. Whatever other sort of smog there might be, I'd seen a green cloud growing larger. It grew larger right here over the

29

compound. And I was supposed to stay here? I wanted to talk to Firner.

In his office a crisis headquarters had been set up. Through the door I could see policemen in green, firemen in blue, chemists in white, and some grey gentlemen from the management.

'What actually happened?' I asked Frau Buchendorff.

'We had a little glitch on site, nothing serious. But the authorities foolishly turned on the smog alarm, and that caused some excitement.'

'I got myself some little scratches at your little glitch.'

'What were you up ... ah, you were on your way to Schneider. He's not here today, by the way.'

'Am I the only injured person? Were there any deaths?'

'What are you thinking of, Herr Self? A few first-aid cases, that's all. Is there anything else we can do for you?'

'You can get me out of here.' I had no desire to battle my way through to Firner and be saluted with a 'Greetings, Herr Self.'

A policeman sporting several badges of rank emerged from the office.

'You're driving back to Mannheim, aren't you, Herr Herzog? Would you mind taking Herr Self with you? He got a few scratches and we don't want to keep him waiting here any longer.'

Herzog, a vigorous type, took me with him. Gathered in front of the gates to the Works were some police vans and reporters.

'Do avoid having your photograph taken with that bandage, please.'

I had absolutely no desire to be photographed. As we drove past the reporters I bent down to reach for the cigarette lighter, which was low on the dashboard.

'Why did the smog alarm go off so rapidly?' I asked on our drive through deserted Ludwigshafen.

Herzog proved to be well informed. 'After the spate of smog alarms in the autumn of nineteen eighty-four we in Baden-Württemberg and the Rhineland-Palatinate started an experiment with new technology on a new legal basis, with overriding authority over both states. The idea is to record the emissions directly, to correlate with the weather report, rather than just setting off the smog alarm when it's already too late. Today the model had its baptism of fire. Until now we've only had dry runs.'

'And how is cooperation with the Works? I gathered that the police were being turned away at the gate.'

'That's a sore point. The chemical industry is fighting the new law tooth and nail. At the moment there's a complaint about infringement of the constitution before the Federal Constitutional Court. Legally we could have entered the plant, but we don't want to rock the boat at this stage.'

The smoke of my cigarette was irritating Herzog, and he rolled down the window. 'Oh Lord,' he said, rolling it up straight away, 'could you please stub out your cigarette.' A pungent odour had penetrated the car, my eyes began to stream, on my tongue was a sharp taste, and we both had a coughing fit.

'It's just as well my colleagues outside have their breathing apparatus on.' At the exit to the Konrad Adenauer Bridge we passed a roadblock. Both police officers stopping traffic were wearing gas masks. At the edge of the approach were fifteen or twenty vehicles. The driver of the first one was in the midst of talking with the police officers. With a colourful cloth pressed to his face, he looked funny.

'What's going to happen with the rush-hour traffic this evening?'

Herzog shrugged. 'We'll have to wait and see how the chlorine gas develops. We hope, in the course of the afternoon, to be able to get out the workers and the RCW employees. That would considerably relieve the problem of rush-hour traffic. Some may have to spend the night at their workplace. We'd inform them of this via radio and loudspeaker vans. I was surprised before how quickly we cleared the streets.'

'Are you considering evacuation?'

'If the chlorine gas concentration doesn't decrease by half in the next twelve hours we'll have to clear east of Leuschnerstrasse and maybe also Neckarstadt and Jung-busch as well. But the meteorologists are giving us grounds for hope. Where should I let you off?'

'If the carbon monoxide concentration in the air permits it, I'd be delighted if you'd drive me to Richard-Wagner-Strasse and let me off at my front door.'

'The carbon monoxide concentration alone wouldn't have been enough for us to set off any smog alarm. It's the chlorine that's bad. With that I prefer to know people are safely at home or in their office, not, at any rate, out on the street.'

He drew up in front of my building. 'Herr Self,' he added, 'aren't you a private detective? I think my predecessor had something to do with you – do you remember the case with the senior civil servant and the sailboat?'

'I hope we're not sharing a case again now,' I said. 'Do you know anything yet about the origins of the explosion?'

'Do you have a suspicion, Herr Self? You certainly didn't just happen to be at the site of the occurrence. Had attacks been anticipated on the RCW?'

'I don't know anything about it. My job is innocuous by comparison and takes a quite different direction.'

'We'll see. I might have to call you down to headquarters to ask you a few more questions.' He looked skywards. 'And now pray for a gusty wind, Herr Self.'

I walked up the four flights of stairs to my apartment. My arm had started to bleed again. But something else was worrying me. Was my job really going in a quite different direction? Was it coincidence that Schneider hadn't come to work today? Had I cast off the idea of blackmail too quickly? Had Firner not told me everything after all?

8

Yes, well then

I washed down the chlorine taste with a glass of milk and tried to change the bandage. The telephone interrupted me.

'Herr Self, was that you leaving the RCW with Herzog? Have the Works called you in for the investigation?'

Tietzke, one of the last honest journalists. When the *Heidelberger Tageblatt* folded, he'd got a job with the *Rhine Neckar Chronicle* by the skin of his teeth, but his status there was tricky.

'What investigation? Don't get any wrong ideas, Tietzke. I had other business at the RCW and I'd be grateful for you not to have seen me there.'

'You've got to tell me a little bit more if I'm not supposed simply to write what I saw.'

'With the best will in the world I can't talk about the job. But I can try to get you an exclusive interview with Firner. I'll be calling him this afternoon.'

It took half the afternoon before I caught Firner between two conferences. He could neither confirm sabotage nor rule it out. Schneider, according to his wife, was in bed with an ear infection. So Firner, too, had been interested in why Schneider hadn't come to work. He reluctantly agreed to receive Tietzke the next morning. Frau Buchendorff would get in touch with him.

Afterwards I tried calling Schneider. No one picked up, which could mean anything or nothing. I lay down on my bed. In spite of the pain in my arm I managed to fall asleep and woke up again in time for the news. It was reported that the chlorine gas cloud was rising in an easterly direction and that any danger, which had never really existed anyway, would be over in the course of the evening. The curfew, which had never really existed either, would be lifted at ten o'clock that night. I found a piece of gorgonzola in the fridge and used it to make a sauce for the tagliatelle I'd brought back from Rome two years ago. It was fun. It took a curfew to make me cook again.

I didn't need a watch to know when ten o'clock came around. Out on the streets a din broke out as if a Mannheim football team had won the German championship. I put on my straw hat and walked to the Rose Garden. A band calling itself Just For Fun was playing golden oldies. The basins of the terraced fountains were empty, and the young folk were dancing in them. I foxtrotted a few steps – gravel and joints crunched.

The next morning in my letterbox I found a postal door-to-door delivery from the Rhineland Chemical Works that contained a perfectly worded statement on the incident. 'RCW protects life,' I discovered, also that a current focus of research was the conservation of the German woodlands. Yes, well then. The delivery included a small plastic cube with a healthy fir-seed suspended in it. How cute. I showed the object to my tomcat and put it on the mantelpiece above the fireplace.

Out on my stroll around the neighbourhood I picked up my week's provision of Sweet Aftons, bought a warm meatloaf sandwich, with mustard, from the butcher on the marketplace, visited my Turk with the good olives, watched the Green Party members at their info-stand on Parade-Platz fruitlessly trying to disturb the harmony between the RCW and the population of Mannheim and

Ludwigshafen. Among the bystanders I noticed Herzog being supplied with fliers.

In the afternoon I sat in Luisenpark. It costs something, just like Tivoli. So at the beginning of the year, for the first time, I'd acquired a year's pass. I wanted to get my money's worth out of it. When I wasn't watching pensioners feeding the ducks I read Keller's *Green Henry*. Frau Buchendorff's first name had led me to the Judith in the book.

At five o'clock I went home. Sewing a button onto my dinner jacket took me a good half-hour with my dodgy arm. I took a taxi from the Wasserturm to the RCW restaurant. There was a banner stretched over the entrance with Chinese characters on it. On three masts flew the flags of the People's Republic of China, the Federal Republic of Germany, and the RCW, flapping in the wind. To the right and left of the entrance were two Rhineland maidens in folk costume, looking about as authentic as Barbie dolls dressed as Munich beer-maids. The procession of cars was in full swing. It all looked so upright and dignified.

9

Groping the décolleté of the economy

Schmalz was standing in the foyer.

'How's your little son doing?'

'Good, thank you. I would like to talk and thank you later. I'm tied up now.'

I went up the stairs and through the open double-doors into the large function suite. People were clustered in small groups, the waitresses and waiters were serving champagne, orange juice, champagne with orange juice, Campari with orange juice, and Campari with soda. I ambled around a bit. It was like any other reception before the speeches were given and the buffet is opened. I sought familiar faces and found the red-haired girl with the freckles. We smiled at each other. Firner drew me into a circle and introduced me to three Chinese men whose names were made up of various combinations of San, Yin, and Kim, as well as Herr Oelmüller, head of the computer centre. Oelmüller was trying to explain computerized data protection in Germany to the Chinese. I don't know what they found so funny about that but in any event they laughed like the Hollywood Chinese in a Pearl S. Buck adaptation.

Then came the speeches. Korten was brilliant. He covered everything from Confucius to Goethe, left out the Boxer Uprising and the Cultural Revolution, and touched on the former RCW branch in Tsingtao solely to weave in the compliment to the Chinese that the last head of branch

37

there had learned a new process for the production of ultramarine from the Chinese.

The Chinese delegation leader replied no less elegantly. He recounted his university years in Karlsruhe, took his hat off to German culture and the economy, from Böll to Schleyer, spoke technical jargon I didn't understand, and closed with Goethe's 'The Orient and Occident can no longer be divided'.

After the president of the Rhineland-Palatinate's speech even a less superb buffet would have seemed exciting. For my first helping I chose the saffron oysters in a champagne sauce. Good thing that there were tables. I hate the stand-up receptions where you have to juggle cigarette, glass, and plate – really you should be fed at them. I spotted Frau Buchendorff at a table with a free chair. She was looking charming in her raw-silk, indigo-coloured suit. The buttons of her blouse were there in their entirety.

'May I join you?'

'You can get another chair, unless you plan on perching the Chinese security expert on your lap straight away?'

'Tell me, did the Chinese pick up on the explosion?'

'What explosion? No, seriously, they were up at Castle Eltz first thing yesterday, and then they tried out the new Mercedes on the Nürburg Ring. When they got back, everything was over. Today the press has really been going at it, mainly from the meteorological angle. How's your arm? You're something of a hero – that couldn't get into the papers, of course, though it would have made a lovely story.'

The Chinese lady appeared. She had everything that German men who dream of Asian women could dream of. Whether she was in fact a security expert I wasn't able to establish either. I asked whether there were private detectives in China.

'No plivate plopethy, no plivate detectives,' she

answered, and asked whether there were also female private detectives in the Federal Republic of Germany. This led on to observations about the waning women's movement. 'I've lead almost evelything published in Gehmany in the way of women's books. Why is it that men in Gehmany ahrite women's books? A Chinese man would lose face.'

Fohtunate China.

A waiter brought me the invitation to Oelmüller's table. On the way I selected a second course of sole roulades, Bremen-style.

Oelmüller introduced me to the gentleman at his table, who impressed me with his pedantic skill in arranging his sparse hair over his head: Professor Ostenteich, head of the law department and honorary professor at Heidelberg University. No coincidence that these gentlemen were dining together. Well, back to work. Since my talk with Herzog, a question had been bothering me.

'Could the gentlemen explain the new smog model to me? Herr Herzog of the police talked about it, said it is not entirely uncontroversial. What, for example, am I to understand by the direct recording of emissions?'

Ostenteich felt called upon to lead the discussion. 'That is *un peu délicat*, as the French would say. You should read the expert opinion by Professor Wenzel that most meticulously lays out the relevant distribution of powers, and unmasks the legislative hubris of Baden-Württemberg and the Rhineland-Palatinate. *Le pouvoir arrête le pouvoir* – the Federal law on Emissions Protection blocks any special paths the states might choose. Added to that is freedom of property, protection of entrepreneurial activity, and a company's privacy. The legislator hoped to disregard that with a single stroke of the pen. But *la vérité est en marche*, the Federal Constitutional Court in Karlsruhe still exists, *heureusement*.'

'And how does this new smog alarm model work?' I looked at Oelmüller invitingly.

Ostenteich didn't relinquish his lead quite so easily. 'It's good that you enquire about the technical side of things, too, Herr Self. Herr Oelmüller can explain all that to you in a minute. The crux, *l'essence*, of our problem is: the state and the economy only have a beneficial juxtaposition and cooperation if a certain distance prevails between the two. And, please allow me this rather bold picture: here the state has overstepped itself and groped the décolleté of the economy.' He roared with laughter, and Oelmüller dutifully joined in.

When quiet had again descended, or, as the French would say, *silence*, Oelmüller said, 'Technically the whole thing isn't a problem at all. The basic process of environmental protection is the examination of the vehicles of emissions – water, or air – to check the concentration of harmful substances. If an emission exceeds the accepted levels, one attempts to trace its source and shut it off. So, smog may be created if some factory or other emits more than their allowance. On the other hand, smog may also be created if the level of the emissions at the individual factories remains within the stated limits, but the weather cannot cope.'

'How does whoever's in charge of the smog alarm know what sort of smog he's dealing with? He surely has to react quite differently to each.' The business was beginning to enthrall me. I postponed my next trip to the buffet, and shuffled a cigarette out of the yellow packet.

'Correct, Herr Self, indeed both sorts require a different reaction, but they're difficult to tell apart using conventional methods. It's possible, for example, that traffic has to be stopped and factories have to grind to a halt because a single coal power station that drastically oversteps its accepted emission level can't be identified and stopped in time. What makes the new model irresistible is that, theoretically at least, problems like the one you raised can be avoided. Via sensors, emissions are measured where they originate and transmitted to the Regional Computing Centre that consequently always knows where which emissions are occurring. Not only that, the RCC feeds the emissions data into a simulation of the local weather expected in the next twenty-four hours – we call it a meteorograph – and the smog can be to a certain extent anticipated. An early-warning system that doesn't look as good in practice as it sounds in theory because, quite simply, meteorology is still in its infancy.'

'How do you view yesterday's incident in this respect? Did the model prove its worth?'

'The model worked all right yesterday.' Oelmüller tugged the end of his beard, contemplatively.

'No, no, Herr Self, here I must expand upon the technicians' perspective to present the broader picture. In the old days, quite simply, absolutely nothing would have happened. Yesterday instead we had chaos with all the loudspeaker announcements, police controls, curfews. And to what purpose? The cloud dispersed, without any assistance from environmentalists. Yesterday's event just fanned the flames of fear and destroyed trust and damaged the image of the RCW – *tant de bruit pour une omelette*. I think this is the very case to make clear to the Federal Constitutional Court how disproportionate the new law is.'

'Our chemists are checking whether yesterday's counts really justified the smog alarm,' Oelmüller inserted. 'They immediately began to evaluate the emissions data, which we also record in our MBI, management and business information, system.'

'At least they deigned to grant the industry online

access to the state emissions analysis,' Ostenteich interjected.

'Do you consider it possible, Herr Oelmüller, that the accident and the incidents in the computer system are in some way connected?'

'I've thought about it. Here practically all production processes are controlled electronically, and there are multiple links between the process computers and the MBI system. Manipulations via the MBI system – I can't completely discount it, in spite of all the built-in security measures. Regarding yesterday's accident, however, I don't know enough to say whether a suspicion in that direction makes sense. If so, I would hate to think what could be in store for us.'

Ostenteich's interpretation of yesterday's accident had almost made me forget my arm was still in a sling. I raised my glass to the gentlemen and made my way over to the buffet. With a loin of lamb in its herb crust on my prewarmed plate, I was steering my way to Firner's table when Schmalz came up to me.

'May my wife and I invite the doctor to coffee?' Schmalz had evidently dug out my title and gladly adopted it to neutralize another sibilant.

'That's extremely kind of you, Herr Schmalz,' I thanked him. 'But I'll hope you'll understand that until the end of this case, my time is not my own.'

'Oh, well, another time, maybe.' Schmalz looked downcast, but understood the Works came first.

I looked around for Firner and found him on his way to his table with a plate from the buffet.

He stood still for a moment. 'Greetings, have you found out anything?' He held his plate awkwardly at chest level to hide a red-wine stain on his dinner shirt.

'Yes,' I said simply. 'And you?'

'What's that supposed to mean, Herr Self?'

'Let's imagine there's a blackmailer who wants to demonstrate his superiority, first of all by manipulating the MBI system and then by creating a gas explosion. Then he demands ten million from the RCW. Who in the company would be the first person to get that demand on his desk?'

'Korten. Because he's the only one who could decide about sums of that size.' He frowned and glanced instinctively at the slightly raised table where Korten was sitting with the head of the Chinese delegation, the president, and other heavyweights. I waited in vain for an appeasing remark like 'But Herr Self, whatever are you thinking?' He lowered his plate. The red-wine stain did its bit to reveal a tense and uncertain Firner beneath the veneer of relaxed serenity. As though I were no longer there, he took a few steps towards the open window, lost in thought. Then he pulled himself together, rearranged the plate in front of his chest, nodded curtly at me, and moved in a determined fashion to his table. I went to the toilet.

'Well, my dear Self, making progress?' Korten arrived at the next stall and fumbled with his fly.

'Do you mean with the case or the prostate?'

He peed and laughed. Laughed louder and louder and had to put a hand out on the tiles to support himself, and then it came back to me, too. We'd stood next to each other like this before, in the urinals at the Friedrich Wilhelm. It had been planned as a preparatory measure for playing hookey, and then, when the teacher noticed we were missing, Bechtel was to stand up and say, 'Korten and Self were feeling sick and went to the lavatory – I can go in quickly and check how they are.' But the teacher checked on us himself, found us there having a great time, and, as a punishment, left us standing there for the rest of the lesson, supervised by the janitor.

'Professor Barfeld with the monocle will be here any minute,' snorted Korten. 'Barfing Barfer, here comes Barfing Barfeld.'

I remembered the nickname, and we stood there, trousers open, clapping each other on the shoulder. Tears sprang to my eyes and my belly hurt from all the laughing.

Back then things almost took a nasty turn. Barfeld reported us to the headmaster and I had already envisaged my father raging and my mother weeping and the scholarship evaporating into thin air. But Korten took it all on his shoulders: he had been the instigator and I'd just joined in. So he got the letter home, and his father only laughed.

'I've got to go.' Korten buttoned up his fly.

'What, again?' I was still laughing. But the fun was over and the Chinese were waiting.

Memories of the blue Adriatic

When I returned to the hall it was all drawing to a close. Passing, Frau Buchendorff asked how I was getting home, I couldn't be driving with my arm.

'I took a taxi before.'

'I'd be glad to give you a lift, since we're neighbours. Quarter of an hour by the exit?'

The tables were deserted. Small knots of people formed and dispersed. The red-haired girl was still standing with a bottle at the ready, but everyone had had plenty to drink.

'Hello,' I said to her.

'Did you enjoy the reception?'

'The buffet was good. I'm amazed there's anything left over. But seeing there is – could you pack a little something for a picnic tomorrow?'

'How many in your party?' She bobbed an ironic curtsy.

'For two, if you have time.'

'Oh, can't do that. But I'll have something packed for two nonetheless. Just a moment.'

She disappeared through the swing-doors. When she returned she had with her a largish box. 'You should have seen the face of our chef. I had to tell him that you're peculiar but important.' She giggled. 'Because you've dined with the general director he took it on himself to add a bottle of Forster Bischofsgarten Spätlese.'

When Frau Buchendorff saw me with the carton she raised an eyebrow.

'I've packed the Chinese security expert. Didn't you notice how petite and dainty she is? The delegation leader shouldn't have let her go with me.' In her presence all I could think of were stupid jokes. If this had happened to me thirty years ago I'd have been forced to admit I was in love. But what was I to make of it at an age where falling in love no longer happens?

Frau Buchendorff drove an Alfa Romeo Spider, an old one without the ugly rear spoiler.

'Should I put the roof up?'

'I usually ride my motorbike in swimming trunks, even in winter.' It was getting worse and worse. And on top of it, a misunderstanding – she was putting up the roof. All because I hadn't dared say that I could think of nothing finer than to be on the road on a mellow summer night with a beautiful woman at the wheel of a cabriolet. 'No, leave it, Frau Buchendorff, I like driving in a sports car with the top down on a mellow summer night.'

We drove over the suspension bridge, below us the Rhine and the harbour. I looked up at the sky and the cables. It was a bright and starry-clear night. When we turned off the bridge and before we were submerged in the streets, Mannheim with its towers, churches, and high-rises lay before us for a moment. We had to wait at traffic lights and a heavy motorbike drew up alongside. 'Come on, let's drive out to the Adriatic,' shouted the girl on the back of the bike to her boyfriend, through his helmet against the noise of the engine. In the hot summer of 1946 I'd often been out at the gravel pit, its name imbued with Mannheimers' and Ludwighafeners' yearning for the South. Back then my wife and I were still happy and I enjoyed our companionship, the peace, and the first cigarettes. So, people still went out there, more

46

rapidly and easier these days, a quick dip in the water after the movies.

We hadn't spoken throughout the journey. Frau Buchendorff had driven fast, and with focus. Now she lit a cigarette.

'The blue Adriatic – when I was small we sometimes drove out in our Opel Olympia. There was coffee substitute in the thermos flask, cold cutlets, and vanilla pudding in the preserving jar. My big brother was streetwise, a rocker, as they called it; on his moped he soon went his own way. Back then the notion of going for a quick dip in the night was just getting fashionable. It all seems so idyllic now, looking back – as a child I always suffered those outings.'

We'd reached my house but I wanted to savour a little longer the nostalgia that had engulfed us both.

'In what way suffered?'

'My father wanted to teach me how to swim but had no patience. My God, the amount of water I swallowed.'

I thanked her for the ride home. 'It was a beautiful drive.'

'Goodnight, Herr Self.'

I I

Terrible thing to happen

A glorious Sunday saw the last of the good weather. At our picnic by the Feudenheim Locks my friend Eberhard and I ate and drank much too much. He had brought a miniature wooden crate with three bottles of a very decent Bordeaux, and then we made the mistake of downing the RCW Spätlese, as well.

On Monday I woke up with a blazing headache. On top of that the rain had coaxed out the rheumatism in my back and hips. Perhaps that's why I dealt with Schneider all wrong. He had reappeared, not flushed out by the Works security service, just like that. I was to meet him in a colleague's laboratory; his own had been burnt to a shell in the accident.

When I entered the room he straightened up from the fridge. He was tall and lanky. He invited me with an indeterminate flick of the hand to take a seat on one of the lab stools and remained standing himself, shoulders stooped, in front of the refrigerator. His face was ashen, the fingers of his left hand yellow from nicotine. The immaculate white coat was supposed to hide the decay of the person inside. But the man was a wreck. If he was a gambler then he was the sort who had lost and had no shred of hope left. The sort who fills out a lottery ticket on a Friday, but doesn't bother to look on the Saturday to see if he's won.

'I know why you want to talk to me, Herr Self, but I've nothing to tell you.'

'Where were you on the day of the accident? You'll know that surely. And where did you disappear to?'

'I unfortunately do not enjoy great health and was indisposed in recent days. The accident in my laboratory was a real blow, important records of research were destroyed.'

'That's hardly an answer to my question.'

'What do you really want? Just leave me alone.'

Indeed, what did I really want from him? I was finding it more and more difficult to picture him as the brilliant blackmailer. Broken as he was, I couldn't even imagine him the tool of some outsider. But my imagination had duped me in the past and there was something not right about Schneider. I didn't have that many leads. His, and my own, misfortune that he'd found his way into the security files. And there was my hangover and my rheumatism and Schneider's sulky, whiny manner that was getting on my nerves. If I couldn't intimidate him then I might as well kiss my job goodbye. I gathered myself for a fresh attack.

'Herr Schneider, we are investigating sabotage resulting in damages reaching into the millions and we're acting to prevent further threats. I've encountered nothing but cooperation during my investigation. Your unwillingness to lend your support makes you, I'll be perfectly honest, a suspect. All the more so as your biography contains phases of criminal entanglement.'

'But I put a halt to the gambling years ago.' He lit a cigarette. His hand was trembling. He took some hasty drags. 'But, okay, I was at home in bed and we often unplug the telephone at the weekend.'

'But Herr Schneider. Security was round at your house. There was nobody home.'

'So you don't believe me anyway. Then I won't say another word.'

I'd heard that often enough. Sometimes it helped to convince the other person I believed whatever he said. Sometimes I'd understood how to address the deep-seated trouble at the source of this childish reaction so that everything came gushing out. Today I was capable of neither one nor the other. I'd had it.

'Right, then we'll have to continue our discussion in the presence of Security and your superiors. I'd have liked to spare you that. But if I don't hear from you by this evening . . . Here's my business card.'

I didn't wait for his reaction, and left. I stood under the awning, looked into the rain and lit a cigarette. Was it also raining on the banks of the Sweet Afton? I didn't know what to do. Then I recalled that the boys from Security would have set their trap and I went over to the computer centre to take a look. Oelmüller wasn't there. One of his co-workers whose badge revealed him to be a Herr Tausendmilch showed me on screen the message sent to users about the false data file.

'Should I print it out for you? It's no problem at all.'

I took the printout and went over to Firner's office. Neither Firner nor Frau Buchendorff were there. A typist regaled me on the subject of cacti. I'd had enough for one day and left the Works.

If I'd been younger I'd have driven out to the Adriatic regardless of the rain to swim off my hangover. If I could just have got into my car I'd maybe have done it anyway, regardless of age. But with my injured arm I still couldn't drive. The guard, the same one as on the day of the accident, called a taxi for me.

'Ah, you're the fellow who brought in Schmalz's son on Friday. You're Self? Then I have something for you. He scrabbled beneath the control and alarm desk and came back up with a package that he handed over with ceremony.

'There is a cake inside as a surprise for you. Frau Schmalz baked it.'

I had the taxi take me to the Herschel baths. It was women's only day in the sauna. I had it take me to the Kleiner Rosengarten, my local, and ate a saltimbocca romana. Then I went to the movies.

The first movie showing in the early afternoon has its charm, regardless of what's playing. The audience consists of tramps, thirteen-year-olds, and frustrated intellectuals. When there were still students who lived out of town, they went to the early showing. Pupils who matured earlier used to go to the early showing to make out. But Babs, a friend who's headmistress of a high school, assures me that pupils now make out at school and are all made out by one o'clock.

I'd ended up in the wrong theatre – the cinema had seven of the things – and had to watch *On Golden Pond*. I liked all the actors but when it was over I was glad I no longer had a wife, a daughter, or some little bastard of a grandson.

On the way home I looked in at the office. I picked up a message that Schneider had hanged himself. Frau Buchendorff had spoken with extreme matter-of-factness on the answering machine and asked to be called back immediately.

I poured myself a sambuca.

'Did Schneider leave a note?'

'Yes. We have it here. We think your case is over now. Firner would like to see you to talk about it.'

I told Frau Buchendorff I'd be there straight away, and called a taxi.

Firner was light of heart. 'Greetings, Herr Self. Terrible thing to happen. He hanged himself in the

51

laboratory with an electric cable. A poor trainee found him. We tried everything to revive him of course. No use. Read the suicide note, we have our man.'

He handed me the photocopy of a hastily scrawled sheet of paper, apparently meant for his wife.

My Dorle – forgive me. Do not think you didn't love me enough – without your love I'd have done this a long time ago. I can't go on now. They know everything and leave me no option. I wanted to make you happy and give you everything – may God grant you an easier life than in these past dreadful years. You deserve it so much. I embrace you. Unto death – your Franz.

'You have your man? This leaves everything open. I spoke with Schneider this morning. It's gambling that had him in its clutches and drove him to death.'

'You're a defeatist.' Firner bellowed with laughter in my face, his mouth wide open.

'If Korten thinks the case has been solved, he can of course relinquish my services at any time. I believe, though, that you're jumping to conclusions. And you yourself don't take them that seriously. Or have you already deactivated the computer trap?'

Firner wasn't impressed. 'Routine, Herr Self, routine. Naturally the trap is still in place. But for the time being the matter is over. We just have a few details to clear up. How, above all, Schneider managed to manipulate the system.'

'I'm quite certain you'll be on the phone to me soon.'

'Let's see, Herr Self.' Firner, honest to God, stuck his thumbs into the waistcoat of his three-piece suit and played 'Yankee Doodle' with his remaining fingers.

On the way home in the taxi I thought about Schneider. Was I responsible for his death? Or was Eberhard responsible for bringing so much Bordeaux that I had been hungover today and too gruff with Schneider? Or was it the senior chef, with his Forster Bischofsgarten Spätlese that finished us off? Or the rain and the rheumatism? The chains of cause and guilt went on and on into infinity.

Schneider in his white lab coat was often in my thoughts in the days that followed. I didn't have much to do. Goedecke wanted a further, more detailed report on the disloyal branch manager, and another client came to me not realizing he could have got the same information from the town clerk's office.

On Wednesday my arm was on the mend and I could finally collect my car from the RCW parking lot. The chlorine had eaten into the paint. I'd add that to the bill. The guard greeted me and asked whether the cake had been good. I had left it in the taxi on Monday.

12

Among screech owls

While playing Doppelkopf with my friends, I presented them with the problem of chains of cause and guilt. A couple of times a year we meet on a Wednesday in the Badische Weinstuben, to play cards: Eberhard, the chess grandmaster; Willy, the ornithologist and an emeritus of the University of Heidelberg; Philipp, surgeon at the city hospital; and myself.

At fifty-seven Philipp is our Benjamin, and Eberhard our Nestor at seventy-two. Willy is half a year younger than me. We never get particularly far with our Doppelkopf, we like talking too much.

I told them about Schneider's background, his passion for gambling, and how I'd cast suspicion on him that I didn't really believe in myself but nonetheless had used to take him harshly to task.

'Two hours later the man hangs himself. Not, I think, because of my suspicion, but because he could foresee the uncovering of his continued gambling addition. Am I to blame for his death?'

'You're the lawyer,' said Philipp. 'Don't you have any criteria for this sort of thing?'

'Legally I'm not guilty. But it's the human aspect that interests me.'

The three of them looked at a complete loss. Eberhard ruminated. 'Then I wouldn't be allowed to win at chess any more because my opponent might be sensitive and might take a defeat so to heart that he kills himself over it.'

'So, if you know that defeat is the drop that will make the glass of depression overflow, leave him alone and look for another opponent,' Philipp suggested.

Eberhard wasn't satisfied with Philipp's hypothesis. 'What do I do at a tournament where I can't select my opponent?'

'Well, among screech owls . . .' Willy began. 'It gets clearer by the day why I love screech owls so much. They catch their mice and sparrows, take care of their young, live in their tree-hollows and cavities in the earth, don't need any company, nor a state, are courageous and sharp, true to their family. There's real wisdom in their eyes, and I've never heard any such snivelling outpourings about guilt and expiation from them. Besides, if it's not the legal but the human side that interests you, all people are guilty of all things.'

'Put yourself under my knife. If it slips from my grasp because a nurse is turning me on, is everyone here guilty?' Philipp made a sweeping hand gesture. The waiter understood it as the ordering of another round and brought a pils, a Laufen Gutedel, an Ihring Vulkanfelsen, and a grog for Willy, who was suffering from a cold.

'Well, you'll have us to deal with if you hack up Willy.' I raised my glass to Willy. He couldn't drink back to me, his grog was still too hot.

'Don't worry, I'm not stupid. If I do something to Willy, we won't be able to play Doppelkopf any more.'

'Exactly, let's play another round,' said Eberhard. But before we could start he folded his cards together pensively and laid the little pile on the table. 'Although, seriously, I'm the eldest so it's easiest for me to broach the subject, what's to become of us if one of us . . . if . . . you know what I mean.'

'If there are only three of us left?' Philipp said with a grin. 'Then we'll play Skat.'

'Don't we know another fourth player, someone we could bring in now as a fifth?'

'A priest would be no bad thing at our age.'

'We don't have to play every time, we don't anyway. We could just go out for a meal, or do something with women. I'll bring a nurse for each of you, if you like.'

'Women,' said Eberhard mistrustfully, and took up his hand of cards again.

'The idea of a meal isn't a bad one.' Willy asked for the menu. We all ordered. The food was good and we forgot about guilt and death.

On the way home I noticed that I'd managed to distance myself from Schneider's suicide now. I was just curious as to when I'd next hear from Firner.

13

Are you interested in the details?

It's not often I stay home in the mornings. Not only because I'm out and about a lot, but because I can barely keep away from the office even if there's nothing for me to do there. It's a relic from my time as an attorney. Perhaps it also stems from the fact that as a child I don't remember my father ever spending a workday at home, and back then you worked six days a week.

On Thursday I was the leopard that changed its spots. The previous day my video recorder had come back from the repair shop. I'd rented a couple of Westerns. Even though they are scarcely shown any more I've remained true to them.

It was ten o'clock. I'd put on *Heaven's Gate*: I'd missed it at the cinema and it was unlikely to be shown there again, and I was watching Harvard graduates at the graduation party in their tails. Kris Kristofferson stood a decent chance. Then the telephone rang.

'I'm glad to reach you, Herr Self.'

'Did you think I would be at the blue Adriatic in this weather, Frau Buchendorff?' Outside the rain was pouring down.

'Ever the old charmer. I'll put you through to Herr Firner.'

'Greetings, Herr Self. We believed the case was over, but now Herr Oelmüller tells me that something has happened in the system again. I'd be happy if you could come over, today if possible. What's your schedule like?'

We agreed on 4 p.m. *Heaven's Gate* was about four hours long, and you shouldn't sell yourself too cheaply.

On the drive to the Works I pondered why Kris Kristofferson had cried at the end. Because early wounds never heal? Or because they heal and, one day, are nothing more than a bleached-out memory?

The gateman at the main gates greeted me like an old friend, hand on the brim of his cap. Oelmüller was distanced. The other member of the party was Thomas.

'Remember I told you about the trap that we'd planned and instigated?' said Thomas. 'Well, today it snapped shut . . .'

'But the mouse ran away with the cheese?'

'That's one way of putting it,' Oelmüller said sourly. 'Here is exactly what occurred: yesterday morning the central computer reported that our bait data file had been opened via terminal PKR 137 by a user with the number 23045 ZBH. The user, Herr Knoblauch, is employed in the main accounting department. He was, however, at the time the file was accessed, in a meeting with three gentlemen from the tax authority. And the said terminal is at the other end of the Works at the purification plant and was being serviced by our own technician off-line.'

'Herr Oelmüller means to say that the machine wasn't workable during its inspection,' added Thomas.

'Which means that another user and another terminal are hidden behind Herr Knoblauch and his number. Didn't you figure the culprit would disguise himself?'

Oelmüller took up my question eagerly. 'Oh yes, Herr Self. I've spent the whole of last weekend thinking through how we can catch the culprit regardless. Are you interested in the details?'

'Try me. If it gets too difficult I'll let you know.'

'Good, I'll attempt to keep it comprehensible. We've seen to it that when a special control command is issued by the system, the terminals that are logged on will set a special switch in their working memory. It's not noticeable to the user. The safety precaution was sent to the terminals at the moment the bait data file was accessed. Our intention was that all terminals in dialogue with the system at that second could later be identified by the state of the switch, and this even independent of the terminal number the culprit could have used to disguise himself.'

'Could I imagine it being like a stolen car being identified not by its false licence plate, but by the engine number?'

'Well, yes, somewhat along those lines.' Oelmüller nodded at me encouragingly.

'And how do you explain that, in spite of all this, there was no mouse in the trap?'

Thomas responded. 'At the moment we have no explanation. Something you may be considering – outside intervention – we still discount. The wiring the telecom people installed to trace things is still in place and signalled nothing.'

No explanation. And that from the specialists. My dependence on their expertise bothered me. I could follow what Oelmüller had described. But I couldn't check his premises. Possibly the pair of them weren't particularly bright and it wasn't a big deal to outwit their trap. But what was I supposed to do? Immerse myself in computers? Follow up the other leads? What other leads were there? I was at a loss.

'The whole thing is very embarrassing for Herr Oelmüller and myself,' said Thomas. 'We were sure we'd trap the culprit and stupidly we said so. Time is ticking by and nonetheless the only possibility I see is to go through all our assumptions and conclusions with a fine-toothed comb. Perhaps we should also speak to the man who set up the system, don't you think, Herr Oelmüller? Can you tell us, Herr Self, how you are going to proceed?'

'I've got to sift through everything in my head first.'

'I'd like us to stay in touch. Shall we get together again on Monday morning?'

We were standing and had said our goodbyes, when my thoughts returned to the accident. 'What, incidentally, came out of the investigation of the causes of the explosion? And did the smog alarm function properly?'

'According to the RCC it was right that the smog alarm went off. So far as the cause of the accident is concerned, we have at least arrived at the point where we know it had nothing to do with our computer. I don't have to tell you how relieved I was. A broken valve – the engineers will have to answer for that.'

14

Lousy reception

With good music playing I can always think well. I'd switched the stereo on but hadn't started playing *The Well-Tempered Clavier* as I wanted to fetch a beer from the kitchen first. When I returned, the neighbour on the floor below had turned her radio up loud, making me listen to her current favourite: 'We are living in a material world and I am a material girl . . .'

I trampled on the floor, to no avail. So it was off with the dressing gown, on with the shoes and jacket, and down the stairs I went to ring the doorbell. I intended to ask the 'material girl' if there was no consideration left in her 'material world'. No one answered, nor was any music coming from the flat. Obviously no one was home. The other neighbours were away on holiday and there's nothing but the attic above my flat.

Then I realized that the music was coming from my own loudspeaker. I don't have a radio attached to the system. I fiddled with the amplifier and couldn't get rid of the music. I put on the record. Bach in the *forti* sections easily managed to drown out the sinister other channel, but the *piani* he had to share with the newscaster of South-West Radio. My stereo was apparently screwed up.

Perhaps it was due to the lack of good music that I didn't get much more thinking done that evening. I played through a scenario in which Oelmüller was the culprit. Apart from the psychology it all fitted. He certainly wasn't the rascal or prankster – could he be the blackmailer? According to everything I'd ever gathered about computer criminality, people who worked with a computer would make different use of it for criminal purposes. They would use the system but not make a mockery of it.

The next morning I went to a radio repair shop before breakfast. I'd tried out the stereo again and the interference had gone. That really did annoy me. I can't abide unpredictable machinery. A car may be roadworthy and a washing machine still wash, but if the last, most insignificant indicator light doesn't work with Prussian precision, my mind will know no rest.

I got a competent young man. He had compassion for my lack of technical know-how, almost called me 'Grandpa' in friendly condescension. Of course, I know that radio waves aren't brought to life by the radio – they're always there. The radio merely makes them audible, and the young man explained to me that practically the same circuit that achieves this in the receiver is also present in the amplifier and that, under certain atmospheric conditions, the amplifier may act as a receiver. There was nothing you could do about it, just had to accept it.

On the way from Seckenheimer Strasse to my café in the arcades by the Wasserturm I bought a newspaper. At my kiosk, lying next to *Süddeutsche* is always the *Rhine Neckar Chronicle* and for some reason the abbreviation RNC stuck fast in my head.

When I was sitting in Café Gmeiner, coffee in front of me, awaiting my ham and eggs, I got that feeling of wanting to say something to someone but not remembering what. Was it related to the RNC? It struck me that I hadn't read Tietzke's interview with Firner yet. But that wasn't what I was looking for. Hadn't someone spoken to me yesterday about the RNC? No, Oelmüller had said the

RCC had had reason to trigger the smoke alarm. That was apparently the office responsible for the smog alarm and analysis of emission data. But there was something else I wasn't getting. It had something to do with the amplifier functioning as a receiver.

When the ham and eggs arrived I ordered another coffee. The waitress didn't bring it until I'd asked for a third time. 'Sorry, Herr Self, I've got lousy reception today. I'm miles away. I was taking care of my daughter's boy last night because the young folk have a subscription for the opera and got back late yesterday. Wagner's *Götterdämmerung* went on and on.'

Lousy reception, miles away, long-distance. Of course, that was it, the long-distance reception at the RCC. Herzog had told me about the direct emission model. The same emission data are also recorded in the RCW system, Oelmüller had said. And Ostenteich had spoken of the online connection with the state monitoring system. Somehow the computer centre of the RCW and the RCC had to be connected. Was it possible to penetrate the MBI system via the RCC? And was it possible that the people at RCW had simply forgotten this? I cast my thoughts back and remembered clearly that there had been talk of the terminals in the plant and of telephone lines to the outside when we'd been discussing possible breaches in the system. A cable running between RCC and RCW, as I was now picturing it, had never been mentioned. It belonged neither to the telephone lines nor to the terminal connections. It differed from those by not being a mode of direct communication. Rather a silent flow of data migrated from the various sensors onto tape. Data that interested no one at the plant and could be immediately forgotten unless there happened to be an alarm or an accident. I understood why the musical confusion on my stereo had preoccupied me for so long: the interference came from inside.

I played around with my ham and eggs and the multitude of questions going through my mind. Above all I needed additional information. I didn't want to speak with Thomas, Ostenteich, or Oelmüller now. If they had forgotten an RCW–RCC connection, that would ultimately cause them more concern than the connection itself. I needed to take a look at the RCC and find someone there who could explain system connections to me.

From the phone booth next to the restroom I gave Tietzke a call. The RCC, it transpired, was the Regional Computer Centre in Heidelberg. 'To a certain degree even trans-regional,' said Tietzke, 'as Baden-Württemberg and the Rhineland-Palatinate are hooked up to it. What do you have in mind, Herr Self?'

'Do you ever let up, Herr Tietzke?' I retorted, and promised him the rights to my memoirs.

15

Bam bam, ba bam bam

I drove straight to Heidelberg. In front of the law school I found a parking space. I walked the few steps to Ebert-Platz, the former Wrede-Platz, and found the Regional Computer Centre in the old building with the two entrance pillars where the Deutsche Bank used to be. The doorman sat in the former banking hall.

'Selk from Springer Publishing,' I introduced myself. 'I'd like to talk to one of the gentlemen from emission supervision, the publishing house called ahead.'

He picked up the telephone. 'Herr Mischkey, there's someone here from Springer Publishing, he says he wants to talk to you and has an appointment. Should I send him up?'

I interjected. 'Can I talk to Herr Mischkey myself?' And as the doorman was sitting at a table not screened by glass and since I was already reaching for it, he handed the receiver to me, nonplussed.

'Hello, Herr Mischkey, Selk from Springer Publishing here, you know? We'd like to include a report on the direct emission model in our computer journal, and after talking with the industry I'd like to hear the other side. Will you see me?'

He didn't have much time but invited me up. His room was on the second floor, the door was open, the view opened onto the square. Mischkey was sitting with his back to the door at a computer that had his full concentration and on which he was typing with two fingers at great speed. He called over his shoulder, 'Come on in, I'll be finished in a second.'

I looked around. The table and chairs were awash with computer printouts and magazines from *Computer Weekly* to the American edition of *Penthouse*. On the wall was a blackboard with 'Happy Birthday, Peter' scrawled on it in smudged chalk. Next to that Einstein was sticking his tongue out at me. On the other wall were film posters and a still that I couldn't assign to a particular film. 'Madonna,' he said without looking up.

'Madonna?'

Now he did look up. A distinctive, bony face with deep furrows in the brow, a small moustache, an obstinate chin, all topped with a wild mop of greying hair. His eyes twinkled at me in delight through a pair of intentionally ugly spectacles. Were the national health glasses of the fifties back in fashion? He was wearing jeans and a dark-blue sweater, no shirt. 'I'll call her up on screen for you from my film file.' He beckoned me over, typed in a couple of commands, and the screen filled in a flash. 'You know how it is when you're fishing for a tune that you can't quite remember? Problem of all music and movie buffs? I've solved that with my file, too. Do you want to hear music from your favourite film?'

'*Barry Lyndon*,' I said, and in the space of seconds came the squeaky but unmistakable start of the Sarabande by Handel, bam bam, ba bam bam. 'That's fantastic,' I said.

'What brings you here, Herr Selk? As you can see, I'm very busy at the moment and haven't much time to spare. It's to do with emissions?'

'Exactly, or rather, with a report on them for our computer journal.'

A colleague entered the room. 'Are you messing around with your files again? Do you expect me to deal with the registration data for the church? I must say I find you extremely uncooperative.'

'May I introduce my colleague Grimm? That's really his name, but with two "m's" – Jörg, this is Herr Selk from the computer journal. He wants to write about the office culture in RCC. Keep going, you're being most authentic.'

'Oh, Peter, really . . .' Grimm puffed out his cheeks. I placed them both in their mid-thirties, but one came across like a mature 25-year-old and the other like a man in his fifties who's aged badly. Grimm's grimness was only accentuated by his safari suit and his long, thinning hair. I kept what was left of my hair trimmed short. I wondered whether my hair situation might still get worse at my age, or whether the balding was over, just as getting pregnant is over for post-menopausal women.

'You could have called up the church report on your computer ages ago, by the way. I'm in the middle of the traffic census. It has to go out today. Yes, Herr Selk, it doesn't look good for the two of us. Unless you want to buy me lunch? At McDonald's?'

We arranged to meet at twelve-thirty.

I strolled up the main street, impressive evidence of the city council's will towards destruction in the seventies. It wasn't drizzling at the moment. Yet the weather couldn't make up its mind what to offer for the weekend. I decided to ask Mischkey about the meteorograph. In the Darmstadt shopping centre I came across a record shop. Sometimes I like to sample the zeitgeist, buy the representative record or the representative book, go to see *Rambo II* or watch an election debate between the chancellor and his challenger. There was a special offer on for Madonna. The girl at the till took a look at me and asked if she should gift-wrap it. 'No. Is that the impression I give?'

I walked out of the Darmstadt shopping centre and saw Bismarck-Platz ahead of me. I'd have liked to visit the old man on his pedestal. But the traffic didn't allow it. On the corner I bought a packet of Sweet Aftons, and then time was up.

16

Like an arms race

It was rush hour at McDonald's. Mischkey pushed us skilfully to the front. Following his recommendation, I chose a Fish Mac with mayonnaise, a small portion of fries with ketchup, and a coffee.

Mischkey, tall and lanky, ordered a quarter-pounder with cheese, a large portion of fries, three portions of ketchup, another small hamburger to 'fill the little gap afterwards', an apple pie, two milkshakes, and a coffee.

The full tray cost me almost 25 marks.

'Not expensive, is it? For lunch for two. Thanks for inviting me.'

First of all we couldn't find two seats together. I wanted to move a chair to a free space, but the chair was attached to the floor. I was bemused; neither as an attorney, nor as a private detective, had I ever come across the offence of theft of restaurant chairs. Eventually we installed ourselves at a table with two high school students who eyed Mischkey's assortment enviously.

'Herr Mischkey, the direct emission model file led to the first lawsuit dealing with computers since the national census, the first, also, to reach the Federal Constitutional Court. The computer journal wants a legal report from me since legal journalism is my field. But I've realized I need to figure out more of the technical side, and that's where I'd appreciate some information.'

'Mmm.' He chomped contentedly on his quarter-pounder.

'What sort of data-sharing is there between yourselves and the industrial firms you supervise the emissions for?'

Mischkey swallowed. 'I can tell you a thousand things about that, the transmission technology, the hardware, the software, you name it. What do you want to know?'

'Perhaps as a lawyer I can't formulate the questions precisely enough. I'd like to know, for example, how a smog alarm is triggered.'

Mischkey was in the process of unwrapping the hamburger for that little gap afterwards and drenching it in ketchup. 'That's actually quite banal. Sensors are attached at the points where the harmful substances escape from the plant, and we receive round-the-clock reports on the fallout. We record the levels and simultaneously they go into our meteorograph. The meteorograph is the result of the weather data we get from the German weather service. If emissions are too high or the weather can't cope with them, an alarm sounds in the RCC and the smog alarm machinery chugs into motion – as it did most excellently last week.'

'I've been told the factories receive the same emissions data as you. How does that work technically? Are they also linked to the sensors, like two lamps on a two-way adaptor?'

Mischkey laughed. 'Something like that. Technically it's a bit different. Since there's not one, but lots of sensors in the factories, the individual lines are already brought together within any one factory. From that collection point, if you like, the data come to us via fixed cable. And the factory in question draws its data from the collection point like we do.'

'How secure is that? I was thinking the industry might have an interest in falsifying the data.'

That got Mischkey's attention and he let his apple pie sink down without taking a bite. 'For a non-technician you ask some pretty good questions. And I have things I'd like to say about that. But I think that is for after this apple pie.' He gazed tenderly at the sickly pastry, which was giving off a synthetic cinnamon smell. 'We shouldn't stay here, we should finish our lunch in the café in Akademie-strasse instead.' I groped for a cigarette and couldn't find my lighter. Mischkey, being a non-smoker, couldn't help me.

The way to the café took us through the Horten department store; Mischkey bought the new *Penthouse*. We lost each other briefly in the crowds but found each other again at the exit.

In the café Mischkey ordered a piece of Black Forest gateau, a mixed-fruit tart, and a pastry to accompany his pot of coffee. With cream. Obviously he was a good burner of food. Thin people who can shovel so much down make me envious.

'And what about a good response to my good question?' I asked, picking up the thread.

'Theoretically there are two exposed flanks. First of all you could play around with the sensors, but they're so well sealed that it wouldn't go unnoticed. The other possible breach is the connection between the collection point and the factory's cable. There the politicians agreed to a compromise I consider rotten through and through. For at the end of the day you can't discount the possibility that, from this connection, emissions data may be falsified or, even worse, the programme of the smog alarm systems tampered with. Naturally we've built in security measures that we're constantly fine-tuning, but you can view this as being like an arms race. Every defence system can be out-tricked by a new attack system and vice versa. A never-ending, and never-endingly expensive, spiral.'

I had a cigarette in my mouth and was going through all my pockets looking for the lighter. In vain again, naturally. Then Mischkey, from the right breast pocket of his fine nappa leather jacket, took out two disposable lighters packed in plastic and cardboard, one pink, the other black. He tore open the packet.

'Is pink all right, Herr Selk? Compliments of the department store.' He winked at me, pushed the pink one over the table, and offered me a light from the black one.

'Former public prosecutor deals in stolen lighters.' I could just picture the headlines, and fiddled a bit with the lighter before pocketing it and thanking Mischkey.

'But what about the opposite direction? Would it be possible for someone to penetrate the factory's computer from the RCC?'

'If the factory's cable leads to the computer and not to an isolated data station . . . But actually you should be able to work that out yourself after all I've said.'

'So you really face off like the two superpowers, with offensive and defensive weapons.'

Mischkey tugged at his earlobe. 'Be careful with your comparisons, Herr Selk. If we follow your analogy, capitalist industry can only be the Americans. That leaves us employees of the state in the role of the Russians. As a public servant,' he straightened up, pulled back his shoulders, and made a suitably stately face, 'I must renounce this impertinent insinuation most strongly.' He laughed, slouched down, and gobbled his pastry.

'Something else,' he said. 'Sometimes I'm amused by the thought that the industry that fought for this damaging compromise has damaged itself. One competitor could naturally take advantage of our network to tamper with the system of another. Isn't that sweet, the RCC as the turntable of industrial spying?' He spun his pastry fork on his plate. When it stopped, the prongs were pointing at me.

I suppressed a sigh. Mischkey's amusing, playful reflections suggested an explosion in the circle of suspects. 'An interesting variant. Herr Mischkey, you've been a great help. In case I think of anything else may I give you a call? Here's my card.' I felt around in my wallet for the business card with my private address and telephone number on which I pose as freelance journalist Gerhard Selk.

We shared the route back to Ebert-Platz.

'What does your meteorograph say about the coming weekend?'

'It'll be fine, no smog, not even rain. It looks like a weekend at the pool.'

We said goodbye. I took the Römer roundabout to Bergheimer Strasse to get petrol. Listening to it running through the hose I couldn't help thinking of the cables between the RCW and the RCC and now God knows which factories. If my case was one of industrial espionage, I thought on the motorway, then there was something missing. The incidents in the RCW system, so far as I could recall, didn't add up to a case of espionage. Unless the spy had used them to cover his tracks. In which case, wouldn't his only reason have been that he feared someone was on his trail? And why should he fear that? Did one of the first incidents perhaps risk undoing him? I needed to take another look at the reports. And I needed to call Firner and get hold of a list of the firms connected to the smog alarm system.

I reached Mannheim. It was three o'clock, the blinds of Mannheim Insurance had already closed for the evening. Only the windows that showed an illuminated M at night were still on duty. M as in Mischkey, I thought.

I liked the man. I also liked him as a suspect. Here was

the joker, the puzzle-lover, the gambler I'd been looking for from the beginning. He possessed the necessary imagination, the requisite talent, and was sitting in the right place. But it was no more than a hunch. And if I wanted to nail him with that he'd serenely send me packing.

I'd tail him over the weekend. Right now I had nothing but a feeling and I didn't see how else I could follow the lead. Maybe he'd make a move that would bring me new ideas. Had it been winter I'd have stocked up at the bookshop for the weekend on computer crime. Shadowing someone is a cold and hard business in winter. But in summer it's fine. Mischkey was going to the pool.

17

Shame on you!

Mischkey currently lived in Heidelberg at number 9, Burgweg, drove a Citroën DS cabriolet with the licence plate HD-CZ 985, was unmarried and childless, earned 55,000 marks as a senior civil servant, and had a personal loan from the Co-operative Savings Bank for 30,000 marks, which he was paying back in an orderly fashion: all this I'd been told on Friday by my colleague Hemmelskopf at the credit bureau. On Saturday at 7 a.m. I was at Burgweg.

It is a small stretch of street, closed to traffic, and the upper part of it becomes a footpath leading to the castle. The residents of the five or so houses in the lower part are allowed to park their cars there and have a key for the gate that divides Burgweg from Unteren Faulen Pelz. I was glad to see Mischkey's car. It was a beauty, bottle-green with gleaming chrome and a cream-coloured hood. That's where the loan money had gone. My own car I parked in the hairpin bend of Neue Schlossstrasse from which steep, straight stairs lead to Burgweg. Mischkey's car was facing uphill; if he were to drive off I ought to have time enough to be in Unteren Faulen Pelz when he arrived. I positioned myself in such a way that I could watch the entrance without being visible from the house.

At half past eight a window opened at eye-level in the house I had taken to be the neighbour's and a naked Mischkey stretched out into the already mild morning air.

I just had time to slip behind the advertising column. I peered out. He was yawning, doing some forward bends, and hadn't seen me.

At nine o'clock he left the house, walked to the market by Heiliggeist Kirche, ate two salmon rolls there, drank a coffee in the drugstore in the Kettengasse, flirted with the exotic beauty behind the bar, made a phone call, read the *Frankfurter Rundschau*, had a quick game of power chess, bought some more stuff, went home to drop off the shopping, and came out again with a big bag and got into his car. Now it was time to go swimming, he was wearing a T-shirt with 'Grateful Dead' printed on it, cut-off jeans, Jesus sandals, and had thin, pale legs.

Mischkey had to turn his car but the gate below was open so I had real trouble getting my Opel behind him in time, one car between us. I could hear the music blasting from his stereo at full volume. 'He's a pretender,' sang Madonna.

He took the motorway to Mannheim. There he drove at eighty past the ADAC pavilion and the Administrative Court, along Oberen Luisenpark. Suddenly he braked sharply and took a left. When the oncoming traffic allowed me to turn I could no longer see Mischkey's car. I drove on slowly, and kept an eye out for the green cabriolet. On the corner of Rathenaustrasse I heard loud music die out all of a sudden. I nudged forward. Mischkey was getting out of his car and going into the corner house.

I don't know what struck me, or what I noticed first, the address or Frau Buchendorff's silver car gleaming in front of Christuskirche. I rolled down the right-hand window and leaned over to take a look at the building. Through a cast-iron fence and an overgrown garden I looked up at the first-floor balcony. Frau Buchendorff and Mischkey were kissing.

Of all people, the two of them had to be involved! I

76

didn't like it at all. Tailing someone you know is bad enough, but if you're discovered you can always pretend it's a coincidental meeting and extract yourself reasonably well. Theoretically that could also be the case for two people, but not here. Would Frau Buchendorff introduce me as private detective Self, or Mischkey as freelance journalist Selk? If things progressed to swimming I'd be staying outside. Too bad, I'd been looking forward to it and had packed my Bermudas especially. They were kissing fervently. Was that something else I didn't like?

I assumed they would set off in Mischkey's car. It was waiting with the top down. I drove a little further into Rathenaustrasse and parked so that the garden gate and Citroën were reflected in my back mirror. Half an hour later they drove past me, and I hid behind my newspaper. Then I followed them through what we call the Suez Canal to Stollenwörth-Weiher.

It's in the south of town and has two club swimming pools. Frau Buchendorff and Mischkey went to the Post Office Pool. I stopped my car outside the entrance. How long do young people in love go swimming these days? In my day at Müggel Lake it could go on for hours, probably that hadn't changed much. I had dismissed the idea of swimming but the prospect of sitting in the car, or leaning propped against it for three hours made me cast about for a different solution. Was this pool within sight of the other one? It was worth a shot.

I drove round to the swimming pool opposite and packed my Zeiss binoculars in my swimming bag. I'd inherited them from my father, a regular officer who lost the First World War with them. I bought an entrance ticket, pulled the Bermudas on and my stomach in, and stepped into the sunshine.

I found a space from which I could view the other pool.

The lawn was full of families, groups, couples, and singles, and some of the moms too had dared to bare their breasts.

When I extracted my binoculars from my bag I encountered the first, reproachful eyes. I pointed them at the trees, at the few seagulls there were, and at a plastic duck on the lake. If only I'd taken my ornithology guide, I thought, I could use it to inspire their confidence. Briefly I got the other pool in my sights; so far as distance was concerned I could have easily tailed the two of them. But I wasn't allowed to.

'Shame on you!' said a family father whose paunch hung over his bathing trunks, and his breasts over his paunch. He and his wife were the last thing I'd want to look at, with or without binoculars. 'Stop it right now, you peeping Tom, you, or I'll smash them.'

It was absurd. The men around me didn't know which way to look, whether to see everything or nothing, and I don't think it's too old-fashioned to believe the women knew exactly what they were doing. And there I was, not interested in the whole business at all – not that it couldn't have interested me, but at the moment it really didn't, now I only had my job on my mind. And now of all times I was suspected of lecherousness, accused, convicted, and pronounced guilty.

Such people can only be dealt with using their own weapons. 'Shame on you,' I said. 'With your figure you really ought to wear a top,' and tucked my binoculars into the bag. I also stood up and topped him by a full head. He contented himself by twitching his mouth disapprovingly.

I jumped into the water and swam over to the other pool. I didn't even have to get out; Frau Buchendorff and Mischkey had lain down near the water in the baking sun. Mischkey was just cracking open a bottle of red wine so I figured I had at least an hour. I swam back. My adversary had pulled on a Hawaiian shirt, was solving crosswords with his wife, and left me in peace. I fetched a bockwurst with fries and lots of mustard and read my newspaper.

An hour later I was waiting back at the car in front of the other pool. But it wasn't until six p.m. that the pair of them came through the turn-stile. Mischkey's thin legs were red, Frau Buchendorff had her shoulder-length hair loose and her tan was emphasized by her blue silk dress. Then they drove back to her place in Rathenaustrasse. When they came out again, she had on a boldly checked pair of Capri pants and a knitted leather sweater, and he was in a pale linen suit. They walked the few steps to the Steigenberger Hotel in the Augusta-Anlage. I skulked around in the hotel lobby until I saw them leave the bar with their glasses and make their way to the restaurant. Now I headed for the bar and ordered an Aviateur. The barman looked puzzled, I explained the mixture to him, and he nodded approvingly. We got talking.

'We're pretty damn lucky,' he said. 'There was a couple in here just now, wanted to eat in the restaurant. A card slipped out of the man's wallet and landed on the bar. He tucked it away again immediately but I'd seen what was on it: *Inspecteur de bonne table* with that little Michelin man. He was one of those people, you know, who do those guides. Our restaurant is good, but still, I alerted the maître d' right away, and now the two of them will get service and a meal they'll never forget.'

'And you'll get your star at last, or at least three sets of crossed knives and forks.'

'Let's hope so.'

Inspecteur de bonne table – well, damn. I don't think there are identity cards of that sort. I was simultaneously fascinated by Mischkey's imagination, and uncomfortable with this little con game. Also the state of German gastronomy gave me reason for concern. Did you have to resort to such means to get decent service?

I knew I could call it a day so far as tailing them was concerned. The two of them, after a last calvados, would return either to Frau Buchendorff's or to Mischkey's in Heidelberg. I would take a Sunday morning walk to Christuskirche and quickly ascertain whether both cars, no cars, or only Frau Buchendorff's were in front of the house in Rathenaustrasse.

I went home, gave the cat a can of cat food, and myself a can of ravioli, and went to bed. I read a bit more of *Green Henry* and wistfully pictured myself at Lake Zurich before falling asleep.

18

The impurity of the world

On Sunday morning I took tea and butter cookies back to bed and mulled things over. I was certain: I had my man. Mischkey corresponded in every way to the image I'd formed of the culprit. He was a puzzle-lover, a joker, and a gambler, and his con-man's impulses rounded off his profile. As an employee of the RCC he had the opportunity to penetrate the systems of the interconnected firms, and as Frau Buchendorff's boyfriend he had the motive to select RCW. The raising of the executive assistant salaries was an anonymous friendly gesture to his girlfriend. This circumstantial evidence alone wouldn't stand up in court if everything there was handled by the book. Yet it was convincing enough for me to think less about whether he was the one than about how to convict him.

To confront him in front of witnesses so that he'd fold under the weight of his guilt – ridiculous. To set him a trap, along with Oelmüller and Thomas, this time targeted and better prepared – on the one hand I wasn't sure of success, and on the other I wanted to have this duel with Mischkey myself with my own weapons. No doubt about it, this was one of those cases that packed a personal punch. Perhaps it even offered too personal a challenge. I felt an unhealthy mixture of professional ambition, respect for my opponent, burgeoning jealousy, the classical rivalry of the hunter and the hunted, and even envy for Mischkey's youth. I know much of this is simply the impurity of the world: only fanatics believe they can escape it and only saints do. Yet, it bothers me sometimes. Because so few people admit to it I tend to think I'm the only one who suffers from it. When I was a student at university in Berlin my professor, Carl Schmitt, presented us with a theory that neatly differentiated the political from the personal enemy, and everyone felt justified in their anti-Semitism. Even then I was preoccupied by the question of whether the others couldn't stand their own impurity and had to cover it up, or whether my ability to erect a barrier between the personal and the objective was under-developed.

I made some more tea. Could I get a conviction via Frau Buchendorff? Could I get Mischkey, through her, to tamper once more, this time identifiably, with the RCW system? Or could I make use of Grimm and his obvious desire to put one over on Mischkey? Nothing convincing came to mind. I'd have to rely on my talent for improvisation.

I could spare myself any further tailing, but on my way to the Kleiner Rosengarten, where I sometimes meet friends for lunch on a Sunday, I didn't take my usual route past the Wasserturm and the Ring, but instead walked past the Christuskirche. Mischkey's Citroën was gone and Frau Buchendorff was working in the garden. I crossed to the other side of the street so I wouldn't have to say hello to her.

19
Anyone for tennis?

'Good morning, Frau Buchendorff. How was your week-end?' At half past eight she was still sitting over her newspaper, opened to the sports page, and was reading the latest on our newest tennis marvel. She had the list of roughly sixty businesses linked to the smog alarm system laid out for me in a green plastic folder. I asked her to cancel my appointment with Oelmüller and Thomas. I only wanted to see them after the case was solved, and even then preferably not.

'So you're crazy about our tennis wunderkind, too, Frau Buchendorff?'

'What do you mean, "too"? Like yourself, or like millions of other German women?'

'I do find him fascinating.'

'Do you play?'

'You'll laugh, but I have difficulty finding opponents with whom I don't wipe the floor. In singles, younger players can sometimes beat me just because they're fitter, but in doubles I'm almost invincible with a reasonable partner. Do you play?'

'To brag like you, Herr Self, I play so well that it gives men complexes.' She stood up. 'Allow me to introduce myself. South-west German Junior Champion nineteen sixty-eight.'

'A bottle of champagne against an inferiority complex,' I offered.

'What's that supposed to mean?'

'It means that I'll beat you, but, as a consolation, I'll bring a bottle of champagne. However, as mentioned, preferably in mixed doubles. Do you have a partner?'

'Yes, I have someone,' she said pugnaciously. 'When should we do it?'

'I'd opt for this afternoon at five, after work. Then it won't be hanging over us. But won't it be difficult to get a court?'

'My boyfriend will manage it. He seems to know someone at the court reservation office.'

'Where will we play?'

'At the RCW sports field. It's over in Oggersheim, I can give you a map.'

I hurried to get into the computer centre and had Herr Tausendmilch, 'but this remains between the two of us,' print me out the current status of the tennis court reservations. 'Are you still here at five o'clock?' I asked him. He finished at four-thirty but was young and declared himself willing to make me another printout at five on the dot. 'I'll be glad to tell Firner how efficient you are.' He beamed.

When I got to the main gate I bumped into Schmalz. 'The cake proved palatable?' he enquired. I hoped the taxi driver had eaten it.

'Please pass on my warm thanks to your wife. It tasted quite excellent. How is little Richard?'

'Thank you. Well enough.'

Don't worry, poor Richard. Your father wants you to be extremely well. He just can't risk the sibilant.

In the car I took a look at the printout of the tennis court reservations, although it was already clear to me that I wouldn't find a reservation for Mischkey or Buchendorff. Then I sat in the car for a while, smoking. We actually didn't have to play tennis; if Mischkey turned up at five and a court was reserved for us, I had him. Nonetheless I drove to Herzogenried School to inform Babs, who owed me a favour, that she was duty-bound to play doubles. It was the morning break and Babs was right: kids were carrying on with one another in every corner. Lots of students had their Walkmans on, whether standing alone or in groups, playing, or smooching. Wasn't the outside world enough, or was it so unbearable for them?

I found Babs in the staffroom talking to two student teachers.

'Anyone for tennis?' I interrupted, and took Babs to one side. 'Really, you must play tennis with me this afternoon. I need you urgently.'

She kissed me, reservedly, as is appropriate for a staffroom. 'What an opportunity! Didn't you promise me a springtime excursion to Dilsberg? You only let me clap eyes on you when you want something. Nice to see you, but I'm annoyed.'

That's how she was looking at me, both delighted and pouting. Babs is a lively and generous woman, small and compact, and agile. I don't know many women of fifty who can dress and act so lightly without trying to play young. She has a flat-ish face, a deep furrow above the bridge of her nose, a full, determined, and at times severe mouth, brown eyes beneath hooded lids, and closely cropped grey hair. She lives with her two grown-up children, Röschen and Georg, who are far too comfortable at home to make the leap to independence.

'And you really forgot we went to Edenkoben for Father's Day? If you did, then I'm the one to be annoyed.'

'Oh dear – when and where do I have to play tennis? And do I get to find out why?'

'I'll collect you from home at quarter past four, all right?'

'And you'll take me at seven to choir; we're rehearsing.'

'Gladly. We're playing from five till six at the RCW tennis courts in Oggersheim, mixed doubles with an executive assistant and her boyfriend, the chief suspect in my current case.'

'How thrilling,' said Babs. Sometimes I have the impression she doesn't take my profession seriously.

'If you'd like to know more I can fill you in on the way. And if not, that's all right too, you just have to behave naturally.'

The bell rang. It sounded the way it did in my day. Babs and I went out into the corridor, and I watched the students streaming into the classrooms. They didn't just have different clothes and hairstyles, their faces were different from the faces back then. They struck me as more conflicted and more knowing. But the knowledge didn't make them happy. The children had a challenging, violent, and yet uncertain way of moving. The air vibrated from their shouts and noise. It almost felt threatening and I was cowed.

'How do you survive this, Babs?'

She didn't understand me. Perhaps because of the noise. She looked at me questioningly.

'Okay then, see you this afternoon.' I gave her a kiss. A few students wolf-whistled.

I appreciated the peace of my car, drove to the Horten parking lot, bought champagne, tennis socks, and a hundred sheets of paper for the report I'd have to write that evening.

20

A lovely couple

Babs and I were at the grounds shortly before five. Neither the green nor the silver cabriolet was parked there. It was fine with me to be first. I'd changed into my tennis things at home. I asked them to put the champagne on ice. Then Babs and I perched ourselves on the uppermost step of the flight of stairs leading from the restaurant terrace of the clubhouse to the courts. The parking lot was in view.

'Are you nervous?' she asked. During the drive she hadn't wanted to know more. Now she was just asking out of concern for me.

'Yes. Perhaps I should stop this work. I'm getting more involved in the cases than I used to. This time it's difficult because I find the main suspect very likeable. You'll get to know him in a moment. I think you'll warm to Mischkey.'

'And the executive assistant?'

Could she sense that, in my mind, Frau Buchendorff was more than just a supporting actress?

'I like her, too.'

We had chosen an awkward place on the steps. The people who had played until five went trooping up to the terrace, and the next lot came out of the changing rooms and bustled down the stairs.

'Does your suspect drive a green cabriolet?'

When my view was clear too I saw that Mischkey and Frau Buchendorff had just pulled up. He sprang out of the car, ran round and flung open her door with a deep bow.

87

She got out, laughing, and gave him a kiss. A lovely, vibrant, happy couple.

Frau Buchendorff spotted us when they reached the foot of the stairs. She waved with her right hand and gave Peter an encouraging nudge with the left. He, too, raised an arm in greeting – then he recognized me, and his gesture froze, and his face turned to stone. For a moment the world stopped turning, and the tennis balls were suspended in the air, and it was absolutely still.

Then the film moved on, and the two of them were standing next to us, and we were shaking hands, and I heard Frau Buchendorff say, 'My boyfriend, Peter Mischkey, and this is the Herr Self I was telling you about.' I went through the necessary introduction rituals.

Mischkey greeted me as though we were seeing each other for the first time. He played his part composedly and skilfully, with the appropriate gestures and the correct sort of smile. But it was the wrong role, and I was almost sorry that he played it with such bravado, and would have wished instead for the proper 'Herr Self? Herr Selk? A man of many guises?'

We went over to the groundsman. Court eight was reserved under Frau Buchendorff's name; the groundsman pointed it out to us curtly and ungraciously, involved as he was in an argument with an older married couple who insisted they had booked a court.

'Take a look yourselves, if you please, all the courts are taken and your name isn't on the list.' He tilted the screen so that they could see it.

'I can't allow this,' said the man. 'I booked the court a week in advance.'

His wife had already given up. 'Oh, leave it, Kurt. Maybe you mixed things up again.'

Mischkey and I exchanged a quick glance. He wore a

88

disinterested expression but his eyes told me his game was up.

The match we launched into is one I'll never forget. It was as though Mischkey and I wanted to compensate for what had been lacking in open combat before. I played beyond my capabilities, but Babs and I were properly thrashed.

Frau Buchendorff was in high spirits. 'I have a consolation prize for you, Herr Self. How about a bottle of champagne on the terrace?'

She was the only one to have enjoyed the game uninhibitedly and didn't mask her admiration for her partner and her opponents. 'I hardly recognized you, Peter. You're enjoying yourself today, aren't you?'

Mischkey tried to beam. He and I didn't say much as we drank the champagne. The two women kept the conversation going.

Babs said, 'Actually, that wasn't really a game of doubles. If I weren't so old, I'd hope you two men were battling for me. But as it is, you must be the one they're wooing, Frau Buchendorff.'

And then the two women were on to age and youth, men and lovers, and whenever Frau Buchendorff made some frivolous remark, she gave the silent Mischkey a kiss.

In the changing rooms I was alone with Mischkey.

'How does it go from here?' he asked.

'I'll hand in my report to the RCW. What they'll do with it, I don't know.'

'Can you leave Judith out of it?'

'That's not so easy. She was the bait to a certain extent. How else could I explain how I got on to you?'

'Do you have to say how you got on to me? Isn't it enough if I simply confess that I cracked the MBI system?'

I thought it over. I didn't believe he wanted to make

trouble for me, nor could I see how that would be possible. 'I'll try. But don't pull any fast ones. Otherwise I'll have to submit that other report.'

Back at the car park we joined the two ladies. Was I seeing Frau Buchendorff for the last time? I didn't like the thought.

'See you soon?' was her goodbye. 'How's the case coming along by the way?'

21

You're such a sweetheart

My report for Korten turned out to be short. Nonetheless, it took me five hours and a bottle of Cabernet Sauvignon before my draft was finished at midnight. The whole case replayed in front of me, and it wasn't easy to keep Frau Buchendorff out of it.

I saw the RCW–RCC link as the exposed flank of the MBI system that allowed not only people from the RCC but also other businesses connected to the RCC to access the RCW. I borrowed Mischkey's characterization of the RCC as the turntable of industry espionage. I recommended disconnecting the emission data recording system from the central system.

Then I described, in a sanitized way, the course my investigation had taken, from my discussions and research in the Works to a fictive confrontation with Mischkey at which he had declared himself willing to repeat a confession and to reveal the technical details to the RCW.

With an empty, heavy head I went to bed. I dreamt of a tennis match in a railway carriage. The ticket inspector, in a gas mask and thick rubber gloves, kept trying to pull out the carpet I was playing on. When he succeeded we continued to play on the glass floor, while beneath us the sleepers raced by. My partner was a faceless woman with heavy, hanging breasts. Her movements were so powerful, I was constantly afraid she'd crash through the glass. As she did I woke up in horror and relief.

In the morning I went to the offices of two young lawyers in Tattersallstrasse whose under-burdened secretary sometimes typed for me. The lawyers were playing Amigo on their computers. The secretary promised me the report for eleven o'clock. Then, back in my office, I looked through the mail, mostly brochures for alarm and security systems, and called Frau Schlemihl.

She hemmed and hawed a great deal, but eventually I got my lunchtime meeting with Korten in the canteen. Before I collected the report, I booked a flight on the spot at the travel agent's for that evening to Athens. Anna Bredakis, a friend from university days, had asked that I give her plenty of prior warning. She had to get the yacht she'd inherited from her parents sail-worthy and assemble a crew from amongst her nieces and nephews. But I'd prefer to be in Piraeus, haunting the harbour bars, rather than reading about Mischkey's arrest in the *Mannheimer Morgen* and having Frau Buchendorff connect me to Firner, who'd congratulate me with his silver tongue.

I arrived half an hour late for lunch with Korten, but I couldn't use that to make a point. 'Are you Herr Self?' asked a grey mouse at reception who'd caked on too much rouge. 'Then I'll call the general director straight away. If you'd be so kind as to wait.'

I waited in the reception hall. Korten came and greeted me rather curtly. 'Things not advancing, my dear Self? You need my help?'

It was the tone of a rich uncle greeting his tiresome, debt-producing, and money-begging nephew. I looked at him in bewilderment. He might have a lot of work and be stressed and hassled, but I was hassled, too.

'All I need is for you to pay the bill in this envelope. You could also listen to how I solved your case, but then again you could also let it be.'

'Not so touchy, my dear friend, not so touchy. Why

didn't you tell Frau Schlemihl right away what this is about?' He took my arm and led me into the Blue Salon once again. My eyes searched in vain for the redhead with the freckles.

'So, you've solved the case?'

I briefly summarized my report. When, over the soup, I came onto the slip-ups of his team, he nodded earnestly. 'Now you see why I can't hand over the reins yet. Nothing but mediocrity.' I didn't comment. 'And what sort of man is this Mischkey?'

'How do you imagine someone who orders a hundred thousand rhesus monkeys for your plant and deletes all account numbers that begin with thirteen?'

Korten grinned.

'Exactly,' I said. 'A colourful character, and a brilliant computer expert to boot. If you'd had him in your computer centre, these mess-ups wouldn't have happened.'

'And how did you get on to this brilliant chap?'

'What I choose to say on that is contained in the report. I don't have any wish to expand greatly on that now. Somehow I find Mischkey likeable and I don't find it easy to turn him in. I'd appreciate it if you weren't too severe, not too hard – you know what I mean, don't you?'

'Self, you're such a sweetheart!' Korten laughed. 'You've never learned to do things thoroughly or not at all.' And then, more reflectively, 'But perhaps that's your strength – your sensitivity lets you get inside things and people; it lets you cultivate your scruples, and at the end of the day you do actually function.'

He rendered me speechless. Why so aggressive and cynical? Korten's observation had got me where it hurt, and he knew it and blinked with pleasure.

'Don't worry, my dear Self, we won't cause any

unnecessary trouble. And about what I said – I admire it in you very much, don't get me wrong.'

He was making it even worse and looked me mildly in the face. Even if there was some truth in his words – doesn't friendship mean treading carefully when it comes to the lies the other person builds into his life? But there wasn't any truth in it. I felt a surge of fury.

I didn't want dessert any more. And preferred to have my coffee in the Café Gmeiner. And Korten had a meeting at two.

At eight I drove to Frankfurt and flew to Athens.

Part Two

I

Luckily Turbo likes caviar

In August I was back in Mannheim.

I always enjoy going on vacation and the weeks in the Aegean were spent in a glow of brilliant blue. But now I'm older I enjoy coming home more, as well. After Klara's death I redecorated the apartment. During our marriage I hadn't managed to assert myself against her taste and so, at fifty-six, I caught up on the pleasures of decorating that other people delight in when they're young. I do like my two chunky leather sofas that cost a fortune and also hold their own with the tomcat, the old apothecary shelves where I keep my books and records, and the bunk-bed in my study I had built into the niche. Coming home I also always look forward to Turbo, whom I know is looked after well by the next-door neighbour but who does, in his quiet manner, suffer in my absence.

I'd put down my suitcases and opened the door when, with Turbo clinging to my trouser leg, I beheld a colossal gift hamper that had been placed on the floor of the hallway.

The door to the next-door apartment opened and Frau Weiland greeted me. 'How nice that you're back, Herr Self. My, you're tanned. Your cat has missed you very much, haven't you, puss wuss wuss wuss? Have you seen the hamper yet? It came three weeks ago with a chauffeur from the RCW. Shame about the beautiful flowers. I did consider putting them in a vase, but they'd be dead now anyway. The mail is on your desk as always.'

I thanked her and sought refuge behind the apartment door from her torrent of words.

From *pâté de foie gras* to Malossol caviar it contained every delicacy I like and dislike. Luckily Turbo likes caviar. The attached card, with an artistic rendition of the firm logo, was signed by Firner. The RCW thanked me for my invaluable service.

They'd paid, too. In the mail were account statements, postcards from Eberhard and Willy, and the inevitable bills. I'd forgotten to cancel my subscription to the *Mannheimer Morgen*; Frau Weiland had stacked the papers neatly on the kitchen table. I leafed through them before putting them in a bin bag, and sampled the musty taste of old political excitement.

I unpacked and threw a load in the washing machine. Then I did my shopping, had the baker's wife, the head butcher, and the people in the grocer's shop comment admiringly on my rested appearance, and enquired after news as though all sorts must have happened in my absence.

It was the summer holidays. The shops and the streets were emptier, my driver's eyes picked out parking spaces in the most unlikely of places, and a stillness infused the town. I'd returned from my break with that lightness of spirit that allows you to experience familiar surroundings as new and different. It all gave me a floating sensation that I wanted to savour. I put off my trip to the office until the afternoon. Fearfully, I made my way to the Kleiner Rosengarten: would it have shut down for the holiday? But from a distance I could see Giovanni standing in the garden gate, napkin over his arm.

'You come-a back from the Greek? Greek not good. Come on-a, I make you the gorgonzola spaghetti.'

'*Si*, old Roman, great.' We played our German-converses-with-guest-worker game.

Giovanni brought me the Frascati and told me about a new film. 'That would be a role for you, a killer who could just as easily be a private detective.'

After the spaghetti gorgonzola, coffee, and sambuca, after an hour with the *Süddeutsche* by the Wasserturm, after an ice-cream and another coffee at Gmeiner I gave myself up to the office. It wasn't as bad as all that. My answering machine had announced my absence until today and not recorded any messages. In amongst the newsletters from the Federal Association of German Detectives, a tax notice, advertisements, and an invitation to subscribe to the *Evangelical State Encyclopedia* I found two letters. Thomas was offering me a teaching appointment on the security studies course at the technical college of Mannheim. And Heidelberg Union Insurance asked me to get in touch as soon as I returned from my holiday.

I dusted a little, flicked through the newspapers, got out the bottle of sambuca, the jar with the coffee beans, and poured myself a measure. While I reject the cliché of whisky in the desk of a private detective, there's got to be some sort of bottle. Then I recorded my new message, made an appointment with Heidelberg Union Insurance, put off replying to Thomas's offer, and went home. The afternoon and evening were spent on the balcony, seeing to this and that. The account statements got me calculating and I realized that with the jobs so far I'd almost fulfilled my annual target. And coming after the holiday, too. Most reassuring.

I managed to hold on to my sense of floating into the following week. The insurance fraud case I'd taken on I worked through without getting involved. Sergej Mencke, a mediocre ballet dancer at Mannheim National Theatre, had taken out a high insurance policy on his legs and promptly suffered a complicated break. He'd never dance again. A million was the sum in question and the insurance company wanted to be sure all was above board. The notion that a person could break their own leg repelled me. When I was a small boy, as an example of male willpower, my mother told me how Ignatius of Loyola re-broke his leg himself with a hammer when it healed crookedly. I've always abhorred self-mutilators, the young Spartan who let his belly be mauled by a fox, Mucius Scaevola, and Ignatius of Loyola. But so far as I was concerned, they could all have had a million if it meant them disappearing from the pages of our school-books. My ballet dancer claimed the break occurred when shutting the heavy door of his Volvo; on the evening in question he was running a high fever, had to get through a performance nonetheless, and afterwards wasn't himself. That's why he'd slammed the door although his leg was still hanging out. I sat in my car for a long time trying to imagine whether such a thing was possible. There wasn't much more I could do with the summer break that had scattered his theatre colleagues and friends in every direction.

Sometimes I thought about Frau Buchendorff and about Mischkey. I hadn't found anything about his case in the papers. Once I happened to walk along Rathenau-strasse and the second-floor shutters were closed.

2

Everything was fine with the car

It was pure coincidence that I got her message in time one afternoon in September. Normally I don't listen to any of the calls that come in the afternoon until the evening, or the next morning. Frau Buchendorff had called in the afternoon and asked if she could talk to me after work. I'd forgotten my umbrella so had to go back to the office, saw the signal on the answering machine, and called back. We agreed to meet at five o'clock. Her voice was subdued.

Shortly before five I was in my office. I made coffee, rinsed the cups, tidied the papers on my desk, loosened my tie, undid my top button, pushed my tie up again, and moved the chairs in front of my desk back and forth. Finally they stood where they always stand. Frau Buchendorff was punctual.

'I really don't know if I should have come. Maybe I'm only imagining things.'

She stood, out of breath, next to the potted palm. She smiled uncertainly, was pale, and had shadows beneath her eyes. As I helped her out of her coat her movements were nervous.

'Take a seat. Would you like a coffee?'

'For days I've done nothing but drink coffee. But, yes, please do give me a cup.'

'Milk and sugar?'

Her thoughts were elsewhere and she didn't reply.

Then she fixed me with a look of determination that forced down her scruples and insecurities.

'Do you know anything about murder?'

Carefully I put the cups down and sat myself behind the desk.

'I've worked on murder cases. Why do you ask?'

'Peter is dead, Peter Mischkey. It was an accident, they say, but I simply can't believe it.'

'Oh, my God!' I got up, paced back and forth behind my desk. I felt queasy. In the summer on the tennis court I'd destroyed a part of Mischkey's vitality, and now he was dead.

Hadn't I ruined something for her, too, then? Why had she come to me anyway?

'You met him just that one time playing tennis, and he did play pretty wildly, and it's true, he was also a wild driver, but he never had an accident and drove so confidently with such concentration – what happened doesn't fit.'

So she knew nothing about my meeting with Mischkey in Heidelberg. Nor would she refer to the tennis match that way if she knew I'd turned Mischkey in. It seemed he'd told her nothing, nor had she, in her role as Firner's personal assistant, discovered anything. I didn't know what to make of that.

'I liked Mischkey and I'm terribly sorry, Frau Buchendorff, to learn of his death. But we both know that not even the best of drivers is immune to road accidents. Why don't you believe it was an accident?'

'You know the railway bridge between Eppelheim and Wieblingen? That's where it happened, two weeks ago. According to the police report, Peter skidded out of control on the bridge, broke through the railings, and crashed down onto the tracks. He had his seatbelt on, but the car buried him beneath it. His cervical vertebra was broken and he was killed on the spot.' She sobbed convulsively, brought out a handkerchief, and blew her nose. 'Sorry. He drove that route every Thursday; after his sauna at the Eppelheim baths he rehearsed with his band in Wieblingen. He was musical, you know, played the piano really well. The section over the bridge is straight as an arrow, the roads were dry, and visibility was good. Sometimes it's foggy but not that evening.'

'Are there any witnesses?'

'The police didn't trace any. And it was late, around eleven p.m.'

'Did they check the car?'

'The police say everything was fine with the car.'

I didn't have to enquire about Mischkey. He'd have been taken to the forensic medicine department, and if any alcohol or heart failure or any other failure had been ascertained the police would have told Frau Buchendorff. For a moment a vision of Mischkey on the stone dissection table came to me. As a young attorney I often had to be present at autopsies. I had a sudden image of his abdominal cavity being stuffed with wood shavings and sewn up with large stitches at the end.

'The funeral was the day before yesterday.'

I considered. 'Tell me, Frau Buchendorff, apart from the details of the event, do you have any reason to doubt that it was an accident?'

'In recent weeks I often barely recognized him. He was morose, dismissive, turned in on himself, sat at home a lot, hardly wanted to join me on anything at all. Once he even threw me out, just like that. And he evaded all my questions. Sometimes I thought he had someone else, but then again he'd cling to me with a kind of intensity he hadn't shown before. I was at a complete loss. Once, when I was especially jealous . . . You'll think, perhaps, I'm not coping with my grief and am being hysterical. But what happened that afternoon . . .'

I topped up her cup and looked at her encouragingly.

'It was on a Wednesday that we'd both taken off to spend more time together. The day started badly and it wasn't the case that we wanted to spend more time with one another; actually I wanted him to have more time for me. After lunch he suddenly said that he had to go to the Regional Computing Centre for a couple of hours. I knew very well that wasn't the truth and was disappointed and furious and could feel his frostiness and imagined him with someone else and did something that I think is actually pretty lousy.' She bit her lip. 'I followed him. He didn't drive to the RCC, but into Rohrbacher Strasse and up the hill on Steigerweg. It was easy to follow him. He drove to the War Cemetery. I'd been careful to keep an appropriate distance. When I reached the cemetery he'd parked his car and was striding up the broad path in the middle. You know the War Cemetery, don't you, with that path that seems to lead straight to heaven? At the end of it there's a man-size, chiselled block of sandstone that looks like a sarcophagus. He went up to it. None of this made any sense to me and I hid in the trees. When he'd almost reached the block two men stepped out from behind it, suddenly and quietly, as if they'd come out of nothingness. Peter looked from one to the other; he seemed to want to turn to one of them, but didn't know which.

'Then everything went like lightning. Peter turned to his right, the man to his left took two steps, grabbed him from behind, and held him tightly. The guy on the right punched him in the stomach, over and over. It was quite unreal. The men seemed detached somehow, and Peter made no attempt to defend himself. Perhaps he was just as paralysed as I was. And it was over in a flash. As I started to run, the one who'd punched Peter took his glasses from his nose with an almost careful gesture, dropped them, and crunched them beneath his heel. Then just as silently and suddenly, they left Peter and disappeared again behind the sandstone block. I heard them running away through the woods.

'When I reached Peter he had collapsed and was lying awkwardly on his side. I . . . but that doesn't matter. He never told me why he had gone to the cemetery and been beaten up. Nor did he ever ask me why I'd followed him.'

We were both silent. What she'd recounted sounded like the work of professionals and I could understand why she doubted Peter's death was an accident.

'No, I don't think you're being hysterical. Is there anything else that seemed odd to you?'

'Little things. For example, he started smoking again. And let his flowers die. He was apparently strange with his friend Pablo as well. I met him once during that time because I didn't know what else I could do and he was worried, too. I'm glad you believe me. When I tried to tell the police about the thing in the War Cemetery they weren't in the least bit interested.'

'And that's what you want me to do, to carry out the investigations the police neglected?'

'Yes. I can imagine you're not cheap. I can give you ten thousand marks and in exchange I'd like clarity about Peter's death. Do you need an advance?'

'No, Frau Buchendorff. I don't need any advance, nor can I tell you now whether I'll be taking on the case. What I can do is conduct a kind of pre-investigation: I have to ask the obvious questions, check the evidence, and only then will I decide whether to take the case. Do you agree?'

'Good, let's do it that way, Herr Self.'

I noted down some names, addresses, and dates, and promised to keep her informed. I took her to the door. Outside the rain was still falling.

3

A silver St Christopher

My old friend in the Heidelberg police force is Chief Detective Nägelsbach. He's just waiting for retirement; since starting as a messenger at the age of fifteen at the public prosecutor's office in Heidelberg he may have constructed Cologne Cathedral, the Eiffel Tower, the Empire State Building, Lomonossov University, and Neuschwanstein Castle from matches, but the reconstruction of the Vatican, his real dream, is simply too much alongside his police work, and has been postponed for his retirement. I'm curious. I've followed my friend's artistic development with interest. In his earlier works the matches are somewhat shorter. Back then his wife and he removed the sulphur heads with a razor blade; he hadn't known that match factories also distribute headless matches. With the longer matches the later models took on a gothic, towering quality. Since his wife no longer needed to help with the matches she began reading to him as he worked. She started with the first book of Moses and is currently on Karl Kraus's *The Torch*. Chief Detective Nägelsbach is an erudite man.

I'd called him in the morning and when I was with him at ten o'clock in police headquarters he made me a photocopy of the police report.

'Ever since data protection came on the scene no one here knows what he's allowed to give out. I've decided not to know what I'm not allowed to give out,' he said, handing me the report. It was only a few pages long.

'Do you know who oversaw the accident protocol?'

'It was Hesseler. I thought you'd want to talk with him. You're in luck, he's here until noon and I've let him know you'll be coming by.'

Hesseler was sitting at a typewriter, pecking away laboriously. I'll never understand why policemen are not taught to type properly. Unless it's supposed to be a form of torture for the suspects and witnesses to watch a typing policeman. It is torture; the policeman brushes away at the typewriter helplessly and aggressively, looking unhappy and extremely determined – an explosive and fearful mixture. And if you're not induced to make a statement then at least you're deterred from altering the statement once it has been written and completed by the policeman, regardless of how unfamiliar he's rendered it.

'Someone who'd driven over the bridge after the accident called us. His name's in the report. When we arrived the doctor had just turned up and clambered down to the accident vehicle. He saw immediately that nothing could be done. We closed the road and secured the evidence. There wasn't much to secure. There was the skid mark showing that the driver simultaneously braked and swung the steering wheel to the left. As to why he did that there's no indication. Nothing points to the fact that another vehicle was involved, no shattered glass, no trace of body paint, no further skid mark, nothing. A strange accident all right but the driver lost control of his vehicle, that's all.'

'Where is the vehicle?'

'At Beisel's scrapyard, behind the Zweifarbenhaus, the brothel behind the railway station. The professionals examined it. I think Beisel will scrap it soon. The storage fees are already higher than the scrap price.'

I thanked him. I looked in on Nägelsbach to say goodbye.

'Do you know *Hedda Gabler*?' he asked me.

'Why?'

'It cropped up yesterday in Karl Kraus and I didn't understand whether she drowned or shot herself or neither of the above, and whether she did it in the sea or in a vine arbour. Karl Kraus is pretty complicated at times.'

'All I know is that she's one of Ibsen's heroines. Why not read the play next? Karl Kraus can easily be interrupted.'

'I'll have to talk to my wife. It would be the first time we interrupted something.'

Then I drove to Beisel. He wasn't there. One of his workers showed me the shell.

'Do you know what's going to happen with the car? Are you family?'

'I think it'll get scrapped.'

Looking at it from the rear right you'd have thought it was almost unscathed. The top had been down when the accident occurred and closed by the towing company, or by the expert, due to the rain; it was in one piece. On the left-hand side the car was completely crushed at the front and gashed open at the side. The axle and the engine block were twisted to the right, the hood was folded into a V, the windshield and the headrests lay on the back seat.

'Ah, scrapped. You can see, yourself, that there's not much to the car now.' So saying, he peered at the stereo with such obvious furtiveness that it caught my attention. It was completely intact.

'I won't take the stereo from you. But could I look at the car now, alone?' I slipped him a ten-mark note and he left me in peace.

I walked round the car once more. Strange, on the right headlight Mischkey had stuck black sticky tape in the shape of a cross. Again I was fascinated that the right side seemed almost intact. When I took a close look I discovered the blotches. They weren't easily visible against the bottle-green paintwork, nor were there many. But they looked like blood and I wondered how it had got there. Had Mischkey been pulled out of the car on his side? Had Mischkey bled at all? Had someone hurt themselves during the recovery? Perhaps it was unimportant but whether it was blood or not now interested me so much that I scraped off some shavings of paintwork where the stains were into an empty film canister with my Swiss penknife. Philipp would get the sample tested.

I pushed back the top and looked inside. I saw no blood on the driver's seat. The side pockets of the doors were empty. A silver St Christopher was attached to the dashboard. I picked it up; maybe Frau Buchendorff would like to have it even though it had let Mischkey down. The radio and cassette player reminded me of the Saturday I'd followed Mischkey from Heidelberg to Mannheim. There was still a cassette inside that I took out and pocketed.

I don't have much of a clue about the inner workings of cars. So I refrained from staring blankly at the motor or crawling under the wreck. What I'd seen was plenty to give me a picture of the car's collision with the railings and the descent onto the tracks. I retrieved my small automatic camera from my coat pocket and took a couple of pictures. Along with the report Nägelsbach had given me were some photos but they were scarcely recognizable on the Xerox.

4

I sweated alone

Back in Mannheim, the first thing I did was drive to the city hospital. I located Philipp's room, knocked, and went in. He was in the process of hiding his ashtray, complete with smouldering cigarette, in the drawer of his desk. 'Ah, it's you.' He was relieved. 'I promised the senior nurse I'd stop smoking. What brings you round my way?'

'I've a favour to ask you.'

'Ask me over a coffee, let's go to the canteen.' As he strode ahead, white coat billowing, a cheeky one-liner for every pretty nurse, he looked like a lecherous Marcus Welby, MD. In the canteen he whispered something at me about the blonde nurse three tables away. She shot him a look, the look of a blue-eyed barracuda. I'm fond of Philipp but if he's gobbled up one day by a barracuda like that he'll deserve it.

I fetched the film canister from my pocket and placed it in front of him.

'Sure, I can get your film developed in the X-ray lab. But now you're shooting pictures you're not comfortable taking to the photo shop? Well, Gerd, that's a shocker.'

Philipp really did have one thing on the brain. Was it the same with me when I was in my late fifties? I thought back. Following the stale years of marriage to Klara I'd experienced those first years as a widower like a second springtime. But a second spring full of romance – Philipp's pose as the gay Lothario was alien to me.

'Wrong, Philipp. There are some grains of paint in the film canister with something on them and I need to know whether it's blood, if possible which blood group. And it doesn't come from a deflowering on the hood of my car, as you're doubtless thinking, but from a case I'm working on.'

'The one doesn't necessarily contradict the other. But, whatever, I'll see to it. Is it urgent? Do you want to wait?'

'No, I'll give you a call tomorrow. How are things, by the way? Shall we drink a glass of wine sometime?'

We decided to meet on Sunday evening in the Badische Weinstuben. As we were leaving the canteen together he suddenly shot off. An Asian nurse's aid was stepping into the elevator. He made it just before the doors closed.

Back in the office I did what I should have done a long time ago. I called Firner's office, exchanged a few words with Frau Buchendorff, and was put through to Firner.

'Greetings, Herr Self. What's up?'

'I'd like to thank you very much for the hamper that was waiting for me when I got back from holiday.'

'Ah. You were on holiday. Where did it take you?'

I told him about the Aegean, about the yacht, and that I'd seen a ship full of RCW containers in Piraeus. He'd gone walking in the Peloponnese as a student and now had business every so often in Greece. 'We're protecting the Acropolis from erosion, a Unesco project.'

'Tell me, Herr Firner, how did my case proceed?'

'We took your advice and severed our system from the emission data site. We did so immediately after your report and since then haven't had any further annoyances.'

'And what did you do with Mischkey?'

'A few weeks ago we had him here with us for a full day and he had a great deal to say about the system connections, points of entry, and possible security measurements. A capable man.'

'You didn't get the police involved?'

'That didn't strike us as particularly opportune. From the police it gets into the press – we don't like that sort of publicity.'

'And the damages?'

'We considered that, too. If it interests you: some of our people found it unbearable simply to let Mischkey go after calculating the damage he caused at five million. But at the end of the day, fortunately, economic sense triumphed over the legal aspect. Also over the legal reflections of Oelmüller and Ostenteich, who wanted Mischkey's case to be brought before the Federal Court. It wasn't a bad idea: before the Federal Court the Mischkey case would have demonstrated the dangers to which businesses are prey under the new emissions law. But it would have brought undesirable publicity. Besides, we're hearing, via the Economics Ministry, about rumblings from Karlsruhe that would make any further arguments on our part unnecessary.'

'So, all's well that ends well.'

'That would have a somewhat cynical ring to it, I think, in the knowledge that Mischkey went on to die in a car crash. But you're right, for the Works the matter had a happy ending, all things considered. Will we be seeing you here again? I had no idea that the general and yourself were such old friends. He told me about it when my wife and I spent an evening at his home recently. You know his house in Ludolf-Krehl-Strasse?'

I knew Korten's house in Heidelberg, one of the first to be built in the late fifties from the perspective of personal security. I can still remember Korten one evening proudly demonstrating the cable car to me that connects the house, situated high up on the steep cliff above the street, with the entrance gate. 'If there's a power cut, it runs on my emergency power supply.'

Firner and I said our goodbyes with a few niceties. It was four o'clock, too late to make up for the missed lunch, too early to eat dinner. I went to the Herschel baths.

The sauna was empty. I sweated alone, swam alone beneath the high cupola with its Byzantine mosaics, found myself alone in the Irish-Roman steam bath and on the roof terrace. Shrouded in a large, white sheet, I dozed off on my deck chair in the rest room. Philipp was roller-skating through the hospital corridors. The columns he passed were shapely female legs. Sometimes they moved. Philipp avoided them, laughing. I laughed back at him. Then I suddenly saw that it was a scream that gashed his face. I woke up and thought of Mischkey.

5

Hmm, well, what do you mean by good?

The proprietor of Café O had expressed his personality in an interior design that summarized everything that was fashionable at the end of the seventies, from the imitation fin-de-siècle lamps and the hand-operated orange juice squeezer to the little bistro tables with the marble tops. I wouldn't want to know him.

Frau Mügler, the dancer, I recognized by the severe black hair pulled back into a little ponytail, her angular femininity, and her look of sincere engagement. She'd gone as far as she could to look like Pina Bausch. She was sitting at the window, drinking a glass of freshly squeezed orange juice.

'Self. We spoke on the phone yesterday.' She looked at me with raised eyebrows and nodded almost imperceptibly. I joined her. 'Nice of you to take the time. My insurance firm still has some questions regarding Herr Mencke's accident that his colleague may be able to answer.'

'How did you hit on me in particular? I don't know Sergej especially well, haven't been here in Mannheim for long.'

'You're simply the first one back from vacation. Tell me, did Herr Mencke strike you as particularly exhausted and nervous in the last few weeks before the accident? We're looking for an explanation for its strange nature.' I ordered a coffee; she took another orange juice.

'Like I said, I don't know him well.'

'Did anything attract your attention?'

'He seemed very quiet, oppressed at times, but what do you mean by "attract attention"? Perhaps he's always like that, I've only been here six months.'

'Who from the Mannheim National Theatre knows him particularly well?'

'Hanne was closer to him at some point, so far as I know. And he hangs out with Joschka a lot, I think. Maybe they can help you.'

'Was Herr Mencke a good dancer?'

'Hmm, well, what do you mean by good? Wasn't exactly Nureyev, but then I'm no Bausch. Are you good?'

I'm no Pinkerton, I could have replied, but that wouldn't have been appropriate for my role.

'You won't find another insurance investigator like me. Could you give me the last names of Hanne and Joschka?'

I could have saved my breath. She hadn't been there long; don't forget, 'and in the theatre we're all on a first-name-terms basis. What's your first name?'

'Hieronymus. My friends call me Ronnie.'

'I didn't want to know what your friends call you. I think first names have something to do with one's personality.'

I'd love to have run out screaming. Instead I thanked her, paid at the counter, and left quietly.

6

Aesthetics and morality

The next morning I called Frau Buchendorff. 'I'd like to take a look at Mischkey's apartment and things. Could you arrange for me to get in?'

'Let's drive over together after office hours. Shall I pick you up at three-thirty?'

Frau Buchendorff and I took the back roads to Heidelberg. It was Friday, people were home early from work and getting their homes, yards, gardens, cars, and even the pavements ready for the weekend ahead. Autumn was in the air. I could feel my rheumatism coming on and would have preferred to have the top up, but I didn't want to appear old and kept quiet. In Wieblingen I thought about the railway bridge on the way to Eppelheim. I'd go there in the next few days. Now, with Frau Buchendorff, the detour hardly seemed appropriate.

'That's the way to Eppelheim,' she said, pointing past the small church to the right. 'I have the feeling I should take a look at the spot, but I can't do it yet.'

She left the car in the parking lot at Kornmarkt. 'I called ahead. Peter shared the apartment with a friend who works at Darmstadt Technical University. I do have a key but didn't want just to turn up.'

She didn't notice I knew the way to Mischkey's apartment. I didn't try to play dumb. No one answered our ring and Frau Buchendorff opened the front door. The lobby contained cool air from the cellar: 'The cellar goes down two levels into the hillside.' The floor was made of heavy slabs of sandstone. Bicycles were propped against the wall decorated with Delft tiles. The letterboxes had all been broken into at some point. Only a faint light trickled through the stained-glass windows onto the worn stairtreads.

'How old is the house?' I asked as we climbed to the third floor.

'A couple of hundred years. Peter loved it. He had lived here since he was a student.'

Mischkey's part of the apartment consisted of two large interlinking rooms. 'You needn't stay here, Frau Buchendorff, while I'm looking around. We can meet afterwards in a café.'

'Thanks, but I'll manage. Do you know what you're looking for?'

'Hmm.' I was getting my bearings. The front room was the study with a large table at the window, a piano and shelves against the remaining walls. In the shelves files and stacks of computer printouts. Through the window I could see the rooftops of the old town and Heiligenberg. In the second room was a bed with a patchwork quilt, three armchairs from the era of the kidney-shaped table, one of the aforementioned tables, a wardrobe, television, and a stereo system. From the window I looked left up to the castle and right to the advertising column I'd stood behind weeks ago.

'He didn't have a computer?' I asked in astonishment.

'No. He had all sorts of private stuff on the RCC system.'

I turned to the shelves. The books were about mathematics, computing, electronics, and artificial intelligence, films and music. Next to them an absolutely beautiful edition of *Green Henry* and stacks of science fiction. The spines of the files indicated bills and taxes, guarantee certificates and instruction manuals, references and documents, travel, the public census, and computer stuff I barely understood. I reached for the folder of bills and leafed through it. In the references file I discovered that Mischkey had won a prize in his third year of high school. On his desk was a pile of papers that I looked through. Along with private mail, unpaid bills, programming notes, and sheet music, I came across a newspaper cutting.

RCW honoured the oldest fisherman on the Rhine. While he was out fishing yesterday on the river, Rudi Basler, who had turned ninety-five years old, was surprised by a delegation from the RCW headed by General Director Dr H. C. Korten: 'I didn't want to pass up the opportunity of congratulating the grand old man of Rhine-fishing personally. Ninety-five years old and still as fresh as a fish in the Rhine.' Our photo captures the moment in which General Director H. C. Korten shares the happiness of the celebrated man and presents him with a gift hamper . . .

The picture had a clear shot of the gift hamper in the foreground; it was the same one I'd received. Then I found a copy of a short newspaper article from May 1970.

Scientists as forced labourers in the RCW? The Institute for Contemporary History has picked up a hot potato. The most recent monograph from the *Quarterly of Contemporary History* deals with the forced labour of Jewish scientists in German industry from 1940 to 1945. According to this, renowned Jewish chemists among others worked in degrading conditions on the development of chemical war materials. The press officer of the RCW pointed to a planned commemorative publication for their 1972 centenary in which one contribution will deal with the firm's history under National Socialism, including the 'tragic incidents'.

Why had this been of interest to Mischkey?

'Could you come here for a moment?' I asked Frau Buchendorff, who was sitting in the armchair in the other room, staring out of the window. I showed her the newspaper article and asked her what she made of it.

'Yes, recently Peter had started asking for information on this or that about the RCW. He never had before. Regarding the matter of the Jewish scientists I even had to copy the article from our commemorative publication.'

'And where this interest stemmed from he didn't say?'

'No, nor did I push him to tell me anything because talking was often so difficult towards the end.'

I found the copy of the commemorative publication in the file entitled 'Reference Chart Webs'. It was next to the computer printouts. The R, the C, and the W had caught my eye as I was casting a resigned farewell glance at the shelves. The file was full of newspaper and other articles, some correspondence, a few brochures and computer printouts. So far as I could see, all the material was linked to the RCW. 'I can take the file with me, can't I?'

Frau Buchendorff nodded. We left the apartment.

On the homeward journey on the motorway the roof was closed. I sat with the file on my knees and felt like a schoolboy.

Suddenly Frau Buchendorff asked me, 'You were a public prosecutor, Herr Self, weren't you? Why did you actually stop?'

I took a cigarette from the packet and lit it. When the pause grew too long I said, 'I'll answer your question, I just need a moment.' We overtook a truck with a yellow tarpaulin, 'Fairwell' on it in red letters. A great name for a removal firm. A motorbike droned past us.

'At the end of the war I was no longer wanted. I'd been a convinced National Socialist, an active party member, and a tough prosecutor who'd also argued for, and won, the death penalty. There were some spectacular trials. I had faith in the cause and saw myself as a soldier on the legal front. I could no longer be utilized on the other front following my wound at the start of the war.' The worst was over. Why hadn't I simply told Frau Buchendorff the sanitized version? 'After nineteen forty-five I first worked on my in-laws' farm, then in a coal merchant's, and then slowly started doing private investigations. For me, my work as a public prosecutor didn't have a future. I could only see myself as the National Socialist I'd been, and certainly couldn't be again. I'd lost my faith. You probably can't imagine how anyone could believe at all in National Socialism. But you've grown up with knowledge that we, after nineteen forty-five, only got piece by piece. It was bad with my wife, who was a beautiful blonde Nazi and stayed that way till she became a nice, round Economic Miracle German.' I didn't want to say any more about my marriage. 'Around the time of the Monetary Reform they started to draft incriminated colleagues back in. I could have returned to the judiciary then, too. But I saw what the efforts to get reinstated, and the reinstatement itself, did to my colleagues. Instead of feeling guilt they only had a sense that they'd been done an injustice when they were expelled and that this reinstatement was a kind of reparation. That disgusted me.'

'That sounds closer to aesthetics than morality.'

'It's hard to tell the difference any more.'

'Can't you imagine anything beautiful that's immoral?'

'I see what you mean, Riefenstahl, *Triumph of the Will* and so on. But since I've grown older I just don't find the choreography of the masses, the bombastic architecture of Speer and his epigones, and the atomic blast brighter than a thousand suns beautiful any more.'

We had stopped by my door and it was approaching seven. I'd have liked to invite Frau Buchendorff to the Kleiner Rosengarten. But I didn't dare.

'Frau Buchendorff, would you care to dine with me in the Kleiner Rosengarten?'

'That's nice of you, many thanks, but I won't.'

7

A raven mother

Quite against my principles I'd taken the file with me to dinner.

'Working and eating izza no good. The stomach is ruined.'

Giovanni pretended to seize the file. I clung to it tightly. 'We always work, we Germans. Not the dolce vita.'

I ordered calamari with rice. I abstained from spaghetti because I didn't want to get any sauce stains on Mischkey's file. Instead I spilled some Barbera on Mischkey's letter to the *Mannheimer Morgen* with which he'd enclosed an advertisement.

Historian at the University of Hamburg looking for oral evidence from workers and employees of the RCW from the years before 1948 for a study of social and economic history. Discretion and reimbursement of expenses. Replies to box number 379628.

I found eleven responses, some in spidery handwriting, some laboriously typed, that answered the ad with not much more than name, address, and phone number. One response came from San Francisco.

Whether anything had come of the contacts wasn't revealed by the file. It contained no notes by Mischkey at all, no clue as to why he'd put this collection together, and what his intentions were. I found the contribution to the commemorative publication photocopied by Frau Buchendorff, and further on the small brochure of an anti-chemical-industry action group – '100 Years RCW – 100 Years Are Enough' – with essays on work accidents, suppression of strikes, the entanglement of capital and politics, forced labour, union persecution, and party contributions. There was even an essay about the RCW and the church with a picture of the Reich Bishop Müller in front of a large Erlenmeyer retort. It struck me that during my Berlin student days I'd got to know a Fräulein Erlenmeyer. She was very rich and Korten said she came from the family of the aforementioned retort. I'd believed him, the similarity was undeniable. What had become of Reich Bishop Müller? I wondered.

The newspaper articles in the file dated back to 1947. They all bore reference to the RCW but otherwise appeared to be ordered randomly. The pictures, sometimes blurred in the copies, showed Korten first as a simple director, then as general director, showed his forerunner General Director Weismüller, who had retired shortly after 1945, and General Director Tyberg whom Korten had replaced in 1967. The photograph of the hundred-year anniversary had captured Korten receiving Chancellor Kohl's congratulations and next to him he seemed small, delicate, and distinguished. The articles were full of news about finance, careers, and production, and now and again about accidents and slip-ups.

Giovanni cleared my plate away and placed a sambuca in front of me without a word. I ordered a coffee to go with it. At the neighbouring table a woman of around forty was sitting, reading *Brigitte*. From the cover I saw its lead article was 'STERILIZED – AND NOW WHAT?' I gathered my courage.

'Yes, indeed, now what?'

'I'm sorry?' She looked at me in confusion and ordered an amaretto. I asked her if she came here often.

'Yes,' she said. 'After work I always come here to eat.'

'Are you sterilized?'

'Believe it or not, I am sterilized. And after my sterilization I had a child, the sweetest little boy.' She laid down *Brigitte*.

'Incredible,' I said. 'And does *Brigitte* approve of that?'

'The case doesn't crop up. It's more about unhappy women and men who realize they want children after they've been sterilized.' She nipped at her amaretto.

I crunched a coffee bean. 'Doesn't your son like Italian food? What does he do in the evenings?'

'Would you mind if I joined you rather than screeching the answer through the entire restaurant?'

I stood up, pulled back a chair invitingly, and said I'd be delighted if she – well, the usual things you say. She brought a glass with her and lit a cigarette. I looked at her more closely, the somewhat tired eyes, the stubborn mouth, and the tiny wrinkles, the lacklustre ash-blonde hair, the ring in one ear and the Band-Aid on the other. If I didn't watch out I'd be in bed with this woman within three hours. Did I want to watch out?

'To come back to your question – my son is in Rio with his father.'

'What's he doing there?'

'Manuel is eight years old now and goes to school in Rio. His father studied in Mannheim. I almost married him, because of the residence permit. When the child arrived he had to return to Brazil and we agreed he'd take him with him.' I frowned at her. 'Now you consider me a raven mother. But I didn't get sterilized for the fun of it.'

A raven mother, indeed. Or at least an irritating one. According to German fairy tales, raven mothers and fathers push their fledglings from the nest. I never found out whether this does justice to real ravens, but it seemed to apply to her and I didn't have any particular desire to keep flirting. When I remained silent, she asked, 'Why the interest in the sterilization thing anyway?'

'First something clicked in my mind, because of the cover of *Brigitte*. Then you interested me, how composed you were as you dealt with the question. Now it feels too composed, the way you talk about your son. Perhaps I'm too old-fashioned for this kind of composure.'

'Composure can't be imparted. A shame that prejudices are always confirmed.' She took her glass and wanted to leave.

'Could you just say first what RCW brings to mind?' She gave me a frosty look. 'I know, it's a stupid-sounding question. But the RCW has been in my mind all day and I can't see the wood for the trees.'

She responded earnestly. 'A whole lot comes to mind. And I'll tell you, because there's something about you that I like. RCW to me stands for the Rhine Chemical Works, contraception pills, poisoned air and poisoned water, power, Korten—'

'Why Korten?'

'I massaged him. I give massages as it happens.'

'So you are a masseuse?'

'Masseuses are our impure sisters. Korten came for six months with back problems and he spoke a bit about himself and his work during the sessions. Sometimes we got into proper discussions. One time he said, "It's not reprehensible to use people, it's just tactless to let them notice." That stayed in my mind for a long time.'

'Korten was my friend.'

'Why "was"? He's still alive.'

Yes, why 'was'? Had our friendship been buried in the meantime? 'Self, you sweetheart' – again and again the words had gone through my head in the Aegean and sent a shudder down my spine. Submerged memories had resurfaced, blended with fantasy, and forced their way into my sleep. With a cry, I'd awoken from the dream bathed in sweat: Korten and I hiking through the Black Forest – I knew very well that it was the Black Forest in spite of the high cliffs and deep gullies. There were three of us, a classmate was with us, Kimski or Podel. The sky was deep blue, the air heavy and yet surreally clear. Suddenly stones crumbled and bounced away silently down the slope, and we were hanging from a rope that was fraying. Above us was Korten and he looked at me and I knew what he expected of me. Still more of the cliff tumbled silently into the valley; I tried to claw my way up, to secure the rope and pull up the third man. I couldn't do it and tears of helplessness and despair came to my eyes. I got out my penknife and started to cut through the rope beneath me. I have to do it, I have to, I thought, and cut. Kimski or Podel fell into the ravine. I could see it all at once, flailing arms, getting smaller and smaller in the distance, gentle mockery in Korten's eyes, as though it were all a game. Now he could pull me up and when he almost had me at the top, sobbing and bleeding, 'Self, you sweetheart' came once again, and the rope broke . . .

'What's wrong? What's your name, by the way? I'm Brigitte Lauterbach.'

'Gerhard Self. If you didn't come in your own car – may I after this bumpy evening offer you a lift home in my jolting Opel?'

'Yes, please. I'd have taken a taxi otherwise.'

Brigitte lived in Max-Joseph-Strasse. The goodbye peck on the cheek turned into a long embrace.

'Would you like to come up, stupid? With a sterilized and raven mother?'

8

An everyday sort of blood

While she fetched wine from the fridge I stood there in her living room with all the awkwardness of the first time. You're still wary about what might not grate: a canary in a cage, a Peanuts poster on the wall, Yevtushenko in the bookshelves, Barry Manilow on the turntable. Brigitte was guilty of none of the above. Yet the wariness was there – perhaps it's always in one's self?

'Can I make a phone call?' I called through to the kitchen.

'Go right ahead. The phone's in the top drawer of the bureau.'

I opened the drawer and dialled Philipp's number. It rang eight times before he picked up.

'Hello?' His voice sounded oily.

'Philipp, Gerd here. I hope I'm disturbing you.'

'You bet, you crazy dick. Yes, it was blood, blood type O, rhesus negative. An everyday sort of blood, so to speak, age of the sample between two and three weeks. Anything else? Sorry, but I'm tied up here. You saw her yesterday, remember, the little Indonesian in the elevator. She brought her friend along. It's all action.'

Brigitte had come into the room with a bottle and two glasses, poured it, and brought a glass over to me. I'd handed her the extension, and Brigitte looked at me in amusement at Philipp's last sentences.

'Do you know anyone at forensics in Heidelberg, Philipp?'

'No, she doesn't work at forensics. At McDonald's at the Planken, that's where she works. Why?'

'It's not Big Mac's blood type I'm after, but Peter Mischkey's – he was examined by forensics at Heidelberg. And I'd like to know if you can find out. That's why.'

'But it doesn't have to be right now. Come round instead, let's talk about it over breakfast. Bring someone with you though. I'm not slogging my guts out so you can come along and lick the cream.'

'Does she have to be Asian?'

Brigitte laughed. I put my arm round her and she snuggled into me demurely.

'No, my home is like a Mombasa brothel, all races, all classes, all colours, all lines of business. And if you're really coming, bring a bottle.'

He hung up. I put my other arm around Brigitte too. She leant back into my arms and looked at me. 'And now?'

'Now we take the bottle and the glasses and the cigarettes and the music over to the bedroom and lie down in bed.'

She gave me a little kiss-and-send in a bashful voice: 'You go ahead, I'll be right there.'

She went into the bathroom. Amongst her records I found one by George Winston, put it on, left the bedroom door open, switched on the bedside lamp, undressed, and got into her bed. I felt a little embarrassed. The bed was wide and smelled fresh. If we didn't sleep well tonight, the fault would be all ours.

Brigitte came into the bedroom, naked, with only the earring in her right ear and the plaster on her left earlobe. She whistled along to the George Winston. She was heavy round the hips, had breasts which were large and couldn't help but sag a little, broad shoulders, and a protruding collarbone which gave her an air of vulnerability. She slipped beneath the covers and into the crook of my arm.

'What happened to your ear?' I asked.

'Oh,' she laughed in embarrassment, 'combing my hair, I kind of combed the ring out of my ear. It didn't hurt, I just bled like a pig. The day after tomorrow I have an appointment with a surgeon. He'll make a clean wound of the tear and patch it together again.'

'Would you mind me removing your other earring? Otherwise I'll be afraid of tearing it out, too.'

'You're such a passionate guy?' She took it out herself. 'Come on, Gerhard, let me take off your watch.' It was nice to have her bending over me like that, fumbling with my arm. I pulled her down to me. Her skin was smooth and fragrant. 'I'm tired,' she said in a sleepy voice. 'Will you tell me a bedtime story?'

I felt relaxed. 'Once upon a time there was a little raven. Like all ravens he had a mother.' She pinched my side. 'The mother was black and beautiful. She was so black that all the other ravens appeared grey next to her, and she was so beautiful that all the other ravens appeared ugly next to her. She herself didn't realize it. Her son, the little raven, could see and knew it very well. He knew much more besides: that black and beautiful is better than grey and ugly, that raven fathers are as good and as bad as raven mothers, that you can be wrong in the right place and right in the wrong place. One day after school the little raven flew away and got lost. He told himself that nothing could happen to him: in one direction he'd be sure to encounter his father, and in the other his mother. Nonetheless he was afraid. Beneath him he could see a land stretching far and wide with small villages and large, gleaming lakes. It was pretty to look at, but frighteningly unfamiliar to him. He flew and flew and flew . . .' Brigitte's breathing had grown regular. She snuggled comfortably into my arms again and started to snore softly, her mouth slightly open. I carefully withdrew my arm from under her head and put out the light. She turned onto her side. So did I and we lay there like spoons in the cutlery case.

When I woke up it was just after seven and she was still asleep. I crept out of the bedroom, shut the door behind me, looked for and found the coffee machine, got it going, pulled on my shirt and trousers, took Brigitte's set of keys from the bureau, and bought croissants in Lange Rötter-strasse. I was back at her bedside with the tray and coffee and croissants before she woke up.

It was a lovely breakfast. And lovely afterwards together again beneath the covers. Then she had to leave to take care of her Saturday morning patients. I wanted to drop her off at her massage practice in the Collini Centre, but she preferred to walk. We didn't arrange another meeting. But when we embraced at her front door we could hardly pull ourselves apart.

9

Clueless for hours

It was a long time since I'd spent a night with a woman. Afterwards, returning home is like coming back to your own town after a holiday. A short period of limbo before normality kicks in again.

I prepared a special rheumatism tea, purely prophylactic, and lost myself in Mischkey's file once again. On the top was the photocopied newspaper article that had been lying on Mischkey's desk and that I'd shoved in the file. I read the connected commemorative piece entitled 'Twelve Dark Yards'. It touched only briefly on the forced labour of Jewish chemists. Yes, these had existed, but the RCW had also suffered with the Jewish chemists in this oppressive situation. In contrast with other big German businesses, RCW had generously compensated forced labourers immediately after the war. Using South Africa as an example, the author portrayed how alien any kind of mandatory employment situation was to the character of the modern industrial enterprise. Moreover, employment in the plant had lowered the rate of suffering in the concentration camps; the survival rate of the RCW forced labourers was proven to be higher than that of the average concentration camp population. The author dealt extensively with the RCW's participation in the resistance, remembered the condemned communist workers, and depicted in detail the trial of the general director-to-be Tyberg, and his erstwhile colleague Dohmke.

Memories of the trial came back to me. I'd led the inquiry then, while my boss, Södelknecht, the senior public prosecutor, had led the prosecution. The two RCW chemists were sentenced to death for sabotage and for some violation of the Race Laws, which I didn't recall. Tyberg managed to escape; Dohmke was hanged. The whole affair must have been at the end of 1943, beginning of 1944. At the start of the fifties Tyberg returned from the USA after succeeding very quickly there with a chemical company of his own, came back to RCW, and soon thereafter was made general director.

A large part of the newspaper article was devoted to the fire of March 1978. The press had estimated the damages at 40 million marks, no deaths or injuries were reported, and statements from the RCW were printed, according to which the poison released from the burnt pesticides posed absolutely no danger to the human body. I'm fascinated by such findings of the chemical industry: the same poison that annihilates the cockroach, which is supposed to be able to survive a nuclear holocaust, is no more harmful to humans than a barbecue on a charcoal grill. In the *Stadstreicher* magazine I found documentation by the group The Chlorine Greens that the Seveso poisons TCDD, hexachloroethane, and trichloroethylene had been released by the fire. Numerous injured employees were swept off in hush-hush fashion to the company's own treatment clinic in the South of France. Then there was a collection of copies and cuttings about the capital stakes of the RCW and about an inquiry by the Federal Antitrust Office, which dealt with the role of the plant within the pharmaceutical market and which went nowhere.

I sat for hours in front of the computer printouts, clueless. I found data, names, figures, curves, and incomprehensible acronyms such as BAS, BOE, and HST. Were these printouts of the files Mischkey had managed privately at RCC? I needed to talk to Grimm.

At eleven I started to call the numbers on the responses to Mischkey's ad. I was Professor Selk of Hamburg University, wanting to pick up the contacts initiated by his colleague for the social and economic history research project. The people on the other end were dumbfounded; my colleague had told them that their oral testimony wasn't of any use to the research project. I was puzzled; one phone call after the other with the same empty result. From some of them I gathered at least that Mischkey hadn't attached any value to their statements because they'd only started work at the RCW after 1945. They were annoyed because if my colleague had put out an ad that referred to the end of the war they could have saved themselves the trouble of responding. 'Reimbursements of expenses, it said, are we going to get our money from you now?'

I'd just put down the receiver when the phone rang.

'It's impossible to get through to you. What woman have you been talking to all this time?' Babs wanted to make sure I hadn't forgotten we were going to a concert that evening. 'I'm bringing Röschen and Georg. They enjoyed *Diva* so much they don't want to miss Wilhelmenia Fernandez.'

Of course I had forgotten. And while I'd been perusing the file, some little coil in my brain had disconnected so that it could play with the possibility of an evening arrangement incorporating Brigitte. Were there any tickets left?

'Quarter to eight at the Kleiner Rosengarten? I might be bringing someone with me.'

'So it was a lady on the phone. Is she pretty?'

'I like her.'

It was only to be thorough that I wrote to Vera Müller

in San Francisco. There was nothing specific I could ask her. Perhaps Mischkey had asked her specific questions, my letter attempted to find out just that. I picked it up and walked to the main post office on Parade-Platz. On the way home I bought five dozen snails for after the concert. I also got fresh liver for Turbo; I felt guilty about leaving him alone the night before.

Back home I was about to make a sandwich with sardines, onions, and olives. Frau Buchendorff prevented me. She'd had to type something for Firner that morning at the plant, was on her way home through Zollhofstrasse passing the Traber-Pilsstuben, and was quite certain she recognized one of the men from the War Cemetery.

'I'm in a phone-box. He hasn't emerged, I don't think. Could you come over straight away? If he drives off, I'll follow him. Head back home if I'm not here and I'll call you later, when I can.' Her voice cracked.

'My God, girl, don't do anything stupid. It's enough to jot down his registration number. I'm on my way.'

10

It's Fred's birthday

In the stairwell I almost flattened Frau Weiland. Driving off, I nearly took Herr Weiland with me. I drove via the railway station and the Konrad Adenauer Bridge, past blanching pedestrians and reddening traffic lights. When I drew up five minutes later in front of the Traber-Pilsstuben, Frau Buchendorff's car was still facing it in the No Stopping zone. No sign of her, though. I got out and went into the pub. One bar, two or three tables, a jukebox and pinball, maybe ten guests and the proprietress. Frau Buchendorff had a glass of Pils in one hand and a meat patty in the other. I placed myself next to her at the bar. 'Hello there, Judith. You're back in the neighbourhood, are you?'

'Hello, Gerhard. Join us for a beer?'

I ordered two meat patties to go with the beer.

The guy on her other side said in a thick Austrian accent, 'It's the boss's mother who makes these meat things.'

Judith introduced him to me. 'This is Fred. A real Viennese gent. He's got something to celebrate, he was saying. Fred, this is Gerhard.'

He'd already celebrated thoroughly. Lurching and weaving cautiously like all drunks, he took himself off to the jukebox, propped himself up to select records as though there were nothing amiss, came back and sat down between Judith and myself. 'The boss, our Silvia, is from

Austria too. That's why I like celebrating my birthday at her pub. And take a look, I've got my birthday present.' He patted Judith's bottom with the flat of his hand.

'What do you do for a living, Fred?'

'Marble and red wine, import and export. And yourself?'

'I'm in the security business, property and personal security, bouncers, bodyguards, dog trainers, and whatnot. I could use a strong guy like you. You'd have to go easy on the alcohol, though.'

'Well, well, security.' He set down his glass. 'There's nothing more secure than a firm ass. Right, sweetheart?' He now used the hand that had been holding the glass to grope Frau Buchendorff's posterior. Judith's butt.

She turned round and slapped down hard on Fred's fingers, looking at him impishly. It hurt and he withdrew his hands, but he wasn't mad at her.

'And what are you doing here with your security?'

'I'm looking for people for a job. There's money in it, for me, for the people I find, and for the contractor I'm on the lookout for.'

Fred's face registered interest. Maybe because his hands weren't permitted to do anything with Judith's butt for the moment, he tapped my chest with a fleshy index finger. 'Isn't that a bit too big for you, gramps?'

I seized his hand, forced it down, twisting his finger in the process, and looking at him innocently all the while. 'How old are you today, Fred? You're not the man I'm looking for? Never mind, come on, I'll get you a drink.'

Fred's face was contorted with pain. I let go and he hesitated for a moment. Should he lay into me, or drink a beer with me? Then his eyes went to Judith and I knew what was coming.

His 'Fine, a beer' was an overture for the punch that caught me on the left side of my ribcage. But I'd already rammed my knee between his legs. He doubled up, cradling his testicles. When he straightened up, my right fist hit him in the middle of his nose. His hands flew up to shield his face, then he lowered them again and stared incredulously at the blood. I reached for his glass and emptied it over his head. 'Cheers, Fred.'

Judith had stepped to the side, the other clients kept their distance. Only the proprietress joined the battle on the front lines. 'Clear out, if it's trouble you want, clear out,' she said, already jostling me towards the exit.

'But sweetheart, can't you see, we're just having a bit of fun? We're getting on just fine, isn't that right, Fred?'

Fred wiped the blood from his lips. He nodded and looked around for Judith.

A quick survey of her pub convinced the proprietress that peace and order had been restored. 'Well, then, have a schnapps on the house,' she said soothingly. Her establishment was under control.

While she was pouring them, and Fred had slunk off to the toilet, Judith came over to me. She looked at me in concern. 'He was one of the ones at the War Cemetery. Is everything all right?' She spoke softly.

'He may have smashed my ribs, but if you'll call me Gerd, I'll get over it,' I replied. 'Then I'd simply call you Judith.'

She smiled. 'I think you're exploiting the situation, but I don't want to quibble. I was just picturing you in a trench coat.'

'And?'

'You don't need one,' she said.

Fred came back from the toilet. He'd put on a hang-dog expression in front of the mirror and even apologized.

'Not bad shape for your age. Sorry I got out of order. You know, basically it's not easy to grow old without a family and around my birthday I really feel it.'

Beneath Fred's friendly veneer, malice and the crooked charm of a Viennese pimp shone through.

'Sometimes something wild takes over, Fred. The thing with the beer wasn't necessary, but I can't undo it.' His hair was still damp and sticky. 'Don't hold it against me. I only get mad when women are involved.'

'What shall we do now?' asked Judith with an innocent blink of the eyes.

'First we'll take Fred home, then I'll take you home,' I ordained.

The proprietress jumped on the bandwagon. 'Right, Fred, you'll be taken home. You can collect your car tomorrow. Come in a taxi.'

We bundled Fred into my car. Judith followed us.

Fred claimed to live in Jungbusch, 'in Werftstrasse, just next to the old police station, you know', and wanted to be dropped off at the corner.

I couldn't care less where he didn't live. We drove over the bridge.

'That big story of yours, is there anything in it for me? I've done some security stuff before, for a big company round here too,' he said.

'We can talk about it. If you're looking for some action I'd be glad to have you. Just give me a call.'

I fished out a business card from my jacket pocket, a real one, and gave it to him. At the corner I let him out and he headed with a swaying gait towards the next pub. I still had Judith's car in the rear-view mirror. I drove via the Ring and turned round the Wasserturm into the Augusta-Anlage. I'd expected a farewell flash of her lights beyond the National Theatre and then to see nothing more of her. She followed me to Richard–Wagner–Strasse outside my front door and waited, motor running, as I parked.

I got out, locked up, and walked over to her. It was only

seven strides but I gave them everything about superior manliness that I'd picked up in my second youth. I leant down to her window, no rheumatic expense spared, and pointed to the next parking space with my left hand.

'You will come up for a cup of tea, won't you?'

11

Thanks for the tea

While I was making the tea, Judith paced the kitchen, smoking. She was still extremely worked up. 'What a twerp,' she said, 'what a twerp. And he put the fear of God in me at the War Cemetery.'

'He wasn't alone that time. And do you know, if I'd let him get going, I'd have been more frightened myself. He's beaten up quite a few people in his time.'

We took our tea into the sitting room. I thought back to breakfast with Brigitte and was glad that the dishes weren't lying in my kitchen now.

'I still don't know whether I can take on your case. But you should consider whether I really ought to take it on. I've investigated Peter Mischkey's affairs before. I turned him in for breaking into the RCW computer system, as a matter of fact.' I told her everything. She didn't interrupt. Her eyes were full of hurt and reproach. 'I can't accept the way you're looking at me. I did my job, and that sometimes means using people, exposing them, turning them in, even if they're likeable.'

'So what? Why the great confession then? Somehow you're seeking absolution from me.'

I spoke into her wounded, cold face. 'You are my client, and I like things to be straight between my clients and me. Why I didn't tell you the story right away, you might ask. I—'

'I might well ask. But actually I really don't want to

listen to the slick, cowardly falsehoods you might care to tell me. Thanks for the tea.' She grabbed her handbag and stood up. 'What do I owe you for your trouble? Send me a bill.'

I stood up, too. As she was about to open the door in the hallway, I pulled her hand away from the door handle. 'You mean a lot to me. And your interest in clearing up what happened to Mischkey isn't satisfied. Don't leave like this.'

While I'd been talking, she'd left her hand in mine. Now she withdrew it and left without a word.

I shut the door to the apartment. I took the olives out of the fridge and sat on the balcony. The sun was shining, and Turbo, who'd been roaming the rooftops, curled up purring on my lap. It was only because of the olives. I gave him a few. From the street I could hear Judith turning on the ignition of her Alfa. The motor roared, then petered out. Was she coming back? A few seconds later the motor was running again and she drove off.

I succeeded in not thinking about whether I had behaved correctly, and enjoyed every single olive. They were the black Greek ones that taste of musk, smoke, and rich earth.

After an hour on the balcony I went into the kitchen and prepared the herb butter for the snails we'd eat after the concert. It was five o'clock. I called Brigitte and let the phone ring ten times. As I did the ironing I listened to *La Wally* and looked forward to Wilhelmenia Fernandez. From the cellar I fetched a couple of bottles of Alsace Riesling and put them in the fridge.

12

Hare and Tortoise

The concert was in the Mozartsaal. Our seats were in the sixth row, off to the left, so that our view of the singer wasn't obscured by the conductor. Sitting down, I cast a glance around. A pleasantly mixed audience, from elderly ladies and gentlemen right down to kids you could easily picture at a rock concert. Babs, Röschen, and Georg arrived in a silly mood; mother and daughter sticking their heads together and giggling, Georg sticking out his chest and preening. I sat between Babs and Röschen, patting the right knee of one and the left knee of the other.

'I thought you were bringing a woman of your own to pet, Uncle Gerd.' Röschen picked up my hand with the tips of her fingers and let it drop next to her knee. She was wearing a black lace glove that left the fingers free. The gesture was crushing.

'Oh, Röschen, Röschen, when you were a little girl and I rescued you from the Indians, you on my left arm, my Colt in my right hand, you never spoke to me like that.'

'There aren't any Indians any more, Uncle Gerd.'

What had become of my sweet girl? I took a sideways look at her, the postmodern angular haircut, and, hanging down from her ear, the clenched silver fist with the expressive thumb between the index and middle finger, the flattish face she'd inherited from her mother, and the somewhat too small, still childlike mouth.

The conductor was a slimy Mafioso, as short as he was fat. He bowed his permed head to us and drove the orchestra into a medley from *Gianni Schicchi*. The man was good. With the barest movements of his delicate baton he coaxed the most tender tones from the mighty orchestra. I also had to concede it was to his credit he'd placed an exquisite little female timpanist behind the kettledrums, in tails and dress trousers. Could I wait for her by the orchestra exit after the concert and offer my assistance in carrying her kettledrums home?

Then Wilhelmenia came on stage. She'd grown plumper since *Diva*, but looked enchanting in a glittering sequined evening gown. Best of all was *La Wally*. With her the concert ended, with her the diva conquered the audience. It was nice to see young and old united in applause. After two hard-fought-for encores, during which the small timpanist brilliantly made my heart turn somersaults again, we stepped lightly into the night.

'Shall we go on somewhere?' asked Georg.

'Back to my place, if you'd like. I've prepared snails and the Riesling is chilling.'

Babs glowed, Röschen moaned, 'Do we have to walk there?' and Georg said, 'I'll walk with Uncle Gerd, you can take the car.'

Georg is a serious young man. On the way he told me about his law studies where he was embarking upon his fifth term, about the grades he was getting and the criminal case he was working on at the moment. Environmental criminal law – that sounded interesting but it was just the usual camouflage for problems of perpetration, instigation, and being an accessory that I could have been asked forty years ago. Is it lawyers that have so little imagination, or reality?

Babs and Röschen were waiting by the front door. When I'd unlocked, it turned out that the lighting in the stairwell wasn't working. We felt our way up, with frequent stumbles and much laughter. Röschen was a bit afraid of the dark and pleasantly mute.

It turned into a nice evening. The snails were good and so was the wine. My performance was a complete success. When I took the cassette player with its small microphone that made pretty good recordings out of my inside pocket, opened it, and slipped the cassette into the tape deck on my stereo, Röschen recognized the reference immediately and clapped her hands. Georg got it when Wally started to sing. Babs looked at us questioningly. 'Mum, you'll have to check out *Diva* next time it's playing.'

We played Hare and Tortoise, the fashionable board game, and at half past midnight it was at a decisive stage and the wine all gone. I took my torch and went down to the cellar. I don't recall ever going down the main stairway without light before. But my legs had grown so used to the way over the long years that I felt quite secure. Until the second to last flight of stairs. Here the architect, perhaps to make the *belle étage* more impressive, and with higher ceilings, had built fourteen steps instead of the customary twelve. I'd never noticed, nor had my legs taken heed of this detail of the stairway, and after the twelfth step I took a large step out instead of a small step down. My legs buckled, I managed to hold on to the banister, but pain shot up my back. I straightened up, took a tentative next step, and turned on the torch. I got a terrible shock. The wall on the second to last section of stair has a mirror with a stucco frame, and in it I saw a man facing me, shining a beam of light right at me. It took just a fraction of a second for me to recognize myself. But the pain and the fright were enough to send me into the cellar with a hammering heart and unsteady step.

We played until two-thirty. When the taxi collected them and I'd mastered the dark stairs once more and cleaned up the dishes in the kitchen, I stood for the duration of a cigarette by the telephone. I felt an urge to call Brigitte. But the old school won.

13
Do you like it?

I frittered the morning away. In bed I leafed through Mischkey's file and thought again about why he had put it together, sipped at my coffee, and nibbled the pastries I'd bought yesterday in anticipation of Sunday. Then in *Die Zeit* I read a pastoral Op-Ed piece, a melodramatic political summary, the statesmanlike commentary from our ex-chancellor with the worldwide reputation, and the usual stuff from the owner. Once again I knew the lie of the land and so didn't feel the need to expose my mind to the food editor's review of a book on how to cook in a hot-air balloon. Then I smooched with Turbo. Brigitte still wasn't picking up. At half past ten Röschen rang the bell. She'd come to collect the car. I threw my dressing gown on over my nightshirt and offered her a sherry. Her brush-cut was in rack and ruin this morning.

At last I was weary of my pottering and drove over to the bridge between Eppelheim and Wieblingen where Mischkey had met his death. It was a sunny early autumn day; I drove through the villages, the mist was hanging over the Neckar, and although it was a Sunday, potatoes were being harvested, the first leaves were turning, and smoke rose from the inns' chimneys.

The bridge itself didn't tell me anything I didn't know from the police report. I looked down at the tracks that lay some five metres beneath me, and thought of the turned-over Citroën. A local train went by in the direction of

Edingen. When I walked across the car lanes and looked down on the other side I saw the old railway station. A beautiful sandstone building from the turn of the century with three floors, rounded bow windows on the second floor, and a little tower. The station café was apparently still open. I went in.

The room was gloomy, of the ten tables three were occupied, on the right-hand side was a jukebox, pinball, and two video games, on the counter, restored in the old German style, a stunted potted palm and in its shadow the landlady. I sat down at the free table at the window, with a view onto the platform and the railroad embankment, got a menu with *Wiener*, *Jäger* and *Zigeuner-schnitzel*, all served with fries, and asked the landlady what their special was, their *plat du jour*, to use Ostenteich's terms. She could offer *Sauerbraten* with dumplings and red cabbage, and broth with beef marrow. 'First rate,' I said, and ordered a wine from Wiesloch to go with it.

A young girl brought me the wine. She was around sixteen, with a lascivious voluptuousness that was more than the combination of too tight jeans, too tight a blouse, and too red lips. She'd have chatted up any man under fifty. Not me. 'Enjoy,' she said, bored.

When her mother brought me the soup I asked about the accident in September. 'Did you hear it at all?'

'I'd have to ask my husband about that.'

'And what would he say?'

'Well, we were already in bed, and then suddenly there was this smash. And shortly afterwards another. I said to my husband, "Something must have happened out there." He got up straight away and took the tear-gas gun with him, because our game machines are always being broken into. But this time it had nothing to do with the games machines, but with the bridge. Are you from the press?'

'I'm from insurance. Did your husband call the police?'

'My husband didn't know anything at that point. When he found nothing in the dining room he came back up and pulled some clothes on. Then he went out to the platform but he could already hear the ambulance siren. Who else could he have called?'

Her ample, blonde daughter brought the beef and listened attentively. Her mother sent her away to the kitchen.

'Your daughter didn't realize what was happening?' It was obvious they had a problem.

'She doesn't notice anything. Just stares at everything in trousers, if you know what I mean. I wasn't like that at her age.' Now it was too late for her. Her eyes were filled with hungry futility. 'Do you like it?'

'Just like home,' I said.

The bell in the kitchen rang, and she removed her willing flesh from my table. I wolfed down the *Sauerbraten* and the Wieslocher.

On the way to the car I heard quick steps behind me. 'Hey, you!' The kid from the station café was running after me breathlessly. 'You wanted to hear something about the accident. Is there a hundred in it for me?'

'Depends what you've got to say.' She was a hard-boiled little slut.

'Fifty upfront, and before that I don't even start talking.'

I wanted to know and pulled out two fifty notes from my wallet. One of them I gave to her, the other I rolled into a ball.

'So it was like this. That Thursday Struppi drove me home. When we came over the bridge, the delivery van was there. I wondered what it was doing on the bridge. Then Struppi and I, we, well, you know. And when the smash came I told Struppi to leave, as I was pretty sure my father would come any minute. My parents have something against Struppi because he's as good as married. But I love him. So what. Anyhow, I saw the delivery van drive off.'

I gave her the scrunched-up ball. 'What did the delivery van look like?'

'Strange, somehow. You don't see them round our way usually. But I can't tell any more. Its lights weren't on either.'

Her mother was peering out of the café doorway. 'Get over here, Dina. Leave the man in peace!'

'Okay, I'm coming.' Dina walked back at a provocatively slow pace.

Sympathy and curiosity prompted me to meet the man who'd been saddled with this wife and daughter. In the kitchen I came across a thin, sweating little guy juggling pots and pans and casseroles. He'd probably already made several attempts to kill himself with the tear-gas gun.

'Don't do it. The two of them aren't worth it.'

On the drive home I kept an eye open for delivery vans that aren't usually found round here. But I didn't see a thing, it was Sunday after all. If what Dina had told me was correct, there was, God knows, more to Mischkey's death than was contained in the police report.

When we met up in the evening at the Badische Weinstuben Philipp knew that Mischkey's blood group was AB. So it wasn't his blood I'd scraped off the side. What conclusions could be drawn?

Philipp ate his black pudding with relish. He told me about gingerbread hearts, heart transplants, and his new girlfriend, who shaved her pubic hair in the shape of a heart.

14

Let's stretch our legs

I'd spent half the Sunday with a case I didn't have a commission for any more. Private detectives don't do that, on principle.

I looked through the smoked glass out onto the Augusta-Anlage. Decided to decide at the tenth car how to proceed. The tenth car was a Beetle. I crawled behind my desk to write a closing report to Judith Buchendorff. Every end must have its form.

I took a writing pad and a pencil, and jotted down key points. What spoke against it being an accident? There was what Judith had told me, there were the two bangs that Dina's mother had heard, and above all there was Dina's observation. If I were continuing with the case, it was explosive enough to send me on an urgent hunt for the delivery van and its driver. Did the RCW have something to do with my case? Mischkey had done extensive research on it, with whatever intention, and it must be the large plant Fred had worked for once. Had Fred rained down punches that day in the War Cemetery on their behalf? Then I also had the traces of blood on the right side of Mischkey's convertible. And finally there was the feeling that something wasn't right, and various shreds of thought from the previous days. Judith, Mischkey, and a jealous, spurned rival? A different computer-hacking venture of Mischkey's, this time with deadly retaliation? An accident involving the delivery van, the driver of which committed a hit-and-run? I thought of the two bangs – an accident in which a third vehicle was also involved? Suicide? Had it all got too much for Mischkey?

It took me a long time to compose these half-baked things into a conclusive report. And I sat almost as long wondering whether I should write Judith an invoice and what should be in it. I rounded it off to a thousand marks and slapped on sales tax. When I'd typed the envelope, and stamped it and put in the letter and invoice and licked down the envelope, pulled on my coat and was ready to go and post it, I sat down again and poured myself a sambuca with three coffee beans.

It had all got fucked up. I'd miss the case, which had taken a stronger hold on me than work usually did. I'd miss Judith. Why not admit it?

When the letter was in the post box I turned to the case of Sergej Mencke. I called the National Theatre and made an appointment with the ballet director. I wrote to the Heidelberg Union Insurance asking if they'd be willing to foot the bill for a trip to the USA. The two best friends and colleagues of the self-mutilated ballet dancer, Joschka and Hanne, had both accepted engagements in Pittsburgh for the new season and had already left, and I'd never been to the States. I discovered that Sergej Mencke's parents lived in Tauberbischofsheim. The father was an army captain there. The mother said on the telephone I could look in at lunchtime. Captain Mencke ate lunch at home. I called Philipp and asked him whether in the annals of leg-breaks, self-induced breaks and breaks caused by a slammed car door were recorded at all. He offered to present his student with the problem as a dissertation theme. 'Three weeks okay for the results?' It was.

Then I set off for Tauberbischofsheim. I still had enough time to drive slowly through the Neckar valley and to stop for coffee in Amorbach. In front of the castle a school class was making a racket waiting for a guided tour. Can one really imbue children with a sense of the beautiful?

Herr Mencke was a bold man. He'd built himself a house, even though he might get relocated. He opened the door in uniform. 'Step right in, Herr Self. I don't have much time, I've got to head back in a minute.' We sat down in the living room. Jägermeister schnapps was offered, but no one drank.

Sergej was actually called Siegfried and had left his parents' house at the age of sixteen, much to his mother's distress. Father and son had broken ties with one another. The sporty son still wasn't forgiven for having evaded army service with a bogus spinal-chord injury. The path leading to ballet had also met with disapproval. 'Perhaps it's also got a good side, his not being able to dance any more,' his mother mused. 'When I visited him in hospital, he was just like my Sigi again.'

I asked how Siegfried had coped financially since then. There were apparently always some friends, or girlfriends, who supported him. Herr Mencke poured himself a Jägermeister after all.

'I'd have liked to give him something from Granny's inheritance. But you didn't want that.' She turned reproachful eyes on her husband. 'You've just driven him deeper into everything.'

'Leave it, Ella. That isn't of interest to the insurance man. I must be getting back. Come along, Herr Self, I'll see you out.' He stood in the doorway and watched me until I'd driven off.

On the journey home I stopped in at Adelsheim. The inn was full; a few business people, teachers from the boarding school, and at one table three gentlemen who gave me the feeling they were a judge, a prosecutor, and a defence lawyer from the Adelsheim local court, negotiating in peace and quiet without the bothersome presence of the accused. I remembered my days at court.

In Mannheim I met the rush-hour traffic and needed twenty minutes for the five hundred metres through the Augusta-Anlage. I opened the door to the office.

'Gerd,' someone called, and as I turned I saw Judith coming from the other side of the street through the parked cars. 'Can we talk for a moment?'

I locked the door again. 'Let's stretch our legs.'

We walked up Mollstrasse and along Richard-Wagner-Strasse. It took a while before she said anything. 'I overreacted on Saturday. I still don't think it's good you didn't tell me straight away on Wednesday about Peter and you. But somehow I can understand how you felt, and the way I acted as though you're not to be trusted, I'm sorry about that. I can get pretty hysterical since Peter's death.'

I needed a while, too. 'This morning I wrote you a final report. You'll find it along with an invoice in your mail, today or tomorrow. It was sad. It felt as though I was having to tear something out of my heart: you, Peter Mischkey, some better understanding of myself that I was getting from the case.'

'Then, you'll agree to continue? Just tell me what's in your report.'

We'd reached the art museum; a few drops were falling. We went in and, wandering through the nineteenth-century painting galleries, I told her what I'd discovered, my theories, and what I was pondering. In front of Feuerbach's painting of Iphigenia on Aulis she stopped. 'This is a beautiful painting. Do you know the story behind it?'

'I think Agamemnon, her father, has just deposited her as a sacrifice to the goddess Artemis so that a wind will start to blow again and the Greek fleet can set sail for Troy. I love the painting.'

'I'd like to know who that lady was.'

'The model, you mean? Feuerbach loved her very much. Nanna, the wife of a cobbler from Rome. He quit smoking for her sake. Then she ran away from him and her husband with an Englishman.'

We walked to the exit and saw it was still raining. 'What do you plan to do next?' Judith asked.

'Tomorrow I want to talk to Grimm, Peter Mischkey's colleague in the Regional Computer Centre, and with a few people from RCW again.'

'Is there anything I can do?'

'If something comes to mind, I'll let you know. Does Firner actually know about you and Mischkey, and that you've hired me?'

'I haven't said anything to him. But why did he never actually tell me about Peter's involvement in our computer story? To begin with he always kept me up to date.'

'So you never realized that I'd tied up the case?'

'Well yes, a report from you crossed my desk. It was all very technical.'

'You only got the first part. Why, I would like to know. Do you think you can find out?'

She'd try. The rain had stopped, it had grown dark, and the first lights were coming on. The rain had brought the stench from the RCW with it. On the way to her car we didn't talk. There was weariness in Judith's step. As I said goodbye I could also see the deep tiredness in her eyes. She felt my eyes on her. 'I'm not looking good at the moment, right?'

'No, you should go away somewhere.'

'In recent years I've always gone on holiday with Peter. We met each other at Club Med, you know. We should be in Sicily now, we always travelled south in the late autumn.' She started to cry.

I put my arm round her shoulders. I didn't know what to say. She kept crying.

15

The guard still knew me

Grimm was barely recognizable. The safari suit had been exchanged for woollen flannel trousers and a leather jacket, his hair was cut short, his upper lip sported, resplendent, a carefully sculpted pencil moustache, and along with the new look there was a new confidence on display.

'Hello, Herr Self. Or should I say Selk? What brings you here?'

What was I to make of this? Mischkey wouldn't have told him about me. Who else then? Someone from the RCW. A coincidence? 'Good that you know. That makes my job simpler. I need to look at the files Mischkey worked on here. Would you show them to me, please?'

'What? I don't understand. There aren't any files of Peter's here any more.' He looked puzzled, and a shade mistrustful. 'Under whose mandate are you here, actually?'

'Two guesses. So you've deleted the files? Perhaps that's for the best. Tell me what you think of this.' I took the computer printout from my briefcase, the one I'd found in Mischkey's file.

He spread it in front of him on the table and leafed through it for quite a while. 'Where did you get this from? It's five weeks old, was printed here in the building, but has nothing to do with our stock.' He shook his head thoughtfully. 'I'd like to keep this here.' He glanced at his watch. 'I must be off to the meeting now.'

'I'll gladly bring you the printout again. I have to take it with me now.'

Grimm gave it to me, but it felt as though I were wrenching it from him. I put the obviously explosive contraband into my briefcase. 'Who took over Mischkey's responsibilities?'

Grimm looked at me in sheer alarm. He stood up. 'I don't understand, Herr Self ... Let's continue our discussion another time. I really must get to this meeting.' He escorted me to the door.

I stepped out of the building, saw a phone-box on Ebertplatz, and called Hemmelskopf immediately. 'Do you have anything at all at the credit bureau on a Jörg Grimm?'

'Grimm ... Grimm ... If we have something on him, it'll come up on the screen in a second. Just a moment ... There he is, Grimm, Jörg, born nineteenth November nineteen forty-eight, married, two children, resident of Heidelberg, in Furtwänglerstrasse, drives a red Escort, HD-S 735. He had debts once, seems to have made something of himself, though. Just around two weeks ago he paid back the loan at the Cooperative Bank. That was around 40,000 marks.'

I thanked him. That wasn't sufficient for Hemmelskopf, though. 'My wife is still waiting for that ficus tree you promised her in spring. When can you come by?'

I added Grimm to the list of suspects. Two people are involved with one another. One dies, the other gets rich, and the one who gets rich also knows too much – I didn't have a theory, but it seemed fishy.

The RCW had never asked me to return my entry pass. With it I had no problem finding a parking space. The guard still knew me and saluted. I went to the computer centre and sought out Tausendmilch without falling into the hands of Oelmüller. I'd have found it unpleasant having to explain to him what I was doing here. Tausendmilch was alert, keen, and quick on the uptake as ever. He whistled through his teeth.

'These are our data. A curious mixture. And the printout isn't from here. I thought everything was quiet again. Should I try to trace the printout?'

'Leave it. But could you tell me what these data are?'

Tausendmilch sat down at a computer and said, 'I'll have to flip through a bit.'

I waited patiently.

'Here we have a list of people on sick leave from spring and summer nineteen seventy-eight, then registers of our inventions and inventors' royalties, way back to before nineteen forty-five, and here's . . . I can't open it but the abbreviations might also stand for other chemical companies.' He turned the machine off. 'I wanted to thank you very much. Firner called me in and said you'd praised me in your report and that he had plans for me.'

I left a happy person behind. For a moment I could picture Tausendmilch, on whose right hand I'd spotted a wedding ring, coming home after work that day and telling his elegant wife, who had a martini ready for him and in her way was contributing to his rise, about his success today.

At security I sought out Thomas. On the wall of his office hung a half-finished plan of the course for security studies. 'I had something to do in the plant and wanted to discuss your kind offer of a teaching appointment. To what do I owe the honour?'

'I was impressed by how you solved our data-security problem. You taught us some things here, Oelmüller in particular. And it would be indispensable for the curriculum to have a freelancer involved.'

'What would be the subject?'

'The detective's work: from the practical to the ethical. With seminars and a final exam if that's not too much trouble. The whole thing should start in the winter term.'

'I see a problem there, Herr Thomas. According to your concept, and it also seems sensible to me, I can only teach the students by using my experience with real cases. But think of the business here at the Works we were just discussing. Even if I didn't mention any names and I went to lengths to disguise the whole thing a bit, it would be a case of the king's birthday suit.'

Thomas didn't get it. 'Do you mean Herr King in export coordination? But he doesn't have a birthday suit. And besides—'

'You still had some trouble with the case, Firner told me.'

'Yes, things were a bit tough with Mischkey.'

'Should I have been harsher?'

'He was rather uncooperative when you left him with us.'

'After everything I heard from Firner he was given the kid-glove treatment. No talk of police and court and prison – that would only encourage a lack of cooperation.'

'But Herr Self, we didn't tell him that. The problem lay elsewhere. He virtually tried to blackmail us. We never found out whether he really had something up his sleeve, but he made some noise.'

'With the same old stories?'

'Yes, with the same old stories. Threatening to go to the press, to the competition, to the union, to the plant authorities, to the Federal Antitrust Office. You know, it's tough to say this, and I'm sorry about Mischkey's death, but at the same time I'm happy not to be burdened with this problem any more.'

Danckelmann came in without knocking. 'Ah, Herr

Self, you've been the topic of conversation today already. Why are you still involved in this Mischkey business? The case is long since closed. Don't go rattling cages.'

Just as I had been when talking to Thomas, I was on thin ice with Danckelmann. Questions that were too direct could make it crack. But nothing ventured, nothing gained. 'Did Grimm call you?'

Danckelmann ignored my question. 'Seriously, Herr Self, keep your nose out of this story. We don't appreciate it.'

'For me, cases are only over when I know everything. Did you know, for example, that Mischkey took another stroll around your system?'

Thomas pricked up his ears and looked disconcerted. He was already regretting his offer of a teaching appointment.

Danckelmann controlled himself and his voice was tight. 'Curious notion you have of a job. It's over when the client says it's over. And Herr Mischkey isn't strolling anywhere any more. So please . . .'

I'd heard more than I'd dreamed possible and had no interest in a further escalation. Just one more wrong word and Danckelmann would remember my special ID. 'You're absolutely right, Herr Danckelmann. On the other hand, you certainly agree that when security is involved, things can't always be contained within the narrow limits of a job. And don't worry, being a freelancer, I can't afford to invest too much without a fee.'

Danckelmann left the room only partially appeased. Thomas was waiting impatiently for me to be gone. But I still had a treat for him. 'To return to what you were saying, Herr Thomas, I'm happy to accept the teaching appointment. I'll draw up a curriculum.'

'Thank you for your interest, Herr Self. We're around.'

I left security and found myself back in the courtyard

with Aristotle, Schwarz, Mendeleyev, and Kekulé. On the north side of the yard a sleepy autumn sun was shining. I sat down on the top step of a small staircase leading to a walled-up door. I had more than enough to think about.

16

Dad's dearest wish

More and more pieces of the jigsaw puzzle were fitting together. Yet they still didn't add up to a plausible picture. I now understood what Mischkey's file was: a collection of everything he could muster against the RCW. A wretched collection. He must have been playing high-stakes poker to impress Danckelmann and Thomas as much as he obviously had. But what did he want to achieve or prevent by this? The RCW hadn't told him to his face that they had no intention of instituting proceedings against him with the police, court, and prison. Why had they wanted to exert pressure? What were their intentions towards Mischkey, and what was he arming himself against with his feeble insinuations and threats?

My thoughts turned to Grimm. He'd come into money, he'd produced some strange reactions that morning, and I was fairly certain he had talked to Danckelmann. Was Grimm the RCW's man in the RCC? Had the RCW initially assigned this role to Mischkey? We won't go to the police, and you'll ensure our emissions data are always squeaky clean? Such a man would be valuable indeed. The monitoring system would be rendered obsolete and wouldn't interfere with production.

But none of this necessarily made the murder of Mischkey plausible. Grimm as the murderer, wanting to do business with the RCW and to have Mischkey out of the way? Or did Mischkey's material contain some other dynamite that had evaded me thus far, that had provoked the deadly reaction of the RCW? But then Danckelmann and Thomas could scarcely have overlooked such an act, and they wouldn't have spoken so openly to me about the conflict with Mischkey. And while Grimm might make a better impression than in his safari suit, even with his pencil moustache I couldn't picture him as a murderer. Was I looking in completely the wrong direction? Fred might have beaten up Mischkey under contract from the RCW, but also from any other employer, and he could have killed him for them. What did I know about all the ways Mischkey could have entangled himself through his confidence tricks? I'd have to talk to Fred again.

I took my leave of Aristotle. The courtyards of the old factory worked their magic again. I walked through the archway into the next courtyard, its walls glowing in the autumnal red of the Virginia creeper. No Richard playing with his ball. I rang the bell of the Schmalzes' work apartment. The elderly woman, whom I recognized by sight, opened the door. She was dressed in black.

'Frau Schmalz? Hello, the name is Self.'

'Hello, Herr Self. You're joining us for the funeral? The children will be collecting me any minute.'

Half an hour later I found myself in the crematorium of Ludwigshafen Cemetery. The family had included me in the mourning for Schmalz senior as though it were perfectly natural, and I didn't like to say that I'd stumbled upon the funeral preparations just by chance. Along with Frau Schmalz, the young married Schmalz couple, and their son Richard, I was driven to the cemetery, glad to be wearing my dark-blue raincoat and the muted suit. During the drive I learned that Schmalz senior had died of a heart attack four days ago.

'He looked so sprightly when I saw him a few weeks ago.'

The widow sobbed. My lisping friend told me about the circumstances that had led to his death. 'Dad kept on tinkering with old vans and trucks after retiring. He had a part of the old hangar by the Rhine where he could work. Lately he didn't take care. The cut in his hand didn't go that deep but according to the doctor he had heavy bleeding in the brain, too. After that Dad felt a tingling in the left part of the body all the time, he felt terribly unwell, and he didn't want to get out of bed. Then the heart attack.'

The RCW was well represented at the cemetery. Danckelmann gave a speech. 'His life was the Works' security and the Works' security was his life.' In the course of his speech he read out a personal farewell letter from Korten. The chairman of the RCW chess club, where Schmalz senior had played third board on the second team, asked Caissa's blessing on the deceased. The RCW orchestra played 'I Had a Comrade'. Schmalz was so moved, he forgot himself and lisped at me, 'Dad's dearest wish.' Then the flower-wreathed coffin glided into the furnace.

I couldn't get out of the funeral tea. I did manage, however, to avoid sitting next to Danckelmann or Thomas, although Schmalz junior had intended this seat of honour for me. I sat next to the chairman of the RCW chess club and we chatted to each other about the world championship. Over cognac we started a game in our heads. By the thirty-second move I lost my overview. We came round to the subject of the deceased.

'He was a decent player, Schmalz. Although he was a late starter. And you could depend on him in the club. He never missed a practice or a tournament.'

'How often do you practise?'

'Every Thursday. Three weeks ago was the first time Schmalz didn't come. The family said he'd over-exerted himself in the workshop. But you know, I believe the bleeding in the brain happened before then. Otherwise he wouldn't have been in the workshop, he'd have been at practice. He must already have been off-balance then.'

It was like any other funeral meal. It starts with the soft voices, the studied grief on the faces, and the stiff dignity in the bodies, lots of awkwardness, some embarrassment, and a general desire to get it over with as quickly as possible. And one hour later it's only the clothing that distinguishes mourners from any other gathering, not the appetite, nor the noise, nor, with a few exceptions, the expressions and gestures. I did grow a little thoughtful though. What would it be like at my own funeral? In the first row of the cemetery chapel, five or six figures, among them Eberhard, Philipp and Willy, Babs, perhaps Röschen and Georg. But it was possible no one at all would learn of my death and, apart from the priest and the four coffin-bearers, not a soul would accompany me to the grave. I could picture Turbo trotting behind the coffin, a mouse in his mouth. It had a bow tied round it: 'To my dear Gerd from his Turbo.'

17

Against the light

At five I was back in the office, slightly tipsy and in a bad mood.

Fred called. 'Hello there, Gerhard, do you remember me? I wanted to ask you again about the job. Do you already have someone?'

'I've a couple of candidates. But nothing's finalized yet. I can take another look at you. It would have to be straight away, though.'

'That suits me.'

I asked him to the office. Dusk was falling, I switched on the light and let the blinds down.

Fred came cheerfully and trustingly. It was underhand, but I got the first punch in immediately. At my age I can't afford a clean fight in such situations. I caught him in the stomach and didn't waste time removing his sunglasses before hitting his face. His hands flew up and I delivered another punch to his underbelly. When he ventured a half-hearted counterpunch with his right hand, I twisted his arm round behind his back, kicked the hollow of his knees and he sank to the ground. I kept my hold on him.

'Who contracted you to beat up a guy in the War Cemetery in August?'

'Hey, stop. You're hurting me. What's all this about? I don't know exactly, the boss doesn't tell me anything. I . . . aagh . . . let up . . .'

Bit by bit out it came. Fred worked for Hans who got

the jobs and made the arrangements, didn't name any names to Fred, just described the person, place, and time. Sometimes Fred had caught wind of something. 'I did some stuff for the wine king, and once for the union, and for the chemical guys . . . stop it, yes maybe that was it at the War Cemetery . . . stop it!'

'And for the chemical guys you killed him a few weeks later.'

'You're crazy. I never killed anyone. We messed him up a bit, nothing more. Stop, you're pulling my arm off, I swear.'

I didn't manage to hurt him so much that he'd prefer the consequences of an admission of murder to riding out the pain. Besides I found him credible. I let him go.

'Sorry I had to manhandle you, Fred. I can't afford to take anyone on who's mixed up in a murder. He's dead, the guy you took care of back then.'

Fred scrambled to his feet. I showed him the sink and poured him a sambuca. He gulped it down and was in a hurry to leave.

'That's fine,' he mumbled. 'But I've had enough, I'm out of here.' Maybe he found my behaviour acceptable from a professional point of view. But we'd never be best friends.

Another piece to fit in, but the picture was no less blurry. So the confrontation between the RCW and Mischkey had reached the stage of professional hit men. But from the warning beaten into him at the War Cemetery to murder was a huge step.

I sat down at my desk. The Sweet Afton had smoked itself and left nothing but its body of ash. The traffic raced by in the Augusta-Anlage. From the backyard I could hear the shrieks of playing children. There are days in autumn where there's a whiff of Christmas in the air. I wondered what I should decorate my tree with this year. Klärchen

loved the traditional way and decked the tree year in, year
out with shiny silver baubles and tinsel. Since then I've
tried everything from matchbox cars to cigarette packs.
I've got a bit of a reputation for it among my friends, but
I've also set standards I'm stuck with now. The universe
doesn't have an endless supply of little objects that can be
used as Christmas tree decorations. Cans of sardines, for
example, would be ornamental, but are very heavy.

Philipp called and demanded I come and admire his
new cabin cruiser. Brigitte asked what I was planning that
evening. I invited her round to dinner, ran out and bought
a fillet of pork, boiled ham, and endives.

We had braised pork, Italian style. Afterwards I put on
The Man Who Loved Women. I knew the film already and
was curious to see how Brigitte would react to it. When
the womanizer, chasing after beautiful women's legs, ran
in front of a car, she thought it served him right. She
didn't particularly like the film. But when it was over she
couldn't resist posing in front of the floor lamp, as if by
accident, showing her legs off to advantage against the
light.

18

A little story

I dropped Brigitte off at work at the Collini Centre and drank my second coffee at the Gmeiner. I didn't have a smoking gun in the Mischkey case. Naturally I could keep on looking for my stupid little jigsaw pieces, trying them helplessly this way and that, and combining them to make some picture or other. I was fed up with it. I felt young and dynamic after the night with Brigitte.

At the sales counter the boss was fighting with her son. 'The way you're carrying on makes me wonder if you really want to become a pastry cook.' Did I really want to follow my leads the way I was carrying on? I was timid about those that led to the RCW. Why? Was I afraid of discovering I had delivered Mischkey to his death? Had I messed up the trails deliberately out of consideration for myself and Korten and our friendship?

I drove to Heidelberg and the RCC. Grimm wanted to deal with me quickly, on his feet. I sat down and fetched Mischkey's computer printout from my briefcase.

'You wanted to take another look, Herr Grimm. I can leave it with you now. Mischkey really was a helluva guy, broke into the RCW system again although the connection was already cut. I suspect via telephone, or what do you think?'

'I don't know what you're talking about.' He was a bad liar.

'You're a bad liar, Herr Grimm. But that doesn't

matter. For what I've got to tell you it's not important whether you're a good one or a bad one.'

'What?'

He was still standing, looking at me helplessly. I made an inviting gesture. 'Wouldn't you care to take a seat?'

He shook his head.

'I don't have to tell you who the red Ford Escort HD–S 735 sitting in the parking lot down there belongs to. Exactly three weeks ago to the day on the bridge over the railroad between Eppelheim and Wieblingen, Mischkey plummeted in his car onto the tracks after being hit by a red Ford Escort. The witness I managed to unearth even saw that the **number** plate of the red Escort started with HD and ended with 735.'

'And why are you telling me this? You should go to the police.'

'Quite right, Herr Grimm. The witness should have gone to the police, too. I had to explain to him first that a jealous wife is no reason to cover up a murder. In the meantime he's ready to go to the police with me.'

'Yes, well then?' He folded his arms over his chest in a superior manner.

'The chances of finding another red Escort from Heidelberg with a number plate that fits the description are perhaps . . . Ah, work it out yourself. The damage to the red Escort appears to have been minimal and easy to repair. Tell me, Herr Grimm, was your car stolen three weeks ago, or did you lend it to someone?'

'No, of course not, what a lot of rubbish you talk.'

'I would have been surprised anyway. You'll certainly know that when a murder occurs you always ask, who benefits? What do you think, Herr Grimm? Who benefits from Mischkey's death?'

He snorted contemptuously.

'Then allow me to tell you a little story. No, no, don't

get impatient, it's an interesting little story. You still won't sit down? Well, once upon a time there was a large chemical plant and a Regional Computing Centre that was supposed to keep an eye on the chemical plant. It was in the chemical plant's interest that they didn't keep too careful an eye on it. Two people in the Regional Computer Centre were crucial for monitoring the chemical plant. An awful lot of money was at stake. If only they could buy off one of these supervisors! What wouldn't they give for that! But they would only buy off one because they only needed one. They sound out both. A little later one is dead and the other pays off his loan. Do you want to know how high the loan was?'

Now he did sit down. To compensate for this mistake he acted outraged. 'It's appalling what you're ascribing not only to me but to our most respected and venerable chemical enterprise. I'd best pass this on to them; they can defend themselves better than a minor employee like me.'

'I can well believe that what you'd most like to do is run to the RCW. But at the moment the story concerns only you, the police, myself, and my witness. The police will be interested in knowing your whereabouts at the time, and like most people, you too, three weeks *post festum*, won't be able to provide a solid alibi.'

If there'd been a visit with his poor wife and his doubtless disgusting children at his parents-in-laws' Grimm would have come out with that. Instead he said, 'There can't be a witness who saw me, because I wasn't there.'

I had him where I wanted him. I didn't feel any fairer than I had yesterday with Fred, but just as good. 'Right, Herr Grimm, nor is there a witness who saw you there. But I have someone who will say he saw you there. And what do you think will happen then? The police have a corpse, a crime, a culprit, a witness, and a motive. It may

171

be that the witness finally cracks during the trial, but long before that you're finished. I don't know what they give you for taking bribes these days, but along with it comes detention awaiting trial for murder, suspension from work, disgrace for your wife and children, the contempt of society.'

Grimm had turned pale. 'What is this? What are you doing to me? What have I done to you?'

'I don't like the way you let yourself be bought. I can't stand you. Moreover there's something I want you to tell me. And if you don't want me to ruin you, you'd better play along.'

'What do you want?'

'When did the RCW contact you for the first time? Who recruited you, and who is, so to speak, the person who runs you? How much have you received from the RCW?'

He recounted the whole thing, from the initial contact Thomas had opened with him after Mischkey's death, to the negotiations over performance and pay, to the programmes, some of which were still only ideas and some of which he'd already written. And he told me about the suitcase with the crisp new notes.

'Stupidly, instead of paying back my loan bit by bit so as not to raise suspicion, I went to the bank straight away. I wanted to save on interest.' He took out a handkerchief and mopped away the sweat, and I asked him what he knew about Mischkey's death.

'So far as I could gather, they wanted to put him under pressure after you had turned him in. They wanted to have the cooperation they're now paying me for, but they wanted it for nothing, in exchange for keeping quiet about his hacking into the system. When he died they were somewhat disgruntled because then they had to pay. Me.'

He could have gone on talking for ever, probably wanted to justify himself, too. I'd heard enough.

'Thank you, that's plenty for now, Herr Grimm. In your place I'd keep our discussion confidential. If the RCW get wind of the fact that I know, you'll be useless to them. Should anything more about Mischkey's death come to mind, call me.' I gave him my card.

'Yes, but – don't you care about what's going on with the emissions control? Or are you going to go to the police anyway?'

I thought about the stink that so often caused me to shut the window. And about what was there, even though we couldn't smell it. Nonetheless it left me indifferent for the time being. I packed away Mischkey's printouts that were lying on Grimm's desk. When I turned to leave, Grimm stretched out his hand towards me. I didn't take it.

19

Energy and Stamina

In the afternoon I should have had my appointment with the ballet director. But I didn't feel like it and cancelled. At home I went to bed and didn't wake up until five. I almost never have a siesta. Because of my low blood pressure I find it difficult afterwards to get going again. I took a hot shower and made a strong coffee.

When I called Philipp at the station the nurse said, 'The doctor is already off to his new boat.' I drove through Neckarstadt to Luzenberg and parked in Gerwigstrasse. In the harbour I passed a lot of boats before finding Philipp's. I recognized it by the name. It was called *Faun 69*.

I know next to nothing about sailing. Philipp explained to me that he could sail to London in this boat or to Rome via France, just not venturing too far from the coast. There was water enough for ten showers, space enough in the fridge for forty bottles, and room enough in the bed for one Philipp and two women. After he'd shown me around he switched the stereo on, put on Hans Albers, and uncorked a bottle of Bordeaux.

'Do I get a test-drive, too?'

'Slowly does it, Gerd. Let's empty this little bottle first, and then we'll raise the anchor. I have radar and can set sail any time day or night.'

One bottle turned into two. First of all Philipp told me about his women. 'And what about you, Gerd, how's your love life?'

'Ah, what can I say?'

'Nothing on the go with smart traffic wardens or attractive secretaries, or whatever else you are involved in?'

'On a case I did get to know a woman recently who'd appeal to me, but it's difficult because her boyfriend isn't alive any more.'

'I beg your pardon, but where's the difficulty in that?'

'Oh, well, I can't flirt with a grieving widow, can I? Especially as I'm supposed to be finding out who murdered the boyfriend.'

'Why can't you? Is it your public prosecutor's code of honour, or are you simply afraid she'll turn you down?' He was laughing at me.

'No, no, you couldn't put it like that. And then there's somebody else – Brigitte. I like her too. I don't know what to do with two women.'

Philipp burst out laughing, loudly. 'You're a real philanderer. And what's stopping you from getting closer to Brigitte?'

'I am already . . . with her, I've even . . .'

'And now she's expecting a child by you?' Philipp could hardly contain his mirth. Then he noticed that I wasn't at all inclined to laugh, and enquired seriously about my situation. I told him.

'That's no reason to look so sad. You just need to be aware of what you want. If you're looking for someone to marry, then stay with Brigitte. They're not bad, these women around forty. They've seen everything, experienced everything, they're as sensual as a succubus if you know how to arouse them. And a masseuse, what's more, and you with your rheumatism. The other one sounds like stress. Is that what you want? *Amour fou*? A heaven of passion, then a hell of despair?'

'But I don't know what I want. Probably I want both,

the security and the thrill. At any rate sometimes I want one, sometimes the other.'

He could understand that. We identified with one other there. I'd worked out in the meantime where the Bordeaux was stored and fetched the third bottle. The smoke was thick in the cabin.

'Hey, landlubber, get to that galley and throw the fish from the fridge on the grill!' In the fridge was potato and sausage salad from Kaufhof and next to it deep-frozen fillets of fish. They just had to be popped into the microwave. Two minutes later I was able to return to the cabin with dinner. Philipp had set the table and put on Zarah Leander.

After eating we went up to the bridge, as Philipp called it. 'And where do you hoist the sail?' Philipp knew my silly jokes and didn't react. He also took my question as to whether he could still navigate as a bad joke. We were pretty tight by then.

We sailed under the bridge over the Altrhein and when we'd reached the Rhine we turned upstream. The river was black and silent. On the RCW premises many buildings were lit up, bright flames were shooting out of tall pipes, streetlamps cast a garish light. The motor chugged softly, the water slapped against the boat's side, and from the Works came an almighty, thunderous hissing. We glided past the RCW loading dock, past barges, piers, and container cranes, past railroad lines and warehouses. It was growing foggy and there was a chill in the air. In front of us I could make out the Kurt Schumacher Bridge. The RCW premises grew murky, beyond the tracks loomed old buildings, sparsely lit in the night sky.

Inspiration struck. 'Drive over to the right,' I said to Philipp.

'Do you mean I should dock? Now, there, next to the RCW? Whatever for?'

'I'd like to take a look at something. Can you park for half an hour and wait for me?'

'It's not called parking, it's dropping the anchor, we're on a boat. Are you aware that it's half past ten? I was thinking we'd turn by the castle, chug back, and then drink the fourth bottle in the Waldhof Basin.'

'I'll explain it all to you later over the fourth bottle. But now I have to go in. It has something to do with the case I mentioned earlier. And I'm not the least bit tipsy any more.'

Philipp gave me a searching look. 'I guess you know what you're doing.' He steered the boat to the right and sailed on with a serene concentration I wouldn't have thought him capable of at that point, moving slowly along the quay wall until he came to a ladder attached to it. 'Hang the fenders out.' He pointed to three white plastic, sausage-like objects. I threw them overboard, fortunately they were attached, and he tied the boat firmly to the ladder.

'I'd like to have you with me. But I'd rather know you're here, ready to start. Do you have a flashlight I can use?'

'Aye, aye, sir.'

I clambered up the ladder. I was shivering. The knitted jumper, some American label, I was wearing beneath the old leather jacket to match my new jeans didn't warm me. I peered over the quay wall.

In front of me, parallel to the banks of the Rhine, was a narrow road, behind it tracks with railway carriages. The buildings were in the brick style I was familiar with from the Security building and the Schmalzes' flat. The old plant was in front of me. Somewhere here was Schmalz's hangar.

I turned to the right where the old brick buildings were lower. I tried to walk with both caution and the necessary authority. I stuck to the shadows of the railway carriages.

They came without the Alsatian making a sound. One of them shone a torch in my face, the other asked me for my badge. I fetched the special pass from my wallet. 'Herr Self? What part of your special job brings you here?'

'I wouldn't require a special pass if I had to tell you that.'

But that neither calmed them nor intimidated them. They were two young lads, the sort you find these days in the riot police. In the old days you found them in the Waffen SS. That's certainly an impermissible comparison because these days we're dealing with a free democratic order, yet the mixture of zeal, earnestness, uncertainness, and servility in the faces is the same. They were wearing a kind of paramilitary uniform with the benzene ring on their collar patch.

'Hey, guys,' I said, 'let me finish my job, and you do yours. What are your names? I want to tell Danckelmann tomorrow that you can be relied on. Continue the good work!'

I don't remember their names; they were along the lines of Energy and Stamina. I didn't manage to get them clicking their heels. But one of them returned my pass and the other switched off his torch. The Alsatian had spent the whole time off to one side, indifferent.

When I couldn't see them any more and their steps had died away I went on. The low-slung buildings I'd seen seemed ramshackle. Some of the windows were smashed, some doors hung crooked from their hinges, here and there a roof was missing. The area was obviously earmarked for demolition. But one building had been rescued from decay. It, too, was a one-floor brick building, with Romanesque windows and barrel vaulting made of corrugated iron. If Schmalz's workshop was anywhere round here, then it had to be in this building.

My flashlight found the small service door in the large sliding gate. Both were locked, and the big one could only be opened from the inside. At first I didn't want to try the bank-card trick, but then I thought that on the evening in question, three weeks ago today, Schmalz might no longer have had the strength or the wit to think of details like padlocks. And indeed, using my special pass, I entered the hangar. Next second, I had to close the door. Energy and Stamina were coming round the corner.

I leaned against the cold iron door and took a deep breath. Now I was really sober. And still I knew it was a good idea to have come looking in the RCW grounds. The fact that on the day Mischkey had had his accident Schmalz had hurt his hand, had had a brain haemorrhage, and forgotten to play chess wasn't much in itself. And the fact that he tinkered with delivery vans and the girl at the station had seen a strange delivery van was hardly a hot lead. But I wanted to know.

Not much light shone through the windows. I could make out the outlines of three panel trucks. I turned on the flashlight and recognized an old Opel, an old Mercedes, and a Citroën. You certainly don't see many of those driving about round here. At the back of the hangar was a large workbench. I groped my way over. Amongst the tools were a set of keys, a cap, and a pack of cigarettes. I pocketed the keys.

Only the Citroën was roadworthy. On the Opel the windshield was missing, the Mercedes was up on blocks. I sat down in the Citroën and tried out the keys. One fitted and as I turned it the lights went on. There was old blood on the steering wheel and the cloth on the passenger's seat was bloodstained, too. I took it. As I was about to turn off the ignition, I touched a switch on the dashboard. Behind me I could hear the humming of an electric motor, and in the side-mirror I could see the loading doors open. I got out and went to the back.

20

Not just a silly womanizer

This time I didn't get such a fright. But the effect was still impressive. Now I knew what had happened on the bridge. Both inside surfaces of the rear doors of the delivery van, and the rear opening itself, had been covered with reflective foil. A deadly triptych. The foil was spread smooth, without creases or warps, and I could see myself in it like on Saturday in the mirror that hung in my stairwell. When Mischkey had driven onto the bridge, the delivery van had been parked there with its back doors open. Mischkey, confronted suddenly with the apparent headlights on his side of the road, had swerved to the left and then lost control of his vehicle. Now I recalled the cross on the right headlight on Mischkey's car. It wasn't Mischkey who'd stuck it on, it was old Schmalz, who'd thus been able to know, in the darkness, that he had to open the doors because his victim was coming.

I heard thumps on the door of the hangar. 'Open up, security!' Energy and Stamina must have noticed the beam from my flashlight. Apparently the hangar had been so much Schmalz's sole preserve that not even security had a key. I was glad that my two young colleagues didn't know the bank-card trick. Nonetheless I was sitting in a trap.

I took note of the number on the licence plate and saw that the plates themselves were tied on in a makeshift fashion with wire. I started the engine. Outside the door was being pounded with ever-increasing energy and stamina. I parked the vehicle just a metre from the door, its mirrored rear opened. Then I grabbed a long, heavy spanner from the table. One of my pursuers hurled himself against the door.

I pressed myself against the wall. Now what I needed was a lot of luck. When I estimated the next assault on the door would come, I pushed down the handle.

The door burst open, and the first security guard fell through it, landing on the ground. The second one stormed in after him with raised pistol and raked to a halt in fright in front of his own mirror image. The Alsatian had been trained to attack whoever was threatening his master with a raised weapon and leapt through the tearing foil. I could hear him howling in pain in the cargo area. The first security man lay dazed on the ground, the second hadn't cottoned on yet. I took advantage of the confusion, zipped out of the gate, and raced in the direction of the boat. I'd made it over the tracks and cleared maybe twenty metres down the road, when I heard Energy and Stamina in renewed pursuit: 'Stop or I'll shoot.' Their heavy boots beat out a fast rhythm on the cobblestones, the panting of the dog was getting closer and closer, and I had no desire to grow acquainted with the application of the regulations on usage of firearms on the plant's premises. The Rhine looked cold. But I had no choice, and jumped.

The dive from a headlong run had enough momentum to let me bob to the surface a good distance away. I turned my head and saw Energy and Stamina standing on the quay wall with the Alsatian, directing their flashlight at the water. My clothes were heavy, and the current of the Rhine is strong, and I could only make headway with difficulty.

'Gerd, Gerd!' Philipp let his boat drift downstream in the shadow of the quayside and called to me in a whisper.

'Here I am,' I whispered back. Then the boat was next to me. Philipp hoisted me up. At that moment Energy and Stamina saw us. I don't know what they planned to do. Fire at us? Philipp started the motor and with a spraying bow wave made for the middle of the Rhine. Exhausted and shivering with cold, I sat on the deck. I pulled the bloodstained cloth from my pocket. 'Could you do me another favour and test the blood group on this? I think I know, blood group O rhesus negative, but better safe than sorry.'

Philipp grinned. 'All that excitement over this damp cloth? But first things first. Go below, take a hot shower, and put on my bathrobe. As soon as we've made it past the water police I'll make you a grog.'

When I came out of the shower we'd reached safety. Neither the RCW nor the police had sent a gunboat after us and Philipp was just in the process of manoeuvring the boat back into the Altrhein channel by Sandhofen. Although the shower had warmed me, I was still shivering. It was all a bit much at my age. Philipp docked at the old mooring and entered the cabin. 'Jeezus,' he said. 'That was quite a fright you gave me. When I heard the guys hammering against the metal I thought something had gone wrong. I didn't know what to do. Then I saw you jump. Hats off!'

'Oh, you know, when you have a killer dog on your tail you don't stop to consider whether the water might be a little on the cold side. Much more important was that you did exactly the right thing at the right time. Without you I'd probably have drowned, with or without a bullet in my head. You saved my life. Boy, am I glad you're not just a silly womanizer.'

Embarrassed, Philipp clattered about in the galley. 'Maybe you want to tell me now what you'd lost at the RCW.'

'Nothing lost, but found some things. Apart from this disgusting wet cloth I found the murder weapon, probably the murderer, too. Which explains the wet cloth.' Over the steaming grog I told Philipp about the corrugated van and its surprising refit.

'But if it was as simple as that to chase your Mischkey off the bridge, what about the injuries to the veteran who was the Works' security guy?' Philipp asked when I was finished with my report.

'You should have become a private detective. You're quick on the uptake. I don't have any answers, unless . . .' I remembered what the owner's wife had told me at the railway restaurant. 'The woman at the old station heard two bangs, one right after the other. Now it's getting clear. Mischkey's car was hanging from the railings on the bridge, Schmalz senior, with a great deal of effort, managed to dislodge it, injuring himself in the process. And the effort killed him two weeks later. Yes, that's how it must have been.'

'One bang as it broke through the railings, the next as it crashed down onto the railroad bank. It all fits together medically, too. When old people strain themselves too much, it can happen that they haemorrhage a little in the brain. It goes unnoticed until the heart gives out.'

I was very tired all of a sudden. 'Still, there's a lot I'm hazy about. Schmalz senior himself didn't come up with the idea to kill Mischkey. And I still can't see a motive. Please take me home, Philipp. We'll have the Bordeaux some other time. I hope you won't get into any trouble on account of my escapades.'

As we turned from Gerwigstrasse into Sandhofenstrasse a patrol car complete with flashing light but without siren went tearing past us towards the harbour basin. I didn't even turn round.

21

Praying Hands

After a feverish night I called Brigitte. She came immediately, brought quinine for my temperature and nose drops, massaged my neck, hung up my clothes to dry that I'd dropped in the hallway the previous evening, prepared something in the kitchen that I was to heat up for lunch, set off, bought orange juice, glucose, and cigarettes, and fed Turbo. She was professional, industrious, and worried. When I wanted her to sit for a little on the edge of the bed, she had to leave.

I slept almost the whole day. Philipp called and confirmed the blood group, O, and the rhesus negative factor. Through the window a rumble of traffic from the Augusta-Anlage and the shouts of playing children drifted into the twilight of my room. I remembered back to sick days as a child, the desire to be outside playing with the other children, and simultaneously the pleasure in my own weakness and all the maternal pampering. In a feverish semi-sleep I kept running from the panting dog and Energy and Stamina. I was making up for the fear I hadn't felt yesterday where everything had happened too quickly. I had wild thoughts about Mischkey's murder and why Schmalz had done it.

Towards evening I was feeling better. My temperature had gone down and I was weak, but I felt like eating the beef broth with pasta and vegetables that Brigitte had prepared, and smoking a Sweet Afton afterwards. How should work on the case proceed? Murder belonged in police hands, and even if the RCW, as I could well imagine, pulled a veil of oblivion over yesterday's incident I'd never find out anything more from anyone in the Works. I called Nägelsbach. He and his wife had finished dinner and were in the studio.

'Of course you can come by. You can listen to *Hedda Gabler*, too, we're in the third act just now.'

I stuck a note on the front door, to reassure Brigitte in case she came to check on me again. The drive to Heidelberg was bad. My own slowness and the quickness of the car made uneasy companions.

The Nägelsbachs live in one of the Pfaffengrunder settlement houses of the twenties. Nägelsbach had turned the shed, originally meant for chickens and rabbits, into a studio with a large window and bright lamps. The evening was cool and the Swedish wood-burning stove held a few crackling logs. Nägelsbach was sitting on his high stool, at the big table on which Dürer's *Praying Hands* were taking shape in matchstick form. His wife was reading aloud in the armchair by the stove. It was a perfect idyll that met my eyes when I came through the garden gate straight to the studio and looked through the window before knocking.

'My word, what a sight you are!' Frau Nägelsbach vacated the armchair for me and took another stool for herself.

'You must really have something on your mind to come here in this state,' was Nägelsbach's greeting. 'Do you mind if my wife stays? I tell her everything, work-wise, too. The rules of confidentiality don't apply to childless couples who only have one another.'

As I recounted my tale, Nägelsbach worked on. He didn't interrupt me. At the end of my narration he was silent for a little while, then he switched off the lamp above his workplace, turned his high stool towards us, and said to his wife: 'Tell him.'

'With what you've just told us, maybe the police will get a search warrant for the old hangar. Maybe they'll find the Citroën still there. But there'll be nothing remarkable or suspicious about it. No reflective foil, no deadly triptych. That was pretty, by the way, how you described that. Right, and then the police can interrogate a few of the security people and the widow Schmalz and whoever else you named, but what is it going to achieve?'

'That's it, and of course I could prime Herzog in particular about the case, and he can try to use his contacts with security, only it won't change a thing. But you know all that yourself, Herr Self.'

'Yes, that's where my thinking has brought me too. Nonetheless I thought you might have an idea of something the police could do, that . . . oh, I don't know what I thought. I haven't been able to resign myself to the case ending like this.'

'Do you have any idea of a motive?' Frau Nägelsbach turned to her husband. 'Couldn't we get further that way?'

'I can only imagine from what I know thus far that something went wrong. Just like that story you read to me recently. The RCW is having trouble with Mischkey, and it's getting more and more bothersome, and then someone in control says, "That's enough," and his subordinate gets a fright and in his turn passes the baton: "See to it Mischkey is quietened down, exert yourself," and the person this is said to wants to show his dedication and prods and encourages his own subordinate to think of something, and it can be unusual, and at the end of this long chain someone believes he's supposed to knock off Mischkey.'

'But old Schmalz was a pensioner and not even part of the chain any more,' his wife offered.

'Hard to say. How many policemen do I know who still feel like policemen after retirement?'

'Dear God,' she interrupted him, 'you're not going to—'

'No, I won't. Perhaps Schmalz senior was one of those who still thought of himself as being in service. What I mean is there needn't be a motive for murder in the classical sense here. The murderer is simply the instrument without a motive, and whoever had the motive wasn't necessarily thinking about murder. That's the effect, and indeed the purpose, of commanding hierarchies. We know that in the police, too, and in the army.'

'Do you think more could be done if old Schmalz were still alive?'

'Well, to begin with, Herr Self wouldn't have got as far. He wouldn't have found out at all about Schmalz's injury, wouldn't have looked in the hangar, and certainly wouldn't have found the murder vehicle. All traces would have been removed long before. But, all right, let's imagine we'd come by this knowledge in a different way. No, I don't think we'd have got anything out of old Schmalz. He must have been a tough old nut.'

'But this just isn't okay, Rudolf. Listening to you, the only person you can get in this chain of command is the last link. And the others are all supposedly innocent?'

'Whether they're innocent is one question and whether you can get them is another. Look, Reni, I don't know of course whether something really went wrong, or whether it's not the case that the chain was so well oiled that everyone knew what was meant without it being spoken out loud. But if it was oiled like that, it certainly can't be proved.'

'Should Herr Self be advised to talk to one of the big cheeses at the RCW? To get a sense of how that person conducts himself?'

'So far as prosecution goes, that won't help either. But you're right, it's the only remaining thing he can do.'

It was good to watch the pair of them, in this question-and-answer game, making sense of what I was too groggy to work out for myself. So what was left for me was a talk with Korten.

Frau Nägelsbach made some verbena tea and we talked about art. Nägelsbach told me what appealed to him in his reproduction of *Praying Hands*. He found the usual sculpture reproductions no less sickly sweet than I. And that very fact made him want to achieve the sublime sobriety of Dürer's original through the rigorous simplicity of the matches.

As I left he promised to check up on the licence plate of Schmalz's Citroën.

The note for Brigitte was still hanging on the door. When I was lying in bed she called. 'Are you feeling better? Sorry I couldn't come round to see you again. I just didn't manage it. How's your weekend looking? Do you think you'll feel up to coming to dinner tomorrow?' Something wasn't right. Her cheerfulness sounded forced.

22

Tea in the loggia

On Saturday morning I found one message from Nägels-bach on the answering machine and one from Korten. The number on the licence plate on old Schmalz's Citroën had been allotted to a Heidelberg postal worker for his VW Beetle five years ago. Presumably the licence plate I saw originated from this scrapped predecessor. Korten asked whether I wouldn't like to visit them in Ludolf-Krehl-Strasse. I should call him back.

'My dear Self, good to hear you. This afternoon, tea in the loggia? You whipped up quite a storm for us, I hear. And you sound as though you have a cold. It doesn't surprise me, ha ha. Your level of fitness, I'm full of respect.'

At four o'clock I was in Ludolf-Krehl-Strasse. For Inge, if it was still Inge, I had brought an autumn bouquet. I marvelled at the entrance gate, the video camera, and the intercom system. It consisted of a telephone receiver on a long cable that the chauffeur could pick up and pass on to the good ladies and gentlemen in the rear. Just as I wanted to sit back in my car with the receiver I heard Korten with the tortured patience you use for a naughty child. 'Don't be silly, Self! The cable car is on its way for you.'

On the ride up I had a view from Neuenheim over the Rhine plain to the Palatinate Forest. It was a clear day and I could make out the chimneys of the RCW. Their white smoke merged innocently with the blue sky.

Korten, in cords, checked shirt, and a casual cardigan, greeted me heartily. Two dachshunds were leaping around him. 'I've had a table set in the loggia, it won't be too cold for you, will it? You can always have one of my cardigans, Helga knits me one after the other.'

We stood enjoying the view. 'Is that your church down there?'

'The Johanneskirche? No, we belong to the Friedens-kirche parish in Handschuhsheim. I've become an Elder. Nice job.'

Helga came with a coffee pot and I unloaded my flowers. I'd only known Inge fleetingly and didn't know whether she'd died, divorced, or simply left. Helga, new wife or new lover, resembled her. The same cheerfulness, the same false modesty, the same delight over my bouquet. She stayed to have a first slice of apple cake with us. Then: 'You men certainly want to talk among yourselves.' As was right and proper we contradicted her. And as was right and proper she went anyway.

'May I have another slice of apple cake? It's delicious.'

Korten leant back in his armchair. 'I am sure you had good reason for frightening security on Thursday evening. If you don't mind I'd like to know what it was. I was the one who recently introduced you to the Works, if you like, and I'm the one to get all the puzzled looks when your escapades became known.'

'How well did you know Schmalz senior? A personal message from you was read out at his funeral.'

'You weren't looking for the answer to that question in the shed. But fine, I knew him better and liked him better than all the other men in security. Back in the dark years we grew close to some of the simple employees in a way that is no longer possible today.'

'He killed Mischkey. And in the hangar I found proof, the thing that killed him.'

191

'Old Schmalz? He wouldn't hurt a fly. What are you talking yourself into, my dear Self.'

Without mentioning Judith or going into detail, I reported what had happened. 'And if you ask me what any of this has to do with me then I'll remind you of our last talk. I ask you to go gently on Mischkey and shortly afterwards he's dead.'

'And where do you see a reason, a motive, for such action on the part of old Schmalz?'

'We can come back to that in a minute. First I'd like to know if you have any questions about the order of events.'

Korten got up and prowled back and forth heavily. 'Why didn't you call me first thing yesterday morning? Then we might still have discovered something more about what went on in Schmalz's hangar. Now it's too late. It was planned for weeks – yesterday the building complex, along with the old hangar, was demolished. That was also the reason I spoke to old Schmalz myself four weeks ago. We had a little schnapps and I tried to break the news to him that we, unfortunately, couldn't keep the old hangar, nor his apartment.'

'You were round at Schmalz senior's?'

'No, I asked him to come and see me. Naturally I don't usually deliver such messages. But he's always reminded me of the old days. And you know how sentimental I am deep down.'

'And what happened to the delivery van?'

'No idea. The son will have taken care of it. But once again, where do you see a motive?'

'I actually thought you'd be able to tell me.'

'What makes you say that?' Korten's steps slowed. He stood still, turned, and scrutinized me.

'That Schmalz senior personally had no reason to kill Mischkey is clear. But the plant did have some trouble with him, put him under pressure, even had him beaten up; and he did show resistance. And he could have blown your deal with Grimm. You're not going to tell me you knew nothing about all this?'

No, Korten wasn't. He had been aware of the trouble and also of the deal with Grimm. But that was surely not the stuff of murder. 'Unless . . .' he removed his glasses, 'unless old Schmalz misinterpreted something. You know, he was the sort of man who still imagined himself in service, and if his son or another security man told him about the trouble with Mischkey, he might have seen himself as obliged to act as saviour of the Works.'

'What could Schmalz senior have misunderstood with such serious repercussions?'

'I don't know what his son or anyone else might have told him. Or if anyone just plain incited him? I'll get to the bottom of it. It's unbearable to think that my good old Schmalz ended up being exploited like this. And what a tragic end. His great love for the Works and a silly little misunderstanding led him to take a life senselessly and unnecessarily, and also to sacrifice his own.'

'What's the matter with you? Giving life, taking life, tragedy, exploitation – I'm thinking: "It's not reprehensible to use people, it's just tactless to let them notice".'

'You're right, let's get back to the matter at hand. Should we bring in the police?'

That was it? An over-eager veteran of security had killed Mischkey, and Korten didn't even turn a hair. Could the prospect of having the police in the Works frighten him? I tried it out.

Korten weighed up the pros and cons. 'It's not only the fact that it's always unpleasant to have the police in the Works. I feel sorry for the Schmalz family. To lose a husband and father and then to discover he had made a lethal mistake – can we take on the responsibility for that? There's nothing left to atone, he paid with his life. But I'm thinking about reparation. Do you know whether Misch-key had parents he looked after, or other obligations, or whether he has a decent gravestone? Did he leave anyone behind we could do something for? Would you be willing to take care of it?'

I assumed that Judith wouldn't particularly care to have anything of the sort done for her.

'I've investigated plenty in Mischkey's case. If you're serious, Frau Schlemihl can find out what you need to know with a couple of phone calls.'

'You're always so sensitive. You did wonderful work on Mischkey's case. I'm also grateful that you kept going with the second part of the investigation. I need to be aware of such things. May I extend my original contract belatedly and ask you to send a bill?'

He was welcome to the bill.

'Ah, and another thing,' said Korten, 'while we're talking business. You forgot to enclose your special pass with your report last time. Please do pop it in the envelope with the bill this time.'

I took the pass out of my wallet. 'You can have it right now. And I'll be on my way.'

Helga came onto the loggia as though she'd been eavesdropping behind the door, and had picked up the signal for saying goodbye. 'The flowers are truly delight-ful, would you like to see where I've put them, Herr Self?'

'Ah, children, drop the formalities. Self is my oldest friend.' Korten put an arm round both our shoulders.

I wanted out. Instead, I followed the two of them into the sitting room, admired my bouquet on the grand piano, listened to the popping of the champagne cork, and clinked glasses with Helga, over the dropping of formal-ities.

'Why haven't we seen you here more often?' she asked in all innocence.

'Yes, we must change that,' said Korten, before I could respond at all. 'What are your plans for New Year's Eve?'

I thought about Brigitte. 'I'm not sure yet.'

'That's wonderful, my dear Self. Then we'll be in touch with each other again soon.'

23

Do you have a tissue?

Brigitte had prepared beef stroganoff with fresh mush-rooms and rice. It tasted delicious, the wine was at a perfect temperature, and the table was lovingly set. Brigitte was chattering. I'd brought her Elton John's *Greatest Hits* and he was singing of love and suffering, hope and separation.

She held forth on reflexology, acupressure, and Rolfing. She told me about patients, health insurers, and colleagues. She didn't care in the least whether it interested me, or how I was.

'What's going on today? This afternoon I scarcely recognize Korten, and now I'm sitting here with you and the only thing you have in common with the Brigitte I like is the scar on your earlobe.'

She laid down her fork, put her elbows on the table, rested her head on her hands, and began to weep. I went round the table to her, she nuzzled her head into my belly, and just cried all the more.

'What's wrong?' I stroked her hair.

'I . . . oh . . . I, it's enough to drive me to tears. I'm going away tomorrow.'

'Why the tears about that?'

'It's for so terribly long. And so far.' She raised her face.

'How long, then, and how far?'

'Oh . . . I . . .' She pulled herself together. 'Do you have a tissue? I'm going to Brazil for six months. To see my son.'

I sat down. Now I felt ready to weep, too. At the same time I felt angry. 'Why didn't you tell me before?'

'I didn't know things would turn out so nice between us.'

'I don't understand.'

She took my hand. 'Juan and I had intended to take the six months to see whether we couldn't be together after all. Manuel misses his mother all the time. And with you I thought it would just be a short episode and over anyway by the time I left for Brazil.'

'What do you mean, you thought it would be over anyway when you left for Brazil? Postcards from Sugar Loaf Mountain won't change a thing.' I was quite bleak with sadness. She said nothing and stared into space. After a while I withdrew my hand from hers and got up. 'I'd better go now.' She nodded mutely.

In the hallway she leaned against me for one last moment. 'You see, I can't go on being the raven mother that you never liked anyway.'

24

She'd hunched her shoulders

The night was dreamless. I woke up at six o'clock, knew I had to talk to Judith today and thought about what I should tell her. Everything? How would she be able to continue working at RCW and hold on to her old life? But that was a problem I couldn't solve for her.

At nine o'clock I phoned her. 'I've wrapped up the case, Judith. Shall we take a walk by the harbour and I'll fill you in?'

'You don't sound good. What have you found out?'

'I'll pick you up at ten.'

I put coffee on, took the butter out of the fridge, and the eggs and smoked ham, chopped onions and chives, warmed up milk for Turbo, squeezed three oranges for juice, set the table, and made myself two fried eggs on ham and lightly sweated onions. When the eggs were just right I sprinkled them with chives. The coffee was ready.

I sat for a long time over my breakfast without touching it. Just before ten I took a couple of gulps of coffee. I set down the eggs for Turbo and left.

When I rang the bell, Judith came down straight away. She looked pretty in her loden coat with its collar turned up, as pretty as only an unhappy person can be.

We parked the car by the harbour office and walked between the rail tracks and the old warehouses along Rheinkaistrasse. Beneath the grey September sky it all had the peacefulness of a Sunday. The John Deere tractors were parked as though they were waiting for a field chaplain to begin the service.

'Will you please finally start to tell me?'

'Didn't Firner mention my run-in with plant security on Thursday night?'

'No. I think he'd gathered I was with Peter.'

I started with the talk I'd had with Korten yesterday, lingered over the question of whether old Schmalz was the last link of a well-functioning chain of command, had crazily set himself up as the saviour of the plant, or had been used, nor did I spare the details of the murder on the bridge. I made it clear that what I knew, and what could be proved, were leagues apart.

Judith strode along firmly beside me. She'd hunched her shoulders and was holding the collar of her coat closed with her left hand against the north wind. She hadn't interrupted me. But now she said with a small laugh that cut me even further to the quick than her tears would have done: 'Do you know, Gerhard, it's so absurd. When I took you on to find out the truth I thought it would help me. But now I feel more at a loss than ever.'

I envied Judith the purity of her grief. My sadness was pervaded by a sense of weakness, of guilt, because I'd delivered Mischkey to the dogs, albeit unwittingly, a feeling that I'd been used, and a strange pride at having come so far. It also saddened me that the case had initially connected Judith and myself then entangled us so much with one another that we'd never be able to grow closer without a sense of awkwardness.

'You'll send me the bill?'

She hadn't understood that Korten wanted to pay for my investigation. As I explained this to her, she retreated even further into herself and said: 'That fits perfectly. It would also fit if I were to be promoted to Korten's personal assistant. It's all so repulsive.'

Between warehouse number seventeen and number nineteen we turned left and came to the Rhine. Opposite lay the RCW skyscraper. The Rhine flowed past, wide and tranquil.

'What do I do now?'

I had no answers. If she managed tomorrow to lay the folder of letters in front of Firner to sign, as though nothing had happened, she'd come to terms with it.

'And the terrible thing is that Peter is already so far away, inside. I've cleared out everything at home that reminded me of him, because it hurt so much. But now my loneliness feels tidied away, too, and I'm getting cold.'

We walked along the Rhine, following it downstream. Suddenly she turned to me, seized me by the coat, shook me and said: 'We can't just let them get away with it!' With her right arm she made a sweeping gesture encapsulating the Works opposite. 'They shouldn't be let off the hook.'

'No, they shouldn't be, but they will be. Since the beginning of time, people with power have got away with it. And here perhaps it wasn't even the people with power, it was a megalomaniac, Schmalz.'

'But that's exactly what power is, not having to act yourself, but getting some megalomaniac to do it. That can't excuse them.'

I tried to explain to her that I didn't want to excuse anyone, but that I simply couldn't pursue the investigation.

'Then you're just one of the somebodies who does the dirty work for those people with power. Leave me alone now, I'll find my own way back.'

I suppressed the impulse to leave her there, and said instead: 'That's mad, the secretary of the director of the RCW reproaching the detective who carried out a contract for the RCW, for working for the RCW. That's rich.'

We walked on. After a while she put an arm through mine. 'In the old days, if something bad happened, I always had the feeling it would all be okay again. Life, I mean. Even after my divorce. Now I know nothing will ever be the same again. Do you recognize that?'

I nodded.

'Listen, it really would be best if I go on walking here on my own for a bit. You needn't look so worried, I won't do anything silly.'

From Rheinkaistrasse I looked back. She hadn't moved. She was looking over to the RCW at the levelled ground of the old factory. The wind blew an empty cement sack over the street.

Part Three

I

A milestone in jurisprudence

After a long, golden Indian summer, winter started abruptly. I can't remember a colder November.

I wasn't working much then. The investigation in the Sergej Mencke affair advanced at a crawl. The insurance company was hemming and hawing about sending me to America. The meeting with the ballet director had taken place on the sidelines of a rehearsal, and had taught me about Indian dance, which was being rehearsed, but otherwise only revealed that some people liked Sergej, others didn't, and the ballet director belonged to the latter category. For two weeks I was plagued by rheumatism so that I wasn't fit for anything except getting through the bare necessities. Beyond that I went on plenty of walks, frequented the sauna and the cinema, finished reading *Green Henry* – I'd laid it aside in the summer – and listened to Turbo's winter coat grow. One Saturday I bumped into Judith at the market. She was no longer working at RCW, was living off her unemployment money, and helping out at the women's bookshop Xanthippe. We promised to get together, but neither of us made the first move. With Eberhard I re-enacted the matches of the world chess championship. As we were sitting over the last game, Brigitte called from Rio. There was a buzzing and crackling in the line; I could barely make her out. I think she said she was missing me. I didn't know what to do with that.

December began with unexpected days of sultry wind. On 2 December the Federal Constitutional Court pronounced as unconstitutional the direct emissions data gathering introduced by statute in Baden-Württemberg and the Rhineland-Palatinate.

It censured the violation of constitutional rights of business data privacy and establishment and practice of a commercial enterprise, but eventually the statute was annulled for lack of legislative authority. The well-known columnist of the *Frankfurter Allgemeine Zeitung* celebrated the decision as a milestone in jurisprudence because, at last, data privacy had broken free of the shackles of mere civil rights protection and was elevated to the rank of entrepreneurial rights. Only now was the true grandeur of the court's judgment regarding data protection revealed.

I wondered what would become of Grimm's lucrative sideline. Would the RCW continue to pay him a fee, for keeping quiet? I also wondered whether Judith would read the news from Karlsruhe, and what would go through her head as she did. This decision half a year earlier would have meant that Mischkey and the RCW wouldn't have locked horns.

That same day there was a letter from San Francisco in the mail. Vera Müller was a former resident of Mannheim, had emigrated to the USA in 1936, and had taught European literature at various Californian colleges. She'd been retired for some years now and out of a sense of nostalgia read the *Mannheimer Morgen*. She'd been surprised not to hear anything back about her first letter to Mischkey. She'd responded to the advertisement because the fate of her Jewish friend in the Third Reich was sadly interwoven with the RCW. She thought it a period of recent history that should be more widely researched and published, and she was willing to broker contact with Frau Hirsch. But she didn't want to cause her friend any unnecessary excitement and would only establish contact if the research project was both academically sound and fruitful from the aspect of coming to terms with the past. She asked for assurances on this score.

It was the letter of an educated lady, rendered in lovely, old-fashioned German, and written in sloping, austere handwriting. Sometimes in the summer I see elderly American tourists in Heidelberg with a blue tint in their white hair, bright-pink frames on their spectacles, and garish make-up on their wrinkled skin. This willingness to present oneself as a caricature had always alienated me as an expression of cultural despair. Reading Vera Müller's letter I could suddenly imagine such a lady being interesting and fascinating and recognize the wise weariness of completely forgotten peoples in that cultural despair. I wrote to her saying I'd try to visit her soon.

I called the Heidelberg Union Insurance company. I made it clear that without the trip to America all I could do was write a final report and prepare an invoice. An hour later the clerk in charge called to give me the go-ahead.

So, I was back on the Mischkey case. I didn't know what there was left for me to find out. But there it was, this trail that had vanished and had now re-emerged. And with the green light from the Heidelberg Union Insurance I could pursue it so effortlessly that I didn't have to think too deeply about the why and wherefore.

It was three o'clock in the afternoon and I figured out from my diary that it was 9 a.m. in Pittsburgh. I'd discovered from the ballet director that Sergej Mencke's friends were at the Pittsburgh State Ballet, and International Information divulged its telephone number. The girl from the exchange was jovial. 'You want to give the little lady from *Flashdance* a call?' I didn't know the film. 'Is the movie worth seeing? Should I take a look?' She'd seen it three times. With my dreadful English the long-distance call to Pittsburgh was a torture. At least I found out from the ballet's secretary that both dancers would be in Pittsburgh throughout December.

I came to an understanding with my travel agency that I'd receive an invoice for a Lufthansa flight Frankfurt–Pittsburgh, but would actually be booked on a cheap flight from Brussels to San Francisco with a stopover in New York and a side trip to Pittsburgh. At the beginning of December there wasn't much going on over the Atlantic. I got a flight for Thursday morning.

Towards evening I gave Vera Müller a call in San Francisco. I told her I'd written, but that rather suddenly a convenient opportunity had arisen to come to the USA, and I'd be in San Francisco by the weekend. She said she'd announce my visit to Frau Hirsch; she herself was out of town over the weekend but would be glad to see me on Monday. I noted down Frau Hirsch's address: 410 Connecticut Street, Potrero Hill.

2

A crackle, and the picture came up

From the old films I had visions in my mind of ships steaming into New York, past the Statue of Liberty and on past the skyscrapers, and I'd imagined seeing the same, not from the deck of a liner, but through the small window on my left. However, the airport was way out of the city, it was cold and dirty, and I was glad when I'd transferred and was sitting in the plane to San Francisco. The rows of seats were so squashed together that it was only bearable to be in them with the seat reclined. During the meal you had to put your seat-back up; presumably the airline only served a meal so that you would be happy afterwards when you could recline again.

I arrived at midnight. A cab took me into the city via an eight-lane motorway, and to a hotel. I was feeling wretched after the storm the airplane had flown through. The porter who'd carried my suitcase to the room turned on the television; there was a crackle, and the picture came up. A man was talking with obscene pushiness. I realized later he was a preacher.

The next morning the porter called me a cab, and I stepped out into the street. The window of my room looked out onto the wall of a neighbouring building, and in the room the morning had been grey and quiet. Now the colours and noises of the city exploded around me, beneath a clear, blue sky. The drive over the hills of the town, on streets that led upwards and swooped down again straight as an arrow, the smacking jolts of the cab's worn-out suspension when we crossed a junction, the views of skyscrapers, bridges, and a large bay made me feel dizzy.

The house was situated in a peaceful street. Like all the houses it was made of wood. Steps led to the front door. Up I went and rang the bell. An old man opened the door. 'Mr Hirsch?'

'My husband's been dead for six years,' she said in rusty German. 'You needn't apologize, I'm often taken for a man and I'm used to it. You're the German Vera was telling me about, right?'

Perhaps it was the confusion or the flight or the cab ride – I must have fainted and came to when the old woman threw a glass of water at my face.

'You're lucky you didn't fall down the steps. When you're ready, come and I'll give you a whisky.'

The whisky burned inside me. The room was musty and smelt of age, of old flesh and old food. The same smell had suffused my grandparents' house, I suddenly recalled, and just as suddenly I was seized by the fear of growing old that I'm continuously suppressing.

The woman was perched opposite, and scrutinizing me. Shafts of sunlight shone through the blinds onto her. She was completely bald. 'You want to talk to me about Weinstein, my husband. Vera thinks it's important that what happened is told. But it's not a good story. My husband tried to forget it.'

I didn't realize straight away who Karl Weinstein was. But as she started to talk I remembered. She didn't realize she was not only telling his story but also touching upon my own past.

She spoke in an oddly monotonous voice. Weinstein had been professor of organic chemistry in Breslau until 1933. In 1941, when he was put in a concentration camp, his former assistant Tyberg put in a request for him for the RCW laboratories, which was granted. Weinstein was even quite pleased that he could work in his field again and that he was working with someone who appreciated him as a scientist, addressed him as Professor, and politely said goodbye in the evening when he was taken back to the camp along with the other forced labourers of the Works. 'My husband didn't cope well with life, nor was he very brave. He had no idea, or didn't want to know, what was happening around him and what was coming for him, too.'

'Did you go through this time at the RCW as well?'

'I met Karl on the transport to Auschwitz in nineteen forty-one. And then again only after the war. I'm Flemish, you know, and could hide in Brussels to begin with, until they caught me. I was a beautiful woman. They conducted medical experiments on my scalp. I think that saved my life. But in nineteen forty-five I was old and bald. I was twenty-three.'

One day they'd come to Weinstein, someone from the Works and someone from the SS. They'd told him how he must testify before the police, the prosecutor, and the judge. It was a matter of sabotage, a manuscript that he'd supposedly found in Tyberg's desk, a conversation between Tyberg and a co-worker that he'd supposedly overheard.

I could picture Weinstein, as he was led into my office, in his prisoner's clothes, and gave his testimony.

'He hadn't wanted to at first. It was all false and Tyberg hadn't been bad to him. But they showed him they would crush him. They didn't even promise him his life, only that he could survive a little longer. Can you imagine that? Then my husband was transferred and simply forgotten in the other camp. We'd arranged where we would meet should the whole thing ever be over. In Brussels on the Grand Place. I came there simply by chance in the spring of nineteen forty-six, not thinking of him any more. He'd been waiting there for me since the summer of nineteen forty-five. He recognized me immediately although I'd become this bald, old lady. Quite irresistible!' She laughed.

I couldn't bring myself to tell her that I was the one Weinstein had delivered his testimony to. I also couldn't tell her why it was so important to me. But I had to know. And so I asked, 'Are you certain that the testimony your husband gave was false?'

'I don't understand. I've told you what he told me.' Her face turned cold. 'Get out,' she said, 'get out.'

3

Do not disturb

I walked down the hill and came to the docks and warehouses by the bay. Far and wide I could see neither cab nor bus, nor subway station. I wasn't even sure if San Francisco had a subway. I set off in the direction of the skyscrapers. The street didn't have a name, just a number. In front of me a heavy, black Cadillac was crawling along. Every few steps it drew to a standstill, a black man in a pink silk suit got out, trampled a beer or coke can flat, and dropped it into a large blue plastic sack. A few hundred metres ahead I saw a store. As I came closer I saw it was barred like a fortress. I went in looking for a sandwich and a packet of Sweet Aftons. The goods were behind grating and the checkout reminded me of a counter at the bank. I didn't get a sandwich and no one knew what Sweet Aftons were, and I felt guilty even though I hadn't done anything. As I was leaving the store with a carton of Chesterfields, a freight train rattled past me in the middle of the street.

On the piers I came across a car rental and rented a Chevrolet. I was taken by the one-piece front seating. It reminded me of the Horch on whose front seat I was initiated into love by the wife of my Latin teacher. Together with the car I got a town plan with the 49 Mile Drive highlighted. I followed it without trouble, thanks to the signs everywhere. By the cliffs I found a restaurant. At the entrance I had to edge forward in a line before being led to a seat by the window. Mist was curling over the

Pacific. The show captivated me, as though, beyond the rents in the fog, Japan's coast would come into view any second. I ate a tuna steak, potato in aluminum foil, and iceberg lettuce salad. The beer was called Anchor Steam and tasted almost like a smoked beer in the Bamberg Schlenkerla. The waitress was attentive, kept refilling my coffee cup without my having to ask, enquired after my health and where I was from. She knew Germany, too; she'd visited her boyfriend at the US base in Baumholder once.

After the meal I stretched my legs, clambered around on the cliffs, and suddenly saw before me, more beautiful than I remembered it from films, the Golden Gate Bridge. I took off my coat, folded it, put it on a rock, and sat on it. The coast fell away steeply, beneath me bright sailing boats were criss-crossing, and a freight ship ploughed its gentle path.

I had planned to live at peace with my past. Guilt, atonement, enthusiasm and blindness, pride and anger, morality and resignation – I'd brought it all together in an elaborate balance. The past had achieved abstraction. Now reality had caught up with me and was threatening that balance. Of course I'd let myself be manipulated as a prosecutor, I'd learned that much after 1945. One may question whether there is better manipulation and worse. Nevertheless, I didn't think it was the same thing to be guilty of having served a putative great, bad cause, or to be used by someone as a pawn on the chessboard of a small, shabby intrigue I didn't yet understand.

The stuff Frau Hirsch had told me, what did it amount to exactly? Tyberg and Dohmke, whom I'd investigated, had been convicted purely on the strength of Weinstein's false testimony. By any standard, even the National Socialist one, the judgment was a miscarriage of justice and my investigation was wrong. I'd been taken in by a plot made to trap Tyberg and Dohmke. My memory of it started to come back. In Tyberg's desk hidden documents had been found that revealed a promising plan, essential to the war effort, initially pursued by Tyberg and his research group, then apparently abandoned. The accused repeatedly stressed to me and to the court that they couldn't have followed two promising paths of research at the same time. They had only put the other one on a backburner, to return to later. The whole thing was under the strictest secrecy and their discovery had been so exciting that they'd safeguarded it with the jealousy of the scientist. That had been the only reason for the cache in the desk. That might have got them off, but Weinstein reported a conversation between Dohmke and Tyberg in which both agreed to suppress the discovery to bring about a quick end to the war, even at the price of a German defeat. And now this conversation had never actually taken place.

The sabotage story had unleashed outrage at the time. The second charge of racial defilement hadn't convinced me, even then: my investigation hadn't produced any evidence that Tyberg had had intercourse with a Jewish forced labourer. He was sentenced to death on that account, too. I pondered who from the SS and who from the economic side back then could have set up the conspiracy.

There was a constant flow of traffic over the Golden Gate Bridge. Where did everyone want to get to? I drove to the approach, parked my car beneath the monument to the architect, and walked to the middle of the bridge. I was the only pedestrian. I gazed down onto the metallic gleaming Pacific. Behind me limousines whizzed by with a callous regularity. A cold wind blew round the suspension cables. I was freezing.

With some trouble I found the hotel again. It soon

turned dark. I asked the porter where I could get a bottle of sambuca. He sent me along to a liquor store two streets away. I scanned the shelves in vain. The proprietor regretted he didn't have sambuca, but he did have something similar, wouldn't I like to try Southern Comfort? He packed the bottle in a brown paper bag for me, and twisted the paper shut round the neck. On the way back to the hotel I bought a hamburger. With my trench coat, the brown paper bag in one hand, and the burger in the other I felt like an extra in a second-rate American cop film.

Back in the hotel room I lay down on the bed and switched on the TV. My toothbrush glass was wrapped in cellophane, I tore it off and poured myself a shot. Southern Comfort really doesn't bear the slightest resemblance to sambuca. Still, it tasted pleasant and trickled quite naturally down my throat. Nor did the football on TV have the faintest in common with our football. But I understood the principle and followed the match with increasing excitement.

After a while I applauded when my team had made decent headway with the ball. Finally I must have whooped when my team won, because there came a knocking through the wall. I tried to get up and thump back, but the bed kept tipping up at the side I was trying to get out of. It wasn't that important. Main thing was that topping up the glass still went smoothly. I left the last gulp in the bottle for the flight back.

In the middle of the night I woke up. Now I felt drunk. I was lying fully clothed on the bed, the TV was spitting out images. When I switched it off, my head imploded. I managed to take off my jacket before falling asleep again.

When I woke up, for a brief moment I didn't know where I was. My room was cleaned and tidied, the ashtray empty, and the toothbrush glass back in cellophane. My watch said half past two. I sat on the toilet for a long time, clutching my head. When I washed my hands I avoided looking in the mirror. I found a packet of aspirin in my toilet bag, and twenty minutes later the headache was gone. But with every movement the brain fluid slapped hard against the walls of my skull, and my stomach was crying out for food while telling me it wouldn't keep it down. At home I'd have made a camomile tea, but I didn't know the American word, nor where I'd find it, nor how I'd boil the water.

I took a shower, first hot, then cold. In the hotel's Tea Room I got a black coffee and toast. I took a few steps out onto the street. The way led me to the liquor store. It was still open. I didn't begrudge the Southern Comfort the previous night, I'm not one to nurse a grudge. To make this clear I bought another bottle. The proprietor said: 'Better than any of your sambuca, hey?' I didn't want to contradict him.

This time I intended to get drunk systematically. I got undressed, hung the 'Do not disturb' sign outside my door and my suit over the clothes stand. I stuffed my worn undershirt into a plastic bag provided for the purpose and left it out in the corridor. I added my shoes and hoped that I'd find everything in a decent state the next morning. I locked the door from the inside, drew the curtains, turned on the TV, slipped into my pyjamas, poured my first glass, placed bottle and ashtray within reach on the bedside table, laid my cigarettes and folder of matches next to them, and myself in bed. *Red River* was on TV. I pulled the covers up to my chin, smoked, and drank.

After a while the images of the courtroom I'd appeared in, of the hangings I'd had to attend, of green and grey and black uniforms, and of my wife in her League of German Girls outfit began to fade. I could no longer hear the echo of boots in long corridors, no Führer's speeches on the

People's Receiver, no sirens. John Wayne was drinking whisky, I was drinking Southern Comfort, and as he set off to tidy things up I was with him all the way.

By the following midday, the return to sobriety had become a ritual. At the same time it was clear the drinking was over. I drove to the Golden Gate Park and walked for two hours. In the evening I found Perry's, an Italian restaurant I felt almost as comfortable in as the Kleiner Rosengarten. I slept deeply and dreamlessly, and on Monday morning I discovered the American breakfast. At nine o'clock I gave Vera Müller a call. She would expect me for lunch.

At half past twelve I was standing in front of her house on Telegraph Hill with a bouquet of yellow roses. She wasn't the blue-rinsed caricature I'd envisaged. She was around my age and if I had aged as a man as she had as a woman, I'd have had reason to be content. She was tall, slim, angular, wore her grey hair piled high, over her jeans a Russian smock, her spectacles were hanging from a chain, and there was a mocking expression hovering round her grey eyes and thin mouth. She wore two wedding rings on her left hand.

'Yes, I'm a widow.' She had noticed my glance. 'My husband died three years ago. You remind me of him.' She led me into the sitting room through the windows of which I could see Alcatraz. 'Do you take Pastis as an aperitif? Help yourself, I'll just pop the pizza into the oven.'

When she returned I had poured two glasses. 'I had to confess something to you. I'm not a historian from Hamburg, I'm a private detective from Mannheim. The man whose advertisement you answered, not a Hamburg historian either, was murdered and I'm trying to find out why.'

'Do you already know by whom?'

'Yes and no.' I told my story.

'Did you mention your connection to the Tyberg affair to Frau Hirsch?'

'No, I didn't dare.'

'You really do remind me of my husband. He was a journalist, a famous raging reporter, but each time he wrote a piece, he was afraid. It's good, by the way, you didn't tell her. It would have upset her too much, because of her relationship with Karl, too. Did you know, he had an amazing career again, in Stanford? Sarah never adapted to that world. She stayed with him because she thought she owed it to him for his having waited so long. And at the same time he only lived with her out of a sense of loyalty. The two of them never married.'

She led me out onto the kitchen balcony and fetched the pizza. 'One thing I do like about growing older is that principles develop holes. I never thought I'd be able to eat with an old Nazi prosecutor without choking on my pizza. Are you still a Nazi?'

I choked on my pizza.

'All right, all right. You don't look like one to me. Do you sometimes have problems with your past?'

'At least two bottles of Southern Comfort's worth.' I told her how the weekend had been spent.

At six o'clock we were still sitting together. She told me about her start in America. At the Olympic Games in Berlin she'd met her husband and moved with him to Los Angeles. 'Do you know what I found most difficult? Wearing my bathing suit in the sauna.'

Then she had to leave for her night shift with the help line. I went back to Perry's and merely took a six-pack of beer to bed with me. The next morning I wrote Vera Müller a postcard over breakfast, settled the bill, and drove to the airport. In the evening I was in Pittsburgh. There was snow on the ground.

4

Demolishing Sergej

The cabs that took me to the hotel in the evening and to the ballet the next morning were every bit as yellow as those in San Francisco. It was nine, the ensemble was already in the midst of a rehearsal, at ten they took a break and I was directed to the Mannheimers. They were standing in tights and leotards next to the radiators, yoghurt in hand.

When I introduced myself and the subject of my visit, they could hardly believe I'd come all this way just for them.

'Did you know about Sergej?' Hanne turned to Joschka. 'Hey, I mean, I feel just devastated.'

Joschka was startled, too. 'If we can help Sergej in any way . . . I'll have a word with the boss. It should be fine for us to start again at eleven o'clock. That way we can sit down together in the canteen and talk.'

The canteen was empty. Through the window I looked onto a park with tall, bare trees. Mothers were out with their children, Eskimos in padded overalls, romping around in the snow.

'All right, I mean, it's really important for me to share what I know about Sergej. I'd find it, like, absolutely awful, if someone thought . . . if someone got the wrong . . . Sergej, he's so incredibly sensitive. And he's so vulnerable, not at all macho. You see, that's why he couldn't have done it for starters, he was always terribly afraid of injuries.'

Joschka wasn't so sure. He stirred the contents of his Styrofoam cup with a little plastic stick, contemplatively. 'Herr Self, I don't think Sergej maimed himself either. I just can't imagine anyone doing that. But if anyone . . . You know, Sergej was always having crackpot ideas.'

'How can you say such mean stuff?' Hanne interrupted him. 'I thought you were his friend. No way, that makes me, like, really sad.'

Joschka placed his hand on her arm. 'But, Hanne, don't you remember the evening we were entertaining the dancers from Ghana? He told us how, when he was a boy scout, he deliberately cut his hand with the potato peeler to get out of kitchen duty. We all laughed about it, you too.'

'But you got it completely wrong. He only pretended he'd cut himself and wrapped a large bandage around it. If you're going to, like, distort the truth like that . . . I mean, really, Joschka . . .'

Joschka didn't appear convinced, but didn't want to quarrel with Hanne. I enquired about the shape, and mood, Sergej was in during the last few months of the season.

'Exactly,' said Hanne. 'That doesn't fit with your strange suspicion either. He believed completely in himself, he absolutely wanted to add flamenco to his repertoire, and tried to get a scholarship to Madrid.'

'But, Hanne, he didn't get the scholarship, that's the thing.'

'But don't you get it, the fact he applied for it, that had so much power somehow. And his relationship, that was finally going well in the summer with his German professor. You know, Sergej, he isn't gay, but he can also love men. He's absolutely fantastic that way, I think. And not just something brief, sexual, but like, really deep. It's impossible not to like him. He's so . . .'

'Sweet?' I suggested.

'Yeah, sweet. Do you actually know him, Herr Self?'

'Uh, could you tell me who the German professor is you mentioned?'

'Was it really German, not law?' Joschka frowned.

'Oh, crap, you're demolishing Sergej. He was a Germanist, such a cuddly guy. But his name . . . I don't know if I should tell you.'

'Hanne, the two of them hardly made a secret of it considering how they carried on round town. It's Fritz Kirchenberg from Heidelberg. Maybe it's a good idea for you to talk to him.'

I asked them about Sergej's qualities as a dancer. Hanne answered first.

'But that's beside the point. Even if you're not a good dancer you don't have to hack your leg off. I'm not even going to discuss it. And I'm still convinced you're wrong.'

'I don't have any concrete opinion as yet, Frau Fischer. And I'd like to point out that Herr Mencke hasn't lost his leg, merely broken it.'

'I don't know what sort of knowledge you have of ballet, Herr Self,' said Joschka. 'At the end of the day, it's the same with us as it is everywhere else. There are the stars, and the ones who will be stars one day, and then there's the solid middle rank of the ones who've let go of their daydreams of glory but don't have to worry about earning a living. And then there are the rest – the ones who have to live in constant fear of whether there'll be a next engagement, for whom it's certainly over when they start to get older. Sergej belongs to the third group.'

Hanne didn't contradict. She let her defiant expression show how completely out of order she felt this conversation was. 'I thought you wanted to find out something about Sergej, the person. You men have nothing in your heads beyond careers, really.'

'How did Herr Mencke envisage his future?'

'On the side he'd always done ballroom dancing and he told me once he'd like to start a dance school, a perfectly conventional one, for fifteen- and sixteen-year-olds.'

'That also proves he couldn't have done anything to himself. Think it through, Joschka. How's he supposed to become a dance teacher minus a leg?'

'Did you also know about his dancing school plans, Frau Fischer?'

'Sergej played around with lots of ideas. He's so brilliantly creative and has an incredible imagination. He could also imagine doing something completely different, breeding sheep in Provence, or something.'

They had to get back to rehearsal. They gave me their telephone numbers in case other questions came to me, asked whether I had plans for the evening, and promised to set aside a complimentary ticket for me at the door. I watched them go. Joschka moved with concentration and there was a spring in his step, Hanne trod lightly, as though walking on air. Admittedly, she'd talked, like, a lot of nonsense, but she walked with conviction, and I'd have liked to watch her dance that evening. But Pittsburgh was far too cold. I had a car take me to the airport, flew to New York, and got a return flight that same evening to Frankfurt. I think I'm too old for America.

5

So whose goose are you cooking?

Over brunch in Café Gmeiner I drew up a programme for the rest of the week. Outside, the snow was falling in thick flakes. I'd have to root out the scoutmaster of the troop Mencke had belonged to, and speak to Professor Kirchenberg. And I wanted to talk to the judge who'd sentenced Tyberg and Dohmke to death. I had to know whether the sentence had been influenced from above.

Judge Beufer had been elevated to the Appellate Court in Karlsruhe after the war. At the main post office I found his name in the Karlsruhe telephone directory. His voice sounded astonishingly young, and he remembered my name. 'Master Self,' he crooned in his Swabian accent. 'Whatever became of him?' He was willing to have me round for a talk that afternoon.

He lived in Durlach in a house on the hillside with a view of Karlsruhe. I could see the large gasometer with its welcoming inscription 'Karlsruhe'. Judge Beufer opened the door in person. He had a soldier's upright posture, was wearing a grey suit, beneath it a white shirt and a red tie with a silver tie pin. The collar of his shirt had become too large for the old, scraggy neck. Beufer was bald and his face had a heavy downward pull, bags under the eyes, jowls, chin. We'd always joked about his sticking-out ears in the public prosecutor's office. They were more impressive than ever. He looked ill. He must be well over eighty.

'So, he's become a private detective. Isn't he ashamed? He was a good lawyer, after all, a sharp prosecutor. I expected to see him back with us when the worst of it was over.'

We sat in his study and sipped sherry. He still read the *New Legal Weekly*. 'Master Self hasn't simply come to pay his old judge a visit.' His little piggy eyes were twinkling shrewdly.

'Do you remember the case of Tyberg and Dohmke? End of nineteen forty-three, beginning of forty-four. I was leading the investigation, Södelknecht was the prosecutor. And you were presiding over court.'

'Tyberg and Dohmke . . .' He spoke the names softly to himself a few times. 'Yes, of course. They were sentenced to death and Dohmke was executed. Tyberg escaped. He went a long way, that man. And was a true gentleman, or is he still alive? Bumped into him once at a reception in Solitude, joked about old times. He certainly understood we all had to do our duty back then.'

'What I'd like to know – was the court given signals from above regarding the outcome, or was it a perfectly normal trial?'

'Why does that interest him? Whose goose is he cooking, that Master Self?'

The question was bound to come. I told him about a coincidental connection to Frau Müller and my meeting with Frau Hirsch. 'I simply want to know what happened back then, and what role I played.'

'To reopen the trial, what the lady told you is nowhere near enough. If Weinstein were still alive . . . but he isn't. I don't believe it anyway. A lawyer has his gut feeling, and the more clearly I remember, the more certain I am the verdict was right.'

'And were there signals from above? I'm sure you won't misunderstand me, Herr Beufer. We both know that

German judges knew how to preserve their independence even under extraordinary conditions. Nevertheless, now and then some interested party would try to exert influence, and I'd like to know whether there was an interested party in this trial.'

'Oh, Self, why won't he let sleeping dogs lie? But if it's essential for his peace of mind ... Weismüller called me a few times back then, the former general director. His focus was to clear it out of the way and stop people gossiping about RCW. Perhaps the sentencing of Tyberg and Dohmke met with his approval, simply for that reaon. Nothing clears up a case quite so effectively as a quick hanging. Whether there were other reasons he wanted the sentence ... No idea, I don't think so, though.'

'That was it?'

'Weismüller also had some business with Södelknecht. Tyberg's defence counsel had brought forward someone from the RCW as a witness who talked himself blue in the face on the witness stand, and Weismüller intervened on his behalf. Hang on, that man also went a long way, yes, Korten is the name, the current general director. There we have them, the whole merry crew of general directors.' He laughed.

How could I have forgotten? I had been glad not to have to bring my friend and brother-in-law into it myself, but then the defence had hauled him in. I'd been glad because Korten had worked so closely together with Tyberg that his participation in the trial could have cast suspicion on him, or damaged his career at least. 'Was it known at court then that Korten and I are brothers-in-law?'

'My word. I'd never have thought it. But you advised your brother-in-law badly. He spoke out so strongly for Tyberg that Södelknecht almost arrested him on the spot at the hearing. Very decent, too decent. It didn't help Tyberg one bit. It smells just a little fishy when a witness for the defence has nothing to say about the deed and only spouts friendly platitudes about the accused.'

There was nothing left to ask Beufer. I drank the second sherry he poured me, and chatted about colleagues we'd both known. Then I took my leave.

'Master Self, now he's off to follow that sniffing nose again. The quest for justice won't let go of him, eh? Will he show his face again at old Beufer's? Be delighted.'

On top of my car were ten centimetres of fresh snow. I swept it off, was glad to make it safely down the hill, onto the autobahn. And once I was on that, I drove north in the wake of a snowplough. It had turned dark. The car radio reported traffic jams and played hits from the sixties.

6

Potatoes, cabbage, and hot black pudding

In the thick snow I missed the turn-off to Mannheim at the Walldorf intersection. Then the snowplough drove into a parking lot, and I was lost. I made it as far as the Hardtwald service area.

At the stand-up snack bar I waited with my coffee for the driving snow to stop. I stared into the swirling flakes. All at once pictures from the past came vividly alive.

It was on an evening in August or September, 1943. Klara and I had to leave our apartment in Werderstrasse, and had just completed the move to Bahnhofstrasse. Korten was over for dinner. There were potatoes, cabbage, and hot black pudding. He enthused about our new apartment, praised Klara for the meal, and this annoyed me, because he knew what a pitiful cook Klärchen was and it couldn't have escaped him that the potatoes were over-salted and the cabbage burnt. Then Klara left us men with our cigars for a bit of male conversation.

At that time the Tyberg and Dohmke file had just reached my desk. I wasn't convinced by the results of the police investigation. Tyberg was from a good family, had volunteered for the front, and it was only against his will, as his research work was essential to the war effort, that he'd been left behind at the RCW. I couldn't picture him as a saboteur.

'You know Tyberg, don't you? What do you think of him?'

'A man beyond reproach. We were all horrified that he and Dohmke were arrested at work, without anyone knowing why. Member of the national German hockey team in nineteen thirty-six, winner of the Professor Demel Medal, a gifted chemist, esteemed colleague and respected superior – no, I really don't understand what you people at the police and prosecutors are thinking.'

I explained to him that an arrest wasn't a conviction and that in a German court no one was sentenced unless the necessary evidence was at hand. This was an old theme of ours from our student days. Korten had come across a book at a bookstall about famous miscarriages of justice and argued for nights on end with me whether human justice can avoid miscarriages. That was my contention, Korten's position being the opposite, that one has to accept they occur.

A winter evening during our student days in Berlin came to my mind. Klara and I were tobogganing on the Kreuzberg, and were expected back at the Korten household for supper. Klara was seventeen, I'd encountered her and overlooked her, thousands of times, as Ferdinand's little sister. I'd only taken the brat tobogganing with me because she'd begged so. Actually, I was hoping to meet Pauline on the toboggan run, help her up after a fall or protect her from the ghastly Kreuzberg street urchins. Was Pauline there? At any rate, all of a sudden I only had eyes for Klara. She was wearing a fur jacket and a bright scarf, and her blonde curls were flying, and snowflakes melting upon her glowing cheeks. On the way home we kissed for the first time. Klara had to persuade me into going up to supper. I didn't know how to behave towards her in front of her parents and brother.

When I left later she found some pretext to bring me to the front door and gave me a secret kiss.

I caught myself smiling out of the window. In the parking lot a military convoy stopped, also unable to make headway in the snow. My car was swathed in another thick layer. At the counter I fetched a coffee refill and a sandwich. I took up my place at the window again.

Korten and I had also come round to talking about Weinstein that time. An irreproachable man as the accused and a Jew as the prosecution witness – I wondered whether I shouldn't drop the investigation. I couldn't tell Korten about Weinstein's significance, nor could I let the opportunity of learning something about Weinstein slip by.

'What do you actually think about using Jews at the Works?'

'You know, Gerd, that we've always thought differently about the Jewish question. I've never had any truck with anti-Semitism. I find it difficult having forced labourers in the plant, but whether they're Jews or Frenchmen or Germans is all the same. In our laboratory we have Professor Weinstein working with us and it's a crying shame that the man can't be behind a lectern or in his own laboratory. His service to us is invaluable, and if you go by his appearance and cast of mind, you couldn't find anyone more German. A professor of the old school, up until nineteen thirty-three he had a chair in organic chemistry at Breslau. Everything that Tyberg is as a chemist he owes, as his pupil and assistant, to Weinstein. The loveable, scatterbrained academic type.'

'And if I were to tell you that he's the one accusing Tyberg?'

'My God, Gerd. And with Weinstein so fond of his student Tyberg . . . I really don't know what to say.'

A snowplough made its way to the parking lot. The

driver got down and came into the snack bar. I asked him how I could get to Mannheim.

'A colleague has just set off for the Heidelberg intersection. Get going quickly before the lane is blocked again.'

It was seven. At a quarter to eight I was at the Heidelberg intersection and at nine in Mannheim. I had to stretch my legs and revelled in the deep snow. I'd have liked to have driven a troika through Mannheim.

7

What exactly are you investigating now?

At eight I awoke, but I didn't manage to get up. It had all been too much, the night flight from New York, the trip to Karlsruhe, the discussion with Beufer, the memories, and the odyssey along the snow-covered autobahn.

At eleven Philipp called. 'Wow, caught you at last? Where have you been gadding off to? Your dissertation is ready.'

'Dissertation?' I didn't know what he was talking about.

'Door-induced fractures. A contribution to the morphology of auto-aggression. You did commission it.'

'Oh, yes. And now there's a scientific treatise? When can I have it?'

'Anytime. Just come by the hospital and pick it up.'

I got up and made some coffee. The sky was still heavy with snow. Turbo came in from the balcony, powdered white.

My refrigerator was empty and I went shopping. It's nice that they go easier than they used to on sprinkling salt in towns. Instead of wading through brown slush, I walked on crunchy, tightly packed fresh snow. Children were building snowmen and having snowball fights. In the bakery at the Wasserturm I bumped into Judith.

'Isn't it a splendid day?' Her eyes were sparkling. 'Before, when I still had to go to work, the snow always irritated me. Clear the windshield, car doesn't start, drive slowly, get stuck. I was really missing out on something!'

'Come on,' I said, 'let's have a winter walk to the Kleiner Rosengarten. You're invited.'

This time she didn't say no. I felt somewhat old-fashioned next to her; she in her padded jacket, trousers, and high boots that are probably a spin-off of space technology, me in my overcoat and galoshes. On the way I told her about my investigations in the Mencke case and the snow in Pittsburgh. She also asked straight away whether I'd seen the little lady from *Flashdance*. I was getting curious about the film.

Giovanni was wide-eyed. When Judith had gone to the restroom he came up to our table. 'Old lady notsa good? New lady better? Next time you getta Italian lady from me, then you have peace.'

'German man don't needa the peace, need lotsa, lotsa, ladies.'

'Then it's lotsa good food you need.' He recommended the steak pizzaiola preceded by the chicken soup. 'The chef slaughtered the chicken himself this morning.' I ordered the same for Judith and a bottle of Chianti Classico to go with it.

'I was in America for another reason, Judith. The Mischkey case won't leave me in peace. I haven't made any progress. But the trip confronted me with my own past.'

She listened attentively to my report.

'What exactly are you investigating now? And why?'

'I don't know. I'd like to talk with Tyberg, if he's still alive.'

'Oh, he's alive all right. I often wrote letters to him, sent him business reports or birthday presents. He lives on Lake Maggiore, in Monti sopra Locarno.'

'Then I'd also like to speak to Korten again.'

'And what does he have to do with Peter's death?'

'I don't know, Judith. What wouldn't I give to be able

233

to get to the bottom of it? At least Mischkey has got me working on the past. Have you had any further thoughts about the murder?'

She'd considered taking the story to the press. 'I find it simply unbearable for the whole thing to end like this.'

'Do you mean not knowing? It won't improve by going to the press.'

'No. I believe the RCW hasn't really paid. Regardless of the way things went with old Schmalz, it does fall under their responsibility somehow. And besides, perhaps we'll discover more if the press stirs up a hornets' nest.'

Giovanni brought the steaks. We ate for a while in silence. I couldn't warm to the idea of going to the press. After all, I had been commissioned by the RCW to find Mischkey, at least the RCW had paid me for it. All that Judith knew and could go to the papers with she knew from me. My professional loyalty was at stake. I was annoyed I'd accepted Korten's money. Otherwise I'd be free now.

I explained my concern to her. 'I need to consider whether I can change my spots, but I'd prefer you to wait.'

'All right then. I was perfectly happy back then not to have to foot your bill, but I should have known straight away it would come at a price.'

We were finished with dinner. Giovanni brought two sambucas. 'With the compliments of the house.' Judith told me about her life as an unemployed person. To begin with she had enjoyed the freedom, but slowly the problems began. She couldn't expect the Unemployment Office to find her another comparable job. She'd have to get going herself. At the same time she wasn't sure if she wanted to embark on a life as an executive assistant again.

'Do you know Tyberg personally? I last saw him forty years ago and I don't know if I'd recognize him again.'

'Yes, at the RCW centenary, I was assigned as his Girl Friday, to look after him. Why?'

'Would you like to come with me if I visit him in Locarno? I'd like that.'

'So you really want to know. How do you propose to make contact with him?'

I pondered.

'Leave it to me,' she said. 'I'll set it up somehow. When do we go?'

'How soon could you organize a meeting with Tyberg?'

'Sunday? Monday? I can't say. Maybe he's in the Bahamas.'

'Set the date for as soon as possible.'

8

On the Scheffel Terrace

Professor Kirchenberg was willing to see me straight away when he heard it had to do with Sergej. 'The poor boy, and you want to help him. Then come round right now. I'm in the Palais Boisserée all afternoon.'

From the press coverage of a trial involving the German department, I knew it was housed in the Palais Boisserée. The professors considered themselves rightful descendants of the early princely residents. When rebellious students had profaned the palais, an example had been made of them with the help of the law.

Kirchenberg was particularly princely in his professorial manner. He had thinning hair, contact lenses, a gorged, pink face, and, in spite of his tendency to corpulence, he moved with a light-footed elegance. As a greeting he clasped my hand in both of his. 'Isn't it simply shocking what has befallen Sergej?'

I replied with my queries about Sergej's state of mind, career plans, finances.

He leaned back in his armchair. 'Serjoscha has been shaped by his difficult youth. The years between eight and fourteen in Roth, a bigoted garrison town in Franken, were sheer martyrdom for the child. A father who could only live out his homoeroticism in military power postures, a mother as busy as a bee, good-hearted, utterly weak-willed. And the tramp, tramp, tramp,' he drummed his knuckles on the desktop, 'of soldiers marching in and out every day. Listen hard.' With one hand he made a gesture commanding my silence, with the other he kept up the drumming. Slowly the hand grew still. Kirchenberg sighed. 'It's only with me that he's been able to work through those years.'

When I broached the suspicion of self-mutilation, Kirchenberg was beside himself. 'That's so laughable, it's ridiculous. Sergej has a very loving relationship with his body, almost narcissistic. Amid all the prejudices doing the rounds about us gays, surely this much at least is understood, that we take better care of our bodies than the average heterosexual. We are our body, Herr Self.'

'Was Sergej Mencke really gay, then?'

'Such prejudice in your questions,' said Kirchenberg, almost pityingly. 'You've never sat on the Scheffel Terrace reading Stefan George. Do it sometime. Then perhaps you'll feel that homoeroticism isn't a question of being, but rather of becoming. Sergej isn't, he's becoming.'

I took my leave from Professor Kirchenberg and passed Mischkey's apartment on the way to the castle. And I did spend a little time on the Scheffel Terrace. I was cold. Or was I becoming cold? There was no becoming going on, perhaps I couldn't expect it without Stefan George.

In Café Gundel their special Christmas cookies, embossed with local sights, were on display already. I purchased a bagful, intending to surprise Judith with them on the journey to Locarno.

Back in the office everything ran like clockwork. From Information I obtained the telephone number of the Catholic priest's office in Roth; the chaplain was only too happy to interrupt his sermon preparation to inform me that the leader of the Catholic Scout troop in Roth since time immemorial had been Joseph Maria Jungbluth, senior teacher. I reached Senior Teacher Jungbluth immediately thereafter. He said he'd be glad to meet me the next day in the early afternoon to talk about little Siegfried.

Judith had fixed a date with Tyberg for Sunday afternoon, and we decided to travel on Saturday. 'Tyberg looks forward to meeting you.'

9

And then there were three

Mannheim to Nürnberg on the new autobahn should take two hours. The Schwabach/Roth exit comes thirty kilometres before Nürnberg. One day Roth will lie on the Augsburg–Nürnberg autobahn. I won't be around then.

Fresh snow had fallen in the night. On the journey I had the choice of two open lanes, a well-worn one on the right and a narrow one for overtaking. Passing a truck was a lurching adventure. Three and a half hours later, I arrived. In Roth there are a couple of half-timbered houses, a few sandstone buildings, the Evangelical and the Catholic churches, pubs that have adapted themselves to military needs, and lots of barracks. Not even a local patriot could describe Roth as the Pearl of Franken. It was just before one and I picked an inn. In the Roter Hirsch, which had resisted the trend for fast food and had even retained its old furnishings, the proprietor did the cooking himself. I asked the waitress for a typically Bavarian dish. She didn't understand my request. 'Bavarian? We're in Franken.' So I asked her to recommend a typical dish from Franken. 'Everything,' she said. 'Our entire menu is Frankish. Including the coffee.' Helpful breed of folk here. Pot luck. I ordered *Saure Zipfel* with fried potatoes, and a dark beer.

Saure Zipfel are bratwurst, but they're not fried, they're heated up in a stock of vinegar, onions, and spices. And they taste like it, too. The fried potatoes were deliciously crispy. The waitress softened enough to point out the way to Allersberger Strasse where Senior Teacher Jungbluth lived.

Jungbluth opened the door in civilian clothes. In my mind's eye I'd pictured him in long socks, knee-length brown trousers, blue neckerchief, and a wide-brimmed scout's hat. He couldn't recall the scout camp at which the young Mencke wore a real or pretend bandage to shirk washing-up duty. But he remembered other incidents.

'Siegfried liked getting out of chores. In school, as well, where he was in my class in the first and second year. You know, he was a frightened child – and a cringing one. I don't understand much about medicine, beyond first aid, of course, which I need as senior teacher and scoutmaster. But I would think you need a certain level of courage for self-mutilation, and I can't imagine Siegfried having that courage. Now his father, on the other hand, he's made of different stuff.'

He was showing me to the door when he remembered something else. 'Would you like to see some photos?' The pictures in the album were of various combinations of scouts, tents, campfires, bicycles. I saw children singing, laughing, and fooling around, but I could also see in their eyes that the snapshots were engineered by Senior Teacher Jungbluth. 'That's Siegfried.' He pointed to a rather frail blond boy with a reticent look on his face. A few photos later I came across him again. 'What's wrong with his leg?' His left leg was in plaster. 'Right,' said Senior Teacher Jungbluth. 'An unpleasant story. For six months the accident insurance tried to stick me with negligence. But Siegfried just had a careless fall when we were in the stalagmite caves in Pottenstein, and broke his leg. I can't be everywhere at once.' He looked at me seeking agreement. I was glad to concur.

On the way home, I took stock. Not much remained to

be done on the Sergej Mencke case. I still wanted to take a look at Philipp's young scholar's thesis, and I'd saved my visit to Sergej in the hospital for last. I was tired of them all, the senior teachers, the army captains, the gay German professors, the whole ballet scene, and Sergej too, even before I'd seen him. Had I grown weary of my profession? In the Mischkey case I'd already let my professional standards drop, and as for my distaste for the Mencke case, it wouldn't have been there before. Should I call it quits? Did I want to live beyond eighty anyway? I could get my life insurance paid out, that would feed me for twelve years. I decided to talk to my tax adviser and insurance agent in the new year.

I drove westwards, into the setting sun. As far as my eye could see the snow gleamed in a rosy hue. The sky was tinted the blue of pale porcelain. In the Franken villages and small towns I drove past, smoke unfurled from the chimneys. The homely light in the windows rekindled old desires for security. Homesick for Nowhere.

Philipp was still on duty when I looked him up in the station at seven. 'Willy is dead,' he greeted me dejectedly. 'The idiot. To die of a burst appendix these days is just ridiculous. I don't understand why he didn't call me; he must have been in terrible pain.'

'You know, Philipp, I've often had the impression in the years since Hilde's death that he didn't actually have the will to live.'

'These silly husbands and widowers. If he'd just said the word, I know women who'd make him forget any number of Hildes. What's become of your Brigitte, by the way?'

'She's running around in Rio. When's the funeral?'

'A week from today. Two p.m. at the main cemetery in Ludwigshafen. I had to see to it all. There's no one else. Would a red sandstone gravestone with a screech owl on it meet with your approval? We'll pool resources, you, Eberhard, and me, so that he gets planted decently.'

'Have you thought of the announcements? And we'll have to inform the dean of his old faculty. Could your secretary do that?'

'That's fine. I wish I could join you to have a bite to eat. But I can't get away. Don't forget the dissertation.'

And then there were three. I went home and opened a can of sardines. I wanted to try empty sardine cans on my Christmas tree this year and had to start collecting them. It was almost too late to get enough together before Christmas. Should I invite Philipp and Eberhard next Friday for a funeral feast of sardines in oil?

'Door-Induced Fractures' was fifty pages long. The system underlying the work emerged as a combination of doors and breaks. The introduction contained a diagram, the horizontal of which depicted the various fracture-inducing doors, and the vertical the door-induced fractures. Most of the 196 squares contained figures revealing how often the corresponding constellation had cropped up at the city hospital in the last twenty years.

I looked for the line 'car door' and the column 'tibia fracture'. At the point they met I found the number 2 and afterwards in the text the respective case histories. Although all names had been removed I recognized Sergej's in one. The other dated back to 1972. A nervous cavalier, while helping his lady into the car, had shut the door too swiftly. The study could only cite one case of self-mutilation. A failed goldsmith had hoped to gain heaps of gold with his insured, and broken, right thumb. In the furnace cellar he had placed his right hand in the frame of the iron door and slammed it shut with his left. The affair only came apart because, with the insurance money already paid, he had bragged about his coup. He told the police that as a child he'd attached his wobbly milk-teeth to the door handle with a thread and pulled them out. That's what had given him the idea.

The decision to call Frau Mencke and enquire about young Siegfried's methods of tooth extraction was one I put on ice.

Yesterday I'd been too tired to stay up to watch *Flashdance*, borrowed from the video rental on Seckenheimer Strasse. Now I slid in the cassette. Afterwards I danced under the shower. Why hadn't I stayed longer in Pittsburgh?

10

Stop thief

In Basle Judith and I took our first break. We drove off the
autobahn into town and parked on Münster-Platz. It was
covered in snow and was free of aggravating Christmas
decorations. We walked a few steps to Café Spielmann,
found a table by the window, and had a view over the
Rhine and the bridge with the small chapel in the middle.

'Now tell me in detail how you set this up with
Tyberg,' I asked Judith over a bowl of muesli, which was
particularly delicious here, with lots of cream and without
an overabundance of oat flakes.

'During the centenary when I was assigned to him he
invited me to look him up if I was ever in Locarno. I
mentioned this and said I had to chauffeur my elderly
uncle,' she placed a soothing hand on mine, 'to look for a
holiday home there. I added that he knew this elderly
uncle from the war years.' Judith was proud of her
diplomatic move. I was concerned.

'Won't Tyberg throw me out on the spot when he
recognizes me as the former Nazi prosecutor? Wouldn't it
have been better to have told him straight out?'

'I did consider it, but then perhaps he wouldn't even
have let the former Nazi prosecutor over his threshold.'

'And why elderly uncle, actually, and not elderly
friend?'

'That smacks of lover. I think Tyberg was interested in
me as a woman, and perhaps he wouldn't see me if he

thought I was firmly attached to someone else, especially if I brought this someone with me. You are a sensitive private detective.'

'Yes. I'm perfectly willing to face up to the responsibility of having been Tyberg's prosecutor. But should I confess to him in one fell swoop that I'm your lover, not your uncle?'

'Are you asking me?' She said it abruptly yet playfully, and got out her knitting as though settling down to a longer discussion.

I lit a cigarette. 'You've interested me as a woman time and again, and now I wonder whether I was just an old dodderer to you, avuncular and sexless.'

'What are you after now? "You've interested me as a woman time and again." If you were interested in me in the past then leave it. If you're interested in the present then say so. You always prefer taking responsibility for the past rather than for the present.' Knit two, purl two.

'I don't have a problem saying I'm interested in you, Judith.'

'Listen, Gerd, of course I see you as a man, and I like you as a man. It never went far enough for me to make the first move. And certainly not in the past few weeks. But what sort of agonized first move is this, or isn't it one? "I don't have a problem saying I'm interested in you" when you obviously have an enormous problem just squeezing that roundabout, cautious sentence out. Come on, let's get going.' She wrapped the started pullover sleeve round the needles and wound more wool round it.

My mind went blank. I felt humiliated. We didn't exchange a word all the way to Olten.

Judith had found Dvořák's Cello Concerto on the radio and was knitting.

What had actually humiliated me? Judith had only hit me around the head with what I'd felt myself in recent months: the lack of clarity in my feelings towards her. But she'd done it so unkindly by quoting myself back at me that I felt exposed and skewered. I told her so near Zofingen.

She let her knitting sink to her lap and stared out in front of her at the road for a long while.

'When I was an executive assistant I so often encountered men who wanted something from me, but didn't put themselves on the line. They'd like to have something going with me, but at the same time they'd pretend they didn't. They'd arrange things so they could immediately retreat without getting really involved. It seemed to me that was the lie of the land with you, as well. You make the first move, but perhaps it isn't really one, a gesture that costs you nothing and has no risk attached. You talk about humiliation . . . I didn't want to humiliate you. Oh, shit, why are the only little wounds you notice your own?' She turned her head away. It sounded as if she was crying. But I couldn't see.

By Lucerne it was getting dark. When we reached Wassen I didn't want to drive any further. The autobahn was cleared, but it had started snowing. I knew the Hotel des Alpes from earlier Adriatic expeditions. There, still, in Reception was the cage with the Indian mynah bird. When it saw us, it squawked, 'Stop thief, stop thief.'

At dinner we had the creamy *Zürcher Geschnetzeltes* and diced roast potatoes. During the drive we had started to argue about whether success inevitably leads an artist to despise his audience. Röschen had once told me about a concert of Serge Gainsbourg's in Paris where the more contemptuously Gainsbourg treated the audience, the more appreciatively they applauded. Since then this question has preoccupied me, and expanded in my mind into the larger problem of whether one can grow old without despising people either. Judith put up a lengthy resistance to this argument about the link between artistic success and scorn of others. Over the third glass of Fendant she gave in. 'You're right, Beethoven went deaf, after all. Deafness is the perfect expression of contempt for one's environment.'

In my monastic single room I slept a sound, deep sleep. We set off early for Locarno. When we drove out of the Gotthard tunnel, winter was over.

I I

Suite in B minor

We arrived towards midday, took rooms in a hotel by the lake, and lunched in the glassed-in veranda, looking out at the colourful boats. The sun beat warmly through the panes. I was nervous thinking about tea at Tyberg's house. From Locarno a blue cable car goes up to Monti. At the halfway point, where the ascending cabin meets the descending one, there's a station, Madonna del Sasso, a famous pilgrimage church, not beautiful to look at, but in a beautiful location. We walked that far on the Way of the Cross, strewn with large round pebbles. And then we took the cable car to save ourselves the rest of the climb.

We followed the curving street to Tyberg's house on the small square with the post office. We were standing in front of a wall at least three metres high that came down to the street, with cast-iron railings running along it. The pavilion on the corner, and the trees and bushes behind the railings, underscored the elevated situation of the house and garden. We rang the bell, opened the heavy door, went up the steps to the front garden, and there facing us was a simple, red-painted, two-level house. Next to the entrance we saw a garden table and chairs, like the ones in beer-gardens. The table was awash with books and manuscripts. Tyberg unwrapped himself from a camel-hair blanket and came towards us, tall, with a slightly bent forward gait, a full head of white hair, a neat, short-trimmed grey beard, and bushy eyebrows. He was wearing a pair of half-spectacles, over the top of which he was now looking at us with curious brown eyes.

'Dear Frau Buchendorff, lovely that you thought of me. And this is your good uncle. You are also welcome to Villa Sempreverde. We've met before, your niece tells me. No, wait,' he deflected me as I was about to start talking, 'I'll work it out on my own. I'm working on my memoirs at the moment,' he indicated the table, 'and like to practise jogging my memory.'

He led us through the house to the back garden. 'Shall we walk a little? The butler will make tea.'

The garden path followed the mountain upwards. Tyberg enquired after Judith's health, her plans, her work at the RCW. He had a quiet, pleasant manner of putting his questions, and showing his interest to Judith by small observations. Nonetheless I was amazed at how openly Judith, albeit not mentioning my name or role in it all, recounted her departure from the RCW. And just as amazed at Tyberg's reaction. He was neither sceptical regarding Judith's picture of events, nor enraged by any of the participants, from Mischkey to Korten, nor did he express condolence or regret. He simply registered Judith's account attentively.

With tea the butler brought us pastries. We sat in a large chamber with a grand piano that Tyberg referred to as the music room. Discussion had turned to the economic situation. Judith juggled with capital and labour, input and output, the balance of trade, and the gross national product. Tyberg and I connected over the notion of the Balkanization of the Federal Republic of Germany. He agreed so swiftly that to begin with I feared he'd misunderstood me and thought I meant there were too many Turks. But his mind, too, was on the decrease in the number of trains and in their punctuality, and how the post office worked less and continuously less reliably, and the police were getting more shameless by the day.

'Yes,' he said thoughtfully. 'Also there are so many regulations that not even the bureaucrats themselves take them seriously any more, instead they apply them either rigidly or sloppily entirely by whim, and sometimes don't apply them at all. I often wonder what sort of industrial society is going to grow out of all this. Post-democratic feudal bureaucracy?'

I love discussions like this. Unfortunately, although he may read a book now and again, Philipp's sole interest is women, and Eberhard's horizon doesn't go beyond the sixty-four squares. Willy had thought in grand evolutionary perspectives and toyed with the idea that the world, or what humans leave of it, will be taken over by birds in the next millennium.

Tyberg scrutinized me for a long time. 'Of course. Being Frau Buchendorff's uncle doesn't mean you have to be called Buchendorff. You are the retired public prosecutor Doctor Self.'

'Not retired, dropped out in nineteen forty-five.'

'Made to drop out, I bet,' said Tyberg.

I didn't want to explain myself. Judith noticed and jumped in. 'Just leaving doesn't mean much. Most of them went back. Uncle Gerd didn't, not because he couldn't, but because he no longer wanted to.'

Tyberg continued to look at me probingly. I felt ill at ease. What do you say to someone sitting opposite you whom you almost sent to the gallows due to an erroneous investigation? Tyberg wanted to know more. 'So you didn't want to remain a public prosecutor after nineteen forty-five. That's interesting. What were your reasons?'

'When I tried to explain it to Judith once she found my reasons to be more aesthetic than moral. I was disgusted by the attitude of my colleagues during and after their re-employment, the lack of any awareness of their own guilt. All right, I could have got involved again if I'd had a different attitude and kept the guilt in mind. But I'd have felt like an outsider, and so I preferred to stay properly outside.'

'The longer you sit there facing me, the clearer I see you as the young prosecutor. Of course you've changed. But there's still that sparkle in your eyes, more mischievous now, and that cleft in your chin was already a dimple back then. What were you thinking of, to wipe the floor with Dohmke and me like that? I've just been working on the trial in my memoirs.'

'The trial came up again for me recently, as well. That's why I'm glad to be able to talk to you. In San Francisco I met the partner of the late prosecution witness Professor Weinstein and discovered his testimony was false. Someone from the Works and an SS officer put pressure on him. Do you have any idea, or do you even know who could have had an interest in your and Dohmke's disappearance? I hate to have been used as the tool of unknown interests.'

Tyberg rang a bell, the butler appeared, tidied up, and served sherry. Tyberg sat there, frowning, staring into space. 'I started pondering this in prison while I was awaiting trial, and to this day I have found no answer. Time and again I've thought of Weismüller. That was also the reason I didn't want to return to RCW immediately after the war. But I've no confirmation for this notion. I've also been preoccupied for a long time by how Weinstein could have given that testimony. That he made it to my desk, found the manuscript in the drawer, misinterpreted it, and reported me, I found devastating enough. But his testimony about a conversation between Dohmke and myself that never took place was even more devastating. I wondered if it was all for a few advantages at the camp.

Now I hear he was forced. It must have been terrible for him. Did his partner know and tell you that he tried to contact me after the war, and I refused? I was too hurt and he must have been too proud to tell me in his letter about the pressure he'd been under.'

'What happened to your research at the RCW, Herr Tyberg?'

'Korten kept going with it. It was the result anyway of close cooperation between Korten, Dohmke, and myself. The three of us had also made the decision together that we would only pursue the one path to begin with, and put the other on the backburner. The whole thing was our baby, you see, that we jealously hatched and tended and didn't let anyone near. We didn't even let Weinstein into our confidence although he was an important part of our team, scientifically almost on equal footing. But you wanted to know what happened to our research. Since the oil crisis I wonder sometimes if it won't become highly topical again all of a sudden. Fuel synthesis. We'd gone at it a different way from Bergius, Tropsch, and Fischer because from the outset we attributed great significance to the cost factor. Korten continued the development of our process with great dedication, and readied it for production. That work was, quite rightly, the basis of his swift ascent in the RCW even though after the end of the war the process itself was no longer of importance. Korten, I believe, had it patented, though, as the Dohmke-Korten-Tyberg process.'

'I don't know if you realize how dreadful I feel that Dohmke was hanged; and equally how happy I am that you managed to escape. It's mere curiosity, of course, but would you mind telling me how you did it?'

'That's sort of a long story. I want to tell you, but . . . you will stay for dinner, won't you? How about afterwards? I'll just let them know so the butler can prepare the food and make a fire. And until then . . . Do you play an instrument, Herr Self?'

'The flute, but I haven't had any time to play all summer and autumn.'

He stood up, fetched a flute case from the Biedermeier cupboard and had me open it. 'Do you think you can play this?' It was a Buffet. I put it together and played a few scales. It had a wonderfully soft, yet clear tone, jubilant in the high reaches, in spite of my bad intonation after the long break. 'Do you like Bach? How about the Suite in B minor?'

We played until dinner, after the Suite in B minor, Mozart's Concerto in D major. He played the piano confidently and with great expression. I had to bluff my way through some of the fast passages. At the end of the pieces Judith laid her knitting aside and clapped.

We ate duck with chestnut stuffing, dumplings, and red cabbage. The wine was new to me, a fruity Merlot from Tessin. By the fire, Tyberg asked us to keep his story to ourselves. It would be made public soon, but until then discretion would be appreciated. 'I was in Bruchsal Penitentiary, in the death cell waiting for my execution.' He described the cell, the everyday routine on death row, knocking on the wall to communicate with Dohmke in the neighbouring cell, the morning Dohmke was taken away. 'A few days later I was also taken, in the middle of the night. Two members of the SS were demanding my transfer to a concentration camp. And then I realized one of the SS officers was Korten.' That same night he had been taken over the border beyond Lörrach by Korten and the other SS man. On the other side two gentlemen from Hoffmann La Roche were waiting for him. 'The next morning I was drinking chocolate and eating croissants, as though it were the middle of peacetime.'

He could tell a good story. Judith and I listened,

captivated. Korten. Again and again he filled me with amazement, or even admiration. 'But why couldn't this be made public?'

'Korten is more modest than he appears. He emphatically asked me to hush up his role in my escape. I've always respected that, not only as a modest, but also as a wise gesture. The deed wouldn't have sat well with the image of a top industrialist that he was fashioning then. It was only this summer that I revealed the secret. Korten's standing is universally recognized these days, and I think he'll be happy if the story appears in the portrait that *Die Zeit* wants to do next spring when he turns seventy. That's why I told the reporter who was here doing research for the portrait some months ago.'

He put another log on the fire. It was eleven o'clock.

'One other question, Frau Buchendorff, before the evening's over. Would you care to work for me? Since I've been writing my memoirs I've been looking for someone to conduct research for me in the RCW archive, in other archives and in libraries, someone who'll read things over with a critical eye, who'll get used to my handwriting and type the final manuscript. I'd be happy if you could start on the first of January. You would be based mostly in Mannheim, and be here for an occasional week or two. The pay wouldn't be worse than before. Think it over until tomorrow afternoon, give me a call, and if you say yes, we can discuss details tomorrow.'

He escorted us to the garden gate. The butler was waiting with the Jaguar to take us back to the hotel. Judith and Tyberg said goodbye with a kiss to the left and right cheek. When I shook his hand he smiled at me and winked. 'Will we meet again, Uncle Gerd?'

Champagne and sardines on my own

At breakfast Judith asked what I thought of Tyberg's proposal.

'I liked him,' I began.

'I'm sure you did. You were quite a number, you two. When the prosecutor and his victim adjourned for chamber music, I couldn't believe my ears. It's all very well that you like him, so do I, but what do you think of his proposal?'

'Accept it, Judith. I don't believe a better thing could come along for you.'

'And that I interest him as a woman doesn't make the job difficult?'

'But that can happen in any workplace, you'll be able to deal with it. And Tyberg is a gentleman, he won't grope you under your skirt during dictation.'

'What will I do when he's finished with his memoirs?'

'I'll come back to that in a minute.' I stood, went over to the breakfast buffet, and, as a finale, helped myself to a crisp-bread with honey. Well, well, I thought. What kind of security is she after? Back at the table I said, 'He'll find you something. That should be the last of your worries.'

'I'll think it over again on a walk along the lake. Shall we meet for lunch?'

I knew how things would unfold. She'd accept the job, call Tyberg at four, and discuss details with him into the evening. I decided to look for my holiday home, left Judith a message wishing her luck in her negotiations with Tyberg, and drove off along the lake to Brissago, where I was transported by boat to Isola Bella and ate lunch. Afterwards I turned towards the mountains and drove in a wide sweep that took me down by Ascona to the lake once more. There was an abundance of holiday homes, that I could see. But then to reduce my life expectancy so drastically to be able to buy one from my life insurance, no, that didn't appeal to me. Perhaps Tyberg would invite me to stay for the next vacation anyway.

When darkness fell I was back in Locarno, strolling through the festively decorated town. I was looking for sardine cans for my Christmas tree. In a delicatessen beneath the arcades I came across some Portuguese vintage sardines. I took two recent tins, one from last year in glowing greens and reds, the other from two years ago in simple white with gold lettering.

Back at the hotel reception a message was waiting from Tyberg. He'd like to have me picked up for dinner. Instead of calling him and having myself picked up I went to the hotel sauna, spent three pleasant hours there, and lay down in bed. Before falling asleep I wrote Tyberg a short letter, thanking him.

At eleven-thirty Judith knocked at my door. I opened up. She complimented me on my nightshirt, and we agreed on a departure time of eight o'clock.

'Are you content with your decision?' I asked.

'Yes. The work on the memoirs will last two years, and Tyberg has already been giving some thought to afterwards.'

'Wonderful. Then sleep well.'

I'd forgotten to open the window and was awakened by my dream. I was sleeping with Judith who, however, was the daughter I'd never had and was wearing a ridiculous red hula skirt. When I opened a can of sardines for the two of us, Tyberg came out, growing bigger and bigger, until he filled the whole room. I felt stifled and woke up.

I couldn't go back to sleep and was glad when it was time for breakfast, even gladder when we were on the road at last. Beyond the Gotthard tunnel, winter began again, and it took us seven hours to reach Mannheim. I'd actually intended to visit Sergej that day, in hospital after a repeat operation, but I wasn't up to it now. I invited Judith in for some champagne to celebrate her new job, but she had a headache.

So I had champagne and sardines on my own.

13

Can't you see how Sergej is suffering?

Sergej Mencke was lying in a double room in the Oststadt Hospital on the garden side. The other bed was currently unoccupied. His leg was suspended from a kind of pulley and held in place at the correct slant by a metal frame and screw system. He'd spent the last three months, with the exception of a few weeks, in hospital and looked correspondingly miserable. Nonetheless I could clearly see that he was a handsome man. Light, blond hair, a longish, English face with a prominent chin, dark eyes, and a vulnerable, arrogant cast to the lips. Unfortunately his voice was petulant, maybe just as a result of the past months.

'Wouldn't it have been right to come and see me first, instead of bothering my entire social world?'

So he was one of those. A whiner. 'And what would you have told me?'

'That your suspicions are pure fantasy, they're the product of a sick brain. Can you imagine mutilating your own leg like this?'

'Oh, Herr Mencke.' I pulled the chair to his bed. 'There's a lot I wouldn't do myself. I could never cut open my thumb to avoid washing up. And what I, as a ballet dancer without a future, would do to make a million, I really couldn't say.'

'That silly story from scout camp. Where did you dredge that one up from?'

'From bothering your social world. What was the story with the thumb again?'

'That was a completely normal accident. I was carving tent pegs with my pocket knife. Yes, I know what you want to say. I've told the story differently, but only because it's such a nice one, and my youth doesn't provide many stories. And as for my future as a ballet dancer . . . Listen. You don't exactly give the impression of a particularly rosy future yourself, but you wouldn't go breaking a limb because of it.'

'Tell me, Herr Mencke, how did you plan to finance the dance school you've talked about so often?'

'Frederik was going to support me, *Fritz* Kirchenberg, I mean. He has stacks of money. If I'd wanted to cheat the insurance company I'd have thought up something a little cleverer.'

'The car door isn't that silly. But what would have been cleverer?'

'I have no desire to discuss it with you. I only said *if* I'd wanted to cheat the insurance people.'

'Would you be willing to undergo a psychiatric examination? That would really facilitate the insurance company's decision.'

'Absolutely not. I'm not going to have them tag me as mad. If they don't pay up right away, I'm going to a lawyer.'

'If you go to trial you won't be able to avoid a psychiatric examination.'

'Let's wait and see.'

The nurse came in carrying a little dish with brightly coloured tablets. 'The two red ones now, the yellow one before and the blue one after your meal. How are we today?'

Sergej had tears in his eyes as he looked at the nurse. 'I can't go on, Katrin. Nothing but pain and no dancing ever again. And now this gentleman from the insurance company wants to make me out to be a cheat.'

Nurse Katrin laid her hand on his forehead and glowered at me. 'Can't you see how Sergej is suffering? You should be ashamed of yourself! Leave him in peace. It's always the same with insurance companies; first they make you pay through the nose and then they torture you because they don't want to cough up.'

I couldn't add anything to this conversation and fled. Over lunch I noted down keywords for my report to the Heidelberg Union Insurance. My conclusion was neither that of deliberate self-mutilation, nor mere accident. I could only gather together the points that spoke for one or the other. Should the insurance not wish to pay they wouldn't have a bad case.

As I was crossing the street, a car spattered me from head to toe in slushy snow. I was already in a foul mood when I reached my office and the work on the report made me all the more morose. By the evening I'd laboriously dictated two cassettes that I took round to Tattersallstrasse to be typed up. On the way home it struck me I'd wanted to ask Frau Mencke about little Siegfried's tooth-extraction methods. But now I couldn't care less.

14

Matthew 6, verse 26

It was a small huddle of mourners that gathered at the Ludwigshafen Cemetery at 2 p.m. on Friday. Eberhard, Philipp, the vice-dean of the Heidelberg faculty for the sciences, Willy's cleaning lady, and myself. The vice-dean had prepared a speech, which, due to the low turnout, he delivered gracelessly. We discovered that Willy had been an internationally recognized authority in the field of screech owl research. And this with heart and soul: in the war, as an adjunct lecturer at Hamburg at the time, he had rescued the entire family of distraught screech owls from the burning aviary in Hagenbeck Zoo. The minister spoke about Matthew 6, verse 26, about all the birds beneath the heavens. Beneath blue heavens and on crunchy snow we walked from the chapel to the grave. Philipp and I were first behind the coffin. He whispered to me, 'I must show you the photo sometime. I came across it when I was tidying up. Willy and the rescued owls, with singed hair, or feathers respectively, six pairs of eyes looking exhaustedly but happily into the camera. It warmed my aching heart.'

Then we stood by the deep hole. It's like eena, meena, mina, mo. According to age, Eberhard is next, and then it's my turn. For a long time now when someone I'm fond of dies, I've stopped thinking, 'Oh, if only I'd done this or that more often.' And when a contemporary dies it's as though he's just gone on ahead, even if I can't say where to. The minister recited the Lord's Prayer and we all joined in; even Philipp, the most hard-boiled atheist I know, said it aloud. Then each of us cast a small shovelful of earth into the grave, and the minister shook our hands, one by one. A young guy, but convinced, and convincing. Philipp had to return to work straight away.

'You will come by this evening for a funeral meal, won't you?' Yesterday in town I'd bought another twelve little sardine cans and laid the tiny fish in an Escabeche marinade. To go with it there'd be white bread and Rioja. We settled on eight o'clock.

Philipp strode off like a Fury, Eberhard did the honours with the vice-dean, and the cleaning lady, still emitting heartrending sobs, was led gently on the arm of the minister to the exit. I had time and slowly wandered along the cemetery paths. If Klara had been buried here I'd have wanted to visit her now, and commune a bit.

'Herr Self!' I turned around and recognized Frau Schmalz, complete with small trowel and watering can. 'I'm just on my way to the family grave, where Heinrich's urn is at rest now, too. It's looking nice, the grave. Will you come and see?' She looked at me shyly from her narrow, careworn face. She was wearing an old-fashioned black winter coat, black button-up boots, a black fur hat over her grey hair pinned in a bun, and was carrying an imitation-leather handbag that made one wince with pity. In my generation there are female figures, the sight of whom rouses in me a belief in all the pronouncements of all the prophets of the women's lib movement. Not that I've ever read them.

'Are you still living in the old compound at the Works?' I asked her on the way.

'No, I had to get out, it's all torn down. The Works found me somewhere on Pfingstweide. The apartment's fine and everything, very modern, but you know, it is hard after so many years. It takes me a full hour to get to the grave of my Heinrich. Later today my son, thank God, will pick me up in his car.'

We were standing in front of the family grave. It was heaped high with snow. The ribbon from the wreath bequeathed by the Works, and long since decomposed, was fixed to a cane and rose up like a standard by the gravestone. Widow Schmalz put down the watering can and let the trowel drop. 'I can't do anything today with this load of snow.' We stood there, both thinking of old Schmalz. 'These days I hardly get to see my little Richard either. I live too far out. What do you think, is it right that the Works ... Oh God, now that Heinrich's no longer around I'm always thinking such things. He never let me, never let anybody question the Works.'

'How much warning did you have that you had to leave?'

'A good six months. They wrote to us. But then everything went so quickly.'

'Didn't Korten make a point of talking to your husband four weeks before your move, so that it wouldn't be too hard on you?'

'Did he? He never told me about it. He did have a close relationship with the general, you know. From the war, when the SS assigned him to the Works. Since then it was right what they said at the funeral, the Works was his life. He didn't get much out of it, but I was never allowed to say that either. Whether SS officer or security officer, the fight goes on, he used to say.'

'What became of his workshop?'

'He set it up with such love. And he really cared for those vans and trucks. Then it was all got rid of very quickly during the demolition, my son could scarcely retrieve a thing. I think they scrapped it all. I didn't think that was right either. Oh, God.' She bit her lips and made a face as though she'd committed a mortal sin. 'Forgive me, I didn't mean to say anything bad about the Works.' She grasped my arm appeasingly. She held on tightly for a while, staring at the grave. Thoughtfully, she continued, 'But perhaps at the end Heinrich himself didn't think it was right the way the Works was treating us. On his deathbed he wanted to say something to the general about the garage and the vans. I couldn't understand him properly.'

'You'll permit an old man a question, Frau Schmalz. Were you happy in your marriage with Heinrich?'

She gathered up the watering can and trowel. 'That's the sort of thing people ask nowadays. I never thought about it. He was my husband.'

We walked to the parking lot. Young Schmalz was pulling in. He was happy to see me. 'The good doctor. Met mum at dad's grave.' I told him about my friend's funeral.

'I'm grieved to hear that. Painful, taking leave of a friend. I've been there too. I remain grateful for your help with our little Richard. And one day my wife and I would like to have that coffee with you. Mum can come along, too. Any particular cake your favourite?'

'My absolute favourite is sweet damson shortcake.' I didn't say it to be mean. It really is my favourite cake.

Schmalz handled it well. 'Ah, plum with floury-butter crumble. My wife can bake it like no other woman. Coffee maybe in the quiet lull between the impending holiday and New Year?'

I said yes. We'd telephone regarding the exact date.

The evening with Philipp and Eberhard was one of melancholic gaiety. We remembered our last Doppelkopf evening with Willy. We'd joked then about what would come of our games circle if one of us were to die. 'No,' said Eberhard, 'we're not going to look for someone new to make up the four. From now on it's Skat.'

'And then chess, and the last one will meet himself twice a year to play solitaire,' said Philipp.

'It's all very well for you to laugh, you're the youngest.'

'It's nothing to laugh about. Solitaire? I'd rather be dead.'

15

And the race is on

Ever since I moved from Berlin to Heidelberg I've been buying my Christmas trees at the Tiefburg in Handschuhsheim. It's been a long time since they were any different from those elsewhere. But I like the small square in front of the ruined castle with its moat. The tram used to turn around here on squealing tracks; this was the end of the line and Klärchen and I often set off on our walks on the Heiligenberg from here. These days Handschuhsheim has turned trendy and everyone who thinks of themselves as having a modicum of cultural and intellectual flair gathers at the weekly market. The day will come when the only authentic neighbourhoods are places like the suburban slums of the sixties.

I'm particularly fond of silver firs. But so far as my sardine cans went, I felt a Douglas spruce would be more appropriate. I found a beautiful, evenly grown, ceiling-height, bushy tree. Stretching from the right-hand corner on the passenger side to the back left-hand corner, it fitted in neatly over the reclined front seat and the folded-down back seat of my Opel. I found a space in the parking garage by the town hall. I'd made a little list for my Christmas shopping.

All hell was loose on the main street. I battled my way through to Welsch the jeweller and bought earrings for Babs. It'll never happen, but I'd like to have a beer with Welsch one day. He has the same taste as me. For

Röschen and Georg, from the selection at one of those all-pervading gift shops, I chose two of those disposable watches, currently modern among our postmodern youth, made of see-through plastic with a quartz movement and a heat-sealed face. Then I was exhausted. In Café Schafheutle I bumped into Thomas with his wife and three puberty-ridden daughters.

'Isn't a security man supposed to make a gift of sons to his Works?'

'In the security field there's an increasingly attractive range of jobs for women. For our course we're estimating around thirty per cent female participants. Incidentally the conference of Ministers of Culture and Education is going to support us as a pilot project, and so the technical college has decided to establish a separate department for internal security. That means I can introduce myself today as the designated founding dean. I'm leaving the RCW on the first of January.'

I congratulated the right honourable dean on his office, the honour, the prestige, and the title. 'What's Danckelmann going to do without you?'

'It will be difficult for him in the next few years until he retires. But I would like the department to provide consultation too, so he can buy advice from us. You'll remember the curriculum you wanted to send me, Herr Self?'

Evidently Thomas already felt emancipated from RCW and was adapting to his new role. He invited me to join them at their table where the daughters were giggling and the mother was blinking nervously. I looked at my watch, excused myself, and dashed off to Café Scheu.

Then I embarked on round two of checking off my list. What do you give a virile man in his late fifties? A set of tiger-print underwear? Royal jelly? The erotic stories of Anaïs Nin? Finally I bought Philipp a cocktail shaker for his boat bar. Then revulsion for the Christmas din and commercialism swamped me. I was filled with immense discontent with the people and with myself. It would take me hours to shake it off at home. Why on earth had I launched myself into the Christmas mêlée? Why did I make the same mistake every year? Haven't I learned anything in my life? What is the point of the whole thing?

The Opel smelled pleasantly of fir forest. When I'd fought my way through the traffic to the autobahn I heaved a sigh of relief. I shoved in a tape, fished out from way down the pile, as I'd heard the others too often on the journey to and from Locarno. But no music came.

A telephone was picked up, the dialling tone sounded, a number was dialled, and the recipient's phone rang. He answered. It was Korten.

'Hello, Herr Korten. Mischkey here. I'm warning you. If your people don't leave me alone your past is going to explode around your ears. I won't be pressured like this any longer, and I certainly won't be beaten up again.'

'I'd imagined you'd be more intelligent from Self's report. First you break into our system and now you threaten blackmail. I have nothing to say.' Actually Korten should have hung up that very second. But the second came and went, and Mischkey talked on.

'The times are over, Herr Korten, where all it takes is an SS contact and an SS uniform to move people from here to there, to Switzerland and to the gallows.' Mischkey hung up. I heard him take a deep gulp of air, then the click of the tape recorder. Music began. 'And the race is on and it looks like heartache and the winner loses all.'

I turned off the player and pulled over to the hard shoulder. The tape from Mischkey's Citroën. I had simply forgotten it.

16

Anything for one's career?

I couldn't sleep that night. At six o'clock I gave up and busied myself setting up and decorating my Christmas tree. I'd listened to Mischkey's tape over and over. On Saturday I'd been in no state to think and make order in my mind.

I put the thirty empty sardine cans that I had accumulated into the sink of water. They shouldn't still smell of fish on the Christmas tree. I looked at them, my elbows on the edge of the sink, as they sank to the bottom. The lids of some of them had been torn off as they were opened. I'd stick them back on.

Was it Korten, then, who'd made Weinstein discover the hidden documents in Tyberg's desk and report him? I should have thought of it when Tyberg told us that only he, Dohmke, and Korten knew about the stash. No, Weinstein hadn't come across them by accident as Tyberg supposed. They'd ordered him to find the documents in the desk. That was what Frau Hirsch had said. And perhaps Weinstein had never even seen the documents; the important thing was the statement, not the find.

When it started growing light outside I went out onto the balcony and fitted the Christmas tree to the stand. I had to saw and use the hatchet. Its top was too high. I trimmed it in such a way that the tip could be reattached to the trunk with a needle. Then I moved the tree to its place in the sitting room.

Why? Anything for one's career? Yes. Korten couldn't have made such a mark if Tyberg and Dohmke had still been around. Tyberg had spoken of the years following the trial as the basis for his ascendancy. And Tyberg's liberation had been Korten's reinsurance. It had certainly paid off. When Tyberg became general director of the RCW Korten was catapulted to dizzying heights.

The plot – with me as the dupe. Set up and executed by my friend and brother-in-law. And I'd been happy not to have to drag him into the trial. He'd used me with contemptuous calculation. I thought back to the conversation after our move to Bahnhofstrasse. I also thought of the last conversations we'd had, in the Blue Salon and on the terrace of his house. Me, the sweetheart.

My cigarettes had run out. That hadn't happened to me in years. I pulled on my winter coat and galoshes, pocketed the St Christopher that I'd taken from Mischkey's car and only remembered yesterday, walked to the train station, then dropped by to see Judith. It was mid-morning now. She came to the front door in a dressing gown.

'What's the matter with you, Gerd?' She looked at me aghast. 'Come on up, I've just put some coffee on.'

'Do I look that bad? No, I won't come up, I'm in the middle of decorating my tree. Wanted to bring you the St Christopher. I needn't tell you where it's from, I'd completely forgotten it, and I just found it again.'

She took the St Christopher and supported herself against the doorpost. She was fighting back tears.

'Tell me something, Judith, do you remember if Peter went away for two or three days in the weeks in between the War Cemetery and his death?'

'What?' She hadn't been listening, and I repeated my question. 'Away? Yes, how do you know?'

'Do you know where to?'

'South, he said. To recover because it had all been too much for him. Why do you ask?'

'I'm wondering whether he went to Tyberg pretending to be a journalist from *Die Zeit*.'

'You mean looking for material to use against the RCW?' She considered this. 'I wouldn't put it past him. But according to what Tyberg said about the visit, there wasn't anything to unearth.' Shivering, she pulled the dressing gown more tightly around her. 'Are you sure you won't have a coffee?'

'You'll be hearing from me, Judith.' I walked home.

It all fitted together. A despairing Mischkey had attempted to use Tyberg's grand aria about decency and resistance for his own ends against Korten. Intuitively he had recognized the dissonances better than all of us, the connection to the SS, the rescue of Tyberg, not that of Dohmke. He didn't realize how close to the truth he was and how threatening that must have sounded to Korten. Not just sounded – was really, thanks to his dogged research.

Why hadn't I thought of it? If it was so easy to save Tyberg, why, then, hadn't Korten rescued both of them two days earlier while Dohmke was still alive? One was sufficient as reinsurance and Tyberg, the head of the research group, was more interesting than his co-worker Dohmke.

I removed my galoshes and clapped them against each other until all the snow had dropped off. The stairwell smelled of *Sauerbraten*. Yesterday I hadn't bought anything else to eat and I could only make myself two fried eggs. The third egg I whisked over Turbo's food. He'd been driven to distraction in recent days by the sardine odour in the apartment.

The SS man who'd helped Korten to liberate Tyberg had been Schmalz. Together with Schmalz Korten had exerted pressure on Weinstein. Schmalz had killed Mischkey for Korten.

I rinsed the sardine cans clean with hot water and dried them off. Where the lids were missing, I glued them back on. I chose green wool to hang them and threaded it through the curl of the rolled-back lid, or through the ring-pull, or around the hinge where an open lid was attached to its can. As soon as a can was ready I looked for its proper place on the tree; the big ones lower down, the small ones higher up.

I couldn't fool myself. I didn't give a damn about my Christmas tree. Why had Korten allowed his accessory Weinstein to survive? I suppose he hadn't had any influence over the SS, only over Schmalz, the SS officer in the Works, whom he'd seduced and conquered. He couldn't steer things so that Weinstein would be killed back in the concentration camp. But he could safely assume it. And after the war? Even if Korten were to discover that Weinstein had survived the camp, he could count on the fact that anyone who'd had to play a role such as Weinstein's would prefer not to go public.

Now the final words made sense, too, the ones the widow Schmalz repeated from her husband's deathbed. He must have tried to warn his lord and master about the trail he himself hadn't been able to remove, given his physical state. How well Korten had known how to make this man depend on him! The young academic from a good home, the SS officer from a modest background, great challenges and tasks, two men in the service of the Works, each in his place. I could imagine the course of things between them. Who knew better than I how convincing and winning Korten could be?

The Christmas tree was ready. Thirty sardine cans were hanging, thirty white candles were erect. One of the vertically hanging sardine cans was oval and reminded me of the garland of light you get in depictions of the Virgin Mary. I went to the basement, found the cardboard box with Klärchen's Christmas tree decorations and in amongst them the small, willowy Madonna in a blue cloak. She fitted into the can.

17

I knew what I had to do

The next night I couldn't sleep either. Sometimes I dozed off and dreamed of Dohmke's hanging and Korten's performance in court, my leap into the Rhine that I didn't resurface from in my dream, Judith in her dressing gown, fighting back her tears at the doorpost, old, square-set, stout Schmalz climbing down from the statue pedestal in the Heidelberg Bismarckgarten and coming towards me, the tennis match with Mischkey, at which a small boy with Korten's face and an SS uniform threw us the balls, my interrogation of Weinstein, and again and again Korten laughing at me, saying, 'Self, you sweetheart, you sweetheart, you sweetheart . . .'

At five I made a cup of camomile tea and tried to read, but my thoughts wouldn't leave me alone. They kept circling. How could Korten have done it? Why had I been blind enough to let myself be used by him? What should happen now? Was Korten afraid? Did I owe anyone anything? Was there anyone I could tell everything to? Nägelsbach? Tyberg? Judith? Should I go to the media? What was I to do with my guilt?

For a long time the thoughts circled in my mind, faster and faster. As they were accelerating into craziness, they flew apart and formed themselves into a completely new picture. I knew what I had to do.

At nine o'clock I called Frau Schlemihl. Korten had left on vacation at the weekend to his house in Brittany where he and his wife spent Christmas every year. I found the card he'd sent me last Christmas. It showed a magnificent estate of grey stone with a slanting roof and red shutters, the crossbars of which formed an inverted Z. Next to it was a high windmill, and beyond it stretched the sea. I checked the timetable and found a train that would get me in to Paris-Est at five o'clock in the afternoon. I'd have to hurry. I prepared a fresh litter-tray for Turbo, shook an abundant amount of cat food into his dish, and packed my travel bag. I ran to the station, changed money, and bought a ticket, second class. The train was full. Noisy soldiers on home-leave over Christmas, students, late businessmen.

The snow of the last weeks had thawed completely. Dirty greenish-brown countryside whipped by. The sky was grey, and sometimes the sun was visible as a faded disk behind the clouds. I thought about why Korten had feared Mischkey's disclosures. He could, indeed, be prosecuted for Dohmke's murder, which was not subject to a statute of limitations. And even if he went free due to lack of evidence, his comfortable life and the legend he'd become would be destroyed.

There was a car rental in the Gare de l'Est and I took a standard-class car, one of those where every make looks much the same as every other. I left the car at the rental and went out into the hectic evening pulse of the city. In front of the station was an enormous Christmas tree that exuded about as much Christmas spirit as the Eiffel Tower. It was half past five, I was hungry. Most of the restaurants were still closed. I found a brasserie I liked the look of that was bustling in spite of what time it was. I was shown to a small table by the headwaiter and found myself in a row of five other uncommonly early diners. They were all eating *Sauerkraut* with boiled pork and sausages and I chose the same. And with it a half-bottle of Alsace

Riesling. In the twinkling of an eye, a steaming plate, a bottle in a cooler with condensation on its sides, and a basket of white bread were in front of me. When I'm in the mood I like the atmosphere of brasseries, beer-cellars, and pubs. Not today. I finished quickly. At the nearest hotel I took a room and asked to be woken in four hours.

I slept like a stone. When I was roused at eleven by the ringing of the phone I didn't know where I was. I hadn't opened the shutters and the noise of the traffic from the boulevard only made a muffled echo in my room. I showered, brushed my teeth, shaved, and paid. On the way to the Gare de l'Est I drank a double espresso. I had a further five poured into my thermos flask. My Sweet Aftons were running out. I bought a carton of Chesterfield once again.

I had reckoned on six hours for the journey to Trefeuntec. But it took an hour just to get out of Paris and onto the highway to Rennes. There was little traffic, and the driving was monotonous. It was only then that it struck me how mild it was. A green Christmas means a cold Easter. Every so often I'd pass a toll booth and never knew if I should be paying or getting a ticket. Once I pulled off the road to fill up and was astounded by the price of petrol. The lights of the villages were growing sparser. I wondered whether it was because of the late hour or because the country was emptier. To begin with I was happy to have a radio in the car. But then there was only clear reception to one station and after I'd heard the song about the angel walking through the room for the third time, I switched it off. Sometimes the road surface would change and the tyres would sing a new song. At three, just after Rennes, I almost fell asleep, or at least I was hallucinating that there were people running all over the highway. I opened the window, drove to the next rest area, drained my thermos flask, and did ten sit-ups.

As the journey continued, my thoughts turned to Korten's performance at the trial. He had been playing for high stakes. His statement mustn't save Dohmke and Tyberg, yet it had to sound as though that was just what he wanted, without seriously damaging him in the process. Södelknecht had almost had him arrested. How had Korten felt then? Secure and superior because he knew how to pull the wool over everybody's eyes? No, he wouldn't have suffered any twinges of conscience. From my colleagues in the law I knew that there were two means of dealing with the past: cynicism, and a feeling of having always been right and only doing one's duty. In retrospect had the Tyberg affair served the greater glory of the RCW for Korten?

When the houses of Carhaix-Plouguer were behind me, I looked in the rear-view mirror and saw the first streak of dawn. Another seventy kilometres to Trefeuntec. In Plonévez-Porzay the bar and the bakery were already open and I ate two croissants along with my milky coffee. At a quarter to eight I reached the bay of Trefeuntec. I drove the car onto the beach, still wet and firm from the tide. Beneath a grey sky the grey sea rolled in. It crashed against the high coast to the right and left of the bay with dirty white crests. It was even milder than Paris in spite of the strong westerly wind that drove the clouds before it. Shrieking gulls were swept aloft on its current before they dropped in a plummeting dive to the water.

I began the search for Korten's house. I drove a little inland and came to a field-track on the craggy northerly coast. With its bays and cliffs rising from the shore it stretched as far as the eye could see. In the distance I could make out a silhouette, it could be anything under the sun, from a water tower to the large windmill. I left the car behind a wind-buffeted hut and made for the tower.

Before I saw Korten, his two dachshunds saw me. They rollicked towards me, yapping. Then he emerged from a dip. We weren't far from one another but between us was a bay that we each headed round. Along the narrow path that ran along the cliff top, we walked towards one another.

18

Old friends like you and me

'You look terrible, my dear Self. A few days' rest here will do you a world of good. I hadn't expected you yet. Let's walk a bit. Helga's preparing breakfast for nine. She'll be glad to see you.' Korten linked his arm through mine and prepared to continue. He was wearing a light loden coat and looked relaxed.

'I know everything,' I said, stepping away.

Korten looked at me enquiringly. He understood immediately.

'It's not easy for you, Gerd. It wasn't easy for me either, and I was happy not to have to burden anyone with it.'

I stared at him speechlessly. He stepped up to me once more, took my arm, and nudged me along the path. 'You think it had to do with my career. No, in the whole mess of those last years of the war what mattered most was sorting out real responsibility and making clean decisions. Things wouldn't have gone well for our research group. Dohmke consigning himself to the sidelines that way – I was sorry back then. But so many people, better people, lost their lives. Mischkey had his choice too, and dug himself deeper and deeper into trouble.' He stood still and grabbed my shoulders. 'You have to understand, Gerd. The Works needed me to be the way I became in those difficult years. I always had great respect for old Schmalz. He was simple but he could understand these tricky connections.'

'You must be crazy. You murdered two men and you talk about it as though . . . as though . . .'

'Oh, those are big words. Did I murder them? Or was it the judge or the hangman? Old Schmalz? And who headed the investigation against Tyberg and Dohmke? Who set the trap for Mischkey and let it snap shut? We're all entangled in it, all of us, and we have to recognize that and bear it, and do our duty.'

I broke loose from his hold. 'Entangled? Perhaps we all are, but you pulled the strings!' I was shouting into his placid face.

He stood still, too. 'That's just child's stuff – "he did it, he did it." And even when we were children we never really believed it; we knew perfectly well that we were all involved when a teacher was being goaded, or one of our classmates bullied, or the other side in the game was being fouled.' He spoke with utter concentration, patiently, didactically, and my head was dazed and confused. It was true, that's how my sense of guilt had eroded, year by year.

Korten was still talking. 'But, please – I did it. If that's what you need – yes, I did it. What do you think would have happened had Mischkey gone to the press? That sort of thing doesn't end with an old boss being replaced by a new one, and everything goes on as before. I needn't tell you the play his story would have got in the USA, and England and France, or talk about what it would do when we're fighting our competition inch by inch, or about how many jobs would be destroyed, and what unemployment means today. The RCW is a large, heavy ship going at breakneck speed through the drift-ice despite its bulk and if the captain leaves and the steering is loose, it will run aground and be wrecked. That's why I say yes, I did it.'

'Murder?'

'Could I have bribed him? The risk was too high. And

don't tell me that no risk is too high when it's about saving a life. It's not true. Think of road deaths, accidents in the workplace, police who shoot to kill. Think of the fight against terrorism: the police have shot as many people by accident as the terrorists have intentionally – is that a reason to give up?'

'And Dohmke?' I suddenly felt empty inside. I could see us standing there, talking, as though a film were running without a soundtrack. Beneath the grey clouds, a craggy coastline, a mist of dirty spray, a narrow path and the fields beyond, and two older men in heated discussion – hands gesticulating, mouths moving – but the scene is mute. I wished I wasn't there.

'Dohmke? Actually I don't have to comment on that. The years between nineteen thirty-three and nineteen forty-five are supposed to remain a blank – that's the foundation on which our state is built. Fine, we had to – still have to – produce some theatre with trials and verdicts. But in nineteen forty-five there was no Night of the Long Knives, and that would have been the only chance of retribution. Then the foundation was set. You're not satisfied? Okay then, Dohmke couldn't be trusted; he was unpredictable, a talented chemist maybe, but an amateur in everything else. He wouldn't have lasted two minutes at the front.'

We walked on. He hadn't needed to link arms with me again; when he continued I'd stuck by his side.

'Fate may talk that way, Ferdinand, but not you. Steamships that set a course, solid foundations, entanglements in which we're all mere puppets – you can tell me all about the powers and forces in life but none of it alters the fact that you, Ferdinand Korten, and only you—'

'Fate?' Now he was furious. 'We are our own fate, and I don't offload anything on powers and forces. You're the one who never sees things through to the end, nor leaves them well and truly alone. Get Dohmke and Mischkey in a mess, yes, but when what inevitably happens next does, you find your scruples and you don't want to have seen it or been it. My God, Gerd, grow up at last.'

He stumped on. The path had narrowed and I walked behind him, cliffs to the left, a wall to the right. Beyond it, the fields.

'Why did you come?' He turned round. 'To see whether I'd kill you, too? Push you over?' Fifty metres below the sea seethed. He laughed, as though it were a joke. Then he read it in my eyes before I said the words.

'I've come to kill you.'

'To bring them back to life?' he mocked. 'Because you . . . because the perpetrator wants to play judge? Do you feel innocent and exploited? What would you have been without me, without my sister and my parents, before nineteen forty-five, and all my help afterwards? Jump yourself if you can't deal with it.'

His voice cracked. I stared at him. Then that grin came to his face, the one I'd known, and liked, since we were young. It had charmed me into shared escapades and out of fatal situations, understanding, winning, superior.

'Hey, Gerd, this is crazy. Two old friends like you and me . . . Come on, let's have breakfast. I can smell the coffee already.' He whistled to the dogs.

'No, Ferdinand.'

He looked at me with an expression of utter incredulity as I shoved against his chest with both hands. He lost his balance and plummeted down, his coat billowing. I didn't hear a cry. He thudded against a rock before the sea took him with it.

19

A package from Rio

The dogs followed me to the car and frolicked alongside, yapping, until I turned off the field-track, onto the road. My whole body was trembling and yet I felt lighter than I had in a long time. On the road a tractor came towards me. The farmer stared at me. Had he been high enough to see me as I pushed Korten to his death? I hadn't even thought about witnesses. I looked back; another tractor was ploughing its furrows in a field and two children were out on bikes. I drove west. At Point-du-Raz I considered staying – an anonymous Christmas abroad. But I couldn't find a hotel, and the cliff line looked just like Trefeuntec. I was going home. At Quimper I came to a police roadblock. I could tell myself a thousand times that it was an unlikely spot to be searching for Korten's murderer, but I was scared as I waited in the queue for the police to wave me on.

In Paris I made the eleven o'clock night train. It was empty and I had no trouble getting a sleeping car. On Christmas Day towards eight o'clock I was back in my apartment. Turbo greeted me sulkily. Frau Weiland had laid my Christmas mail on the desk. Along with all the commercial Christmas greetings I found a Christmas card from Vera Müller, an invitation from Korten to spend New Year's Eve with him and Helga in Brittany, and from Brigitte a package from Rio with an Indian tunic. I took it as a nightshirt, and went to bed. At half past eleven the telephone rang.

'Merry Christmas, Gerd. Where are you hiding?'

'Brigitte! Merry Christmas.' I was happy, but I could hardly see for weariness and exhaustion.

'You grouch, aren't you pleased? I'm back.'

I made an effort. 'You're kidding. That's really great. Since when?'

'I arrived yesterday morning and I've been trying to reach you ever since. Where have you been hiding?' There was reproach in her voice.

'I didn't want to be here on Christmas Eve. I felt very claustrophobic.'

'Would you like to eat *Tafelspitz* with us? It's already on the stove.'

'Yes . . . who else is coming?'

'I've brought Manu with me. I can't wait to see you.' She blew a kiss down the telephone.

'Me too.' I returned the kiss.

I lay in bed, and felt my way back to the present. To my world in which fate doesn't control steamships or puppets, where no foundations are laid and no history gets made.

The Christmas edition of the *Süddeutsche* lay on the bed. It gave an annual balance sheet of toxic incidents in the chemical industry. I soon laid the paper aside.

The world wasn't a better place for Korten's death. What had I done? Come to terms with my past? Wiped my hands of it?

I arrived far too late for lunch.

20

Come with the Wind!

Christmas Day brought no news of Korten's death, nor did the next. Sometimes I was fearful. Whenever the doorbell rang, I was frightened and assumed the police had arrived to storm the apartment. When I was relaxing happily in Brigitte's arms, alive with her sweet kisses, occasionally I wondered anxiously if this might be our last time together. At times I imagined the scene with Herzog, telling him everything. Or would I prefer to give my statement in front of Nägelsbach?

Most of the time I was easy in myself, fatalistic, and enjoyed the last days of the year, including coffee and plum-with-floury-butter-crumble-cake at the younger Schmalzes'. I liked little Manuel. He tried valiantly to speak German, accepted my morning presence in the bathroom without jealousy, and hoped staunchly for snow. To begin with the three of us went on our expeditions together, visiting the fairytale park on Königstuhl and the planetarium. Then he and I set out on our own. He liked going to the cinema as much as I did. When we came out of *Witness* we both had to fight our tears. In *Splash* he didn't understand why the mermaid loved the guy although he was so mean to her – I didn't tell him that's always the way. In the Kleiner Rosengarten he figured out the game Giovanni and I played, and played along. There was no teaching him a sensible German sentence after that. On the way back from ice skating he took my hand and said, 'You always with us when I come back?'

Brigitte and Juan had decided Manuel should go to high school in Mannheim, starting next autumn. Would I be in prison next autumn? And if not – would Brigitte and I stay together?

'I don't know yet, Manuel. But we'll certainly go to the cinema together.'

The days passed without Korten hitting the headlines, either dead or missing. There were moments when I wished things would come to an end, no matter how. Then once again I was grateful for the time gained. On the 27th Philipp called. He complained he hadn't caught a glimpse of my Christmas tree yet this year. 'And where have you been these last few days?'

That's when I got the idea about a party. 'I have something to celebrate,' I said. 'Come round on New Year's Eve, I'm having a party.'

'Should I bring you round a squeezable little Taiwanese something?'

'No need, Brigitte is back.'

'A-ha, Come with the Wind! But may I bring a little something for me to the party?'

Brigitte had followed the phone call. 'Party? What party?'

'We're celebrating New Year's Eve with your friends and mine. Who would you like to invite?'

On Saturday afternoon I dropped by to see Judith. I caught her in the midst of packing. She was planning to travel to Locarno on Sunday. Tyberg wanted to introduce her to Tessin society in Ascona on New Year's Eve. 'It's nice of you to come round, Gerd, but I'm in a terrible rush. Is it important, can't it wait? I'll be back at the end of January.' She indicated the open suitcases, and the packed ones, two large moving cartons, and a wild confusion of clothes. I recognized the silk blouse that she'd worn when she'd shown me to Firner's office. The button was still missing. 'I can tell you the truth about Mischkey's death now.'

She sat down on a suitcase and lit a cigarette. 'Yes?'

She listened without interrupting. When I'd finished she asked: 'And what happens to Korten now?'

It was the question I had dreaded. I had racked my brains over whether I should only go to Judith once Korten's death was public knowledge. But I mustn't make my actions dependent upon Korten's murder, and without it there was no reason to hush up the solving of the case any longer. 'I'll try to put him on the spot. He'll be back from Brittany at the beginning of January.'

'Oh, Gerd, you can't believe that Korten will break down in mid-sentence and confess?'

I didn't answer. I was reluctant to enter into a discussion about what should happen to Korten.

Judith took another cigarette from the pack and rolled it between the fingertips of both hands. She looked sad, worn out by all the to-ing and fro-ing that had accompanied Peter's murder, also aggravated, as if she wanted finally, finally, to put the whole thing behind her. 'I'll talk to Tyberg. You don't mind, do you?'

That night I dreamed that Herzog was interrogating me. 'Why didn't you go to the police?'

'What could the police have done?'

'Oh, we have impressive possibilities these days. Come on, I'll show you.' Through long corridors, via many stairs, we came to a room that I recognized from castles of the Middle Ages, with pincers, irons, masks, chains, whips, straps, and needles. A hellfire was burning in the grate. Herzog pointed to the rack. 'We'd have made Korten talk on that. Why didn't you trust the police? Now you'll have to go on it yourself.' I didn't struggle and was strapped to it. When I couldn't move, panic surged through me. I must have cried out before I woke. Brigitte had switched on the bedside lamp and turned to me with concern.

'Everything's fine, Gerd. No one's hurting you.'

I kicked myself free of the sheets that were stifling me. 'My God, what a dream.'

'Tell me, then you'll feel better.'

I didn't want to and she was hurt. 'I keep noticing, Gerd, that something's wrong with you. Sometimes you're hardly there.'

I snuggled into her arms. 'It'll pass, Brigitte. It has nothing to do with you. Have patience with an old man.'

It was only on New Year's Eve that Korten's death was reported. A tragic accident at his holiday home in Brittany on the morning of Christmas Eve had caused him to fall from the cliffs into the sea while out walking. The information gathered by the press and radio for Korten's seventieth birthday was now used for obituaries and eulogies. With Korten an epoch had ended, the epoch of the great men of Germany's era of reconstruction. The funeral was to take place at the beginning of January, attended by the president, the chancellor, the economics minister, as well as the complete cabinet of Rhineland-Palatinate. Scarcely anything better could have happened for his son's career. As his brother-in-law I'd be invited, but I wouldn't go. Nor would I send condolences to his wife.

I didn't envy him his glory. Nor did I forgive him. Murder means never having to say you forgive.

I'm sorry, Herr Self

Babs, Röschen, and Georg arrived at seven. Brigitte and I had just been putting the finishing touches to the party preparations, had lit the Christmas tree candles, and were sitting on the sofa with Manuel.

'Here she is, then!' Babs looked at Brigitte with kindly curiosity and gave her a kiss.

'Hats off, Uncle Gerd,' said Röschen. 'And the Christmas tree looks really cool.'

I gave them their presents.

'But Gerd,' said Babs reproachfully, 'I thought we'd decided against Christmas presents this year,' and took out her package. 'This is from the three of us.'

Babs and Röschen had knitted a wine-red sweater to which Georg had attached, at the appropriate spot, an electric circuit with eight lamps in the shape of a heart. When I pulled on the sweater the lamps started to flash to the rhythm of my heartbeat.

Then Herr and Frau Nägelsbach arrived. He was wearing a black suit, complete with stiff wing-collar and bow tie, a pince-nez on his nose, and was the spitting image of Karl Kraus. She was wearing a fin-de-siècle dress. 'Hedda Gabler?' I greeted her cautiously. She gave a curtsy and joined the ladies. He looked at the Christmas tree with disapproval. 'Bourgeois nonsense.'

The doorbell didn't stop ringing. Eberhard arrived with a little suitcase. 'I've come with a few magic tricks.'

Philipp brought Füruzan, a feisty, voluptuous Turkish nurse. 'Fuzzy can belly-dance!' Hadwig, a friend of Brigitte's, had her fourteen-year-old son Jan with her, who immediately took charge of Manuel.

Everyone streamed into the kitchen for the cold buffet. Dusty Springfield's 'I Close My Eyes and Count to Ten' played unnoticed in the living room. Philipp had put on *Hits of the 1960s.*

My study was empty. The telephone rang. I shut the door behind me. Only muffled jollity from the party reached my ears. All my friends were here – who could be calling?

'Uncle Gerd?' It was Tyberg. 'A Happy New Year! Judith told me and I read the newspaper. It appears you've solved the Korten case.'

'Hello, Herr Tyberg. All the best to you for the New Year, too. Will you still write the chapter about the trial?'

'I'll show it to you when you come to visit. Springtime is very nice at Lake Maggiore.'

'I'll be there. Until then.'

Tyberg had understood. It helped to have a secret ally who wouldn't call me to account.

The door burst open and my guests were asking for me. 'Where are you hiding, Gerd? Füruzan is going to do a belly dance for us.'

We cleared the dance floor and Philipp screwed a red lightbulb into the lamp. Füruzan entered from the bathroom in a veil and sequined bikini. Manuel and Jan's eyes popped out of their heads. The music began, supplicating and slow, and Füruzan's first movements were of a gentle, languorous fluidity. Then the tempo of the music increased and with it the rhythm of the dance. Röschen started to clap, everyone joined in. Füruzan discarded the veil, and let a tassel attached to her belly button circle wildly. The floor shook. When the music died away Füruzan ended with a triumphant pose and flung herself into Philipp's arms.

'This is the love of the Turks,' Philipp laughed.

'Laugh all you like. I'll get you. You don't play around with Turkish women,' she said, looking him haughtily in the eye.

I brought her my dressing gown.

'Stop,' called Eberhard as the audience was ready to disperse. 'I invite you to the breathtaking show by the great magician Ebus Erus Hardabakus.' And he made rings spin and link together and come apart again, and yellow scarves turn to red; he conjured up coins and made them disappear again, and Manuel was allowed to check that everything was above board. The trick with the white mouse went wrong. At the sight of it, Turbo leapt onto the table, knocked over the top hat it had supposedly disappeared into, chased it round the apartment, and playfully broke its neck behind the fridge before any of us could intervene. In response Eberhard wanted to break Turbo's neck, but luckily Röschen stopped him.

It was Jan's turn. He recited 'The Feet in the Fire' by Conrad Ferdinand Meyer. Next to me sat an anxious Hadwig, silently mouthing the poem with him. 'Mine is the revenge, saith the Lord,' thundered Jan at the end.

'Fill your glasses and plates and come back,' called Babs. 'It's on with the show.' She whispered with Röschen and Georg and the three of them pushed tables and chairs to the side and the dance floor became a small stage. Charades. Babs puffed out her cheeks and blew, and Röschen and Georg ran off.

'*Gone with the Wind*,' called Nägelsbach.

Then Georg and Röschen slapped one another until Babs stepped between them, took their hands, and joined them together. 'Kemal Atatürk in War and Peace!'

'Too Turkish, Fuzzy,' said Philipp and patted her thigh. 'But isn't she clever?'

It was half past eleven and I went to check there was plenty of champagne on ice. In the living room Röschen and Georg had taken over the stereo and were feeding old records onto the turntable: Tom Waits was singing 'Waltzing Matilda', and Philipp tried to waltz Babs down the narrow corridor. The children were playing tag with the cat. In the bathroom Füruzan was showering away the sweat of her belly dance. Brigitte came through to the kitchen and gave me a kiss. 'A lovely party.'

I almost didn't hear the doorbell. I pressed the buzzer for the front door, but then saw the green silhouette through the frosted glass of the apartment door and knew the visitor was already upstairs. I opened up. In front of me stood Herzog in uniform.

'I'm sorry, Herr Self . . .'

So this was the end. They say it happens just before you're hanged, but now the pictures of the past weeks went shooting through my mind, as if in a film. Korten's last look, my arrival in Mannheim on Christmas morning, Manuel's hand in mine, the nights with Brigitte, our happy group round the Christmas tree. I wanted to say something. I couldn't make a sound.

Herzog went ahead of me into the apartment. I heard the music being turned down. But our friends kept laughing and chattering cheerfully. When I had control of myself again, and went into the sitting room, Herzog had a glass of wine in his hand, and Röschen, a little tipsy, was fiddling with the buttons on his uniform.

'I was just on my way home, Herr Self, when the complaint about your party came through on the radio. I took it upon myself to look in on you.'

'Hurry up,' called Brigitte, 'two minutes to go.' Enough

time to distribute the champagne glasses and pop the corks.

Now we're standing on the balcony, Philipp and Eberhard let off the fireworks, from all the churches comes the ringing of bells, we clink glasses.

'Happy New Year.'